PRAISE FOR
Tread Lightly

"With a pulse-pounding opening, *Tread Lightly* is a gripping tale of resilience, trauma, and belonging. Elizabeth Kemp is an evocative storyteller with a knack for blending genres, combining high-octane thriller with nuanced, introspective commentary."

—**Rhodi Hawk, ITW award-winning author of**
The Wolf of Cinnamon Falls

"Part thriller, part soul-searching journey, this story gripped me from page one. Tierney's voice is so vivid and real, I felt like I was swimming laps beside her."

—**Ann Huchingson, screenwriter**

"Tensions seethe deliciously beneath the glossy surface of suburbia in Elizabeth Kemp's novel, *Tread Lightly*. Former hostage negotiator turned stay-at-home-mom, Tierney Gillespie may have been able to handle hardened criminals in her past job, but a death in the 'burbs tests her skills and PTSD in ways she didn't see coming. A tense and compelling story of surprise attacks, from both past and present."

—**Jordan Rosenfeld, author of *Fallout* and *Women in Red***

"A compelling debut, chock full of suspense."

—Robin Somers, author of *Eleven Stolen Horses* & *Beet Fields*

"*Tread Lightly* introduces an iconic new heroine: Tierney Gillespie . . . [whose] personal and professional struggles ignite an unforgettable and deeply satisfying climax. Fans of Laura Dave and Liane Moriarty will love this debut thriller."

–Diane Schaffer, author of *Mortal Zin*

Tread Lightly

A Novel

ELIZABETH KEMP

Sibylline Press

Published in the United States by Sibylline Press,
an imprint of All Things Book LLC, California.

Sibylline Press is dedicated to publishing the
brilliant work of women authors ages 50 and older.
www.sibyllinepress.com

Sibylline Digital First Edition
eBook ISBN: 9798897409730
Print ISBN: 9798897409747
Library of Congress Control Number: 2025938363

Cover Design: Alicia Feltman
Book Production: Aaron Laughlin

Sibylline
Press

For my family. For everything.

FRIDAY, OCTOBER 8, 1999

Embassy of the United States of America

Dublin, Ireland

Tierney was ten minutes late. She rolled down the Ford Cortina's window and fumes from the freshly-laid asphalt wafted inside. Security recognized her by now, but she still flashed her badge.

Jeffrey was working the evening shift and expecting her. He removed his headset on approach from the guardhouse. "Looking lovely, Sergeant O'Shaughnessy." He passed her the clipboard for a signature, and waved the requisite search mirror underneath her vehicle.

Tierney didn't mind when grandfatherly men commented on her looks, but her smile faded at the realization of being the last unchecked name on the guest list. Norah, her mentor and partner with the Squad, was already waiting inside. Tierney glanced ahead at the traffic cones blocking off spaces in the lot and kicked herself for having spent so much time practicing her speech and choosing an outfit. "Is it already full?"

"Aye, but you're welcome to a spot by the lorries at the end. Not too long of a walk for you young ones."

"Better than street parking, I suppose."

"That it is. Enjoy the festivities." He ambled to the guard-house and activated the ten-foot-high gate.

Tierney entered the compound and could hear the weight of the iron bars rotate back behind her, locking into place. The sedan she still shared with her fellow Irish American roommate since uni followed the path of the newly blackened road. *Not too long of a walk?*

The stick shift was no easy task in the four-inch pumps she'd purchased that afternoon on Grafton Street—compliments of her recent salary bump. She'd never worn heels so high.

As she geared down to round the circular building, she eyed an open spot and glided in. She hopped out, steadied herself, and began the trek to the lobby when she hesitated. *Lipstick.* It was an honorary night for women in law enforcement and every detail needed to be in place. Reaching into the side pocket of her clutch, she found the new shade.

She rotated a nearby parked car's sideview mirror and bent down for a quick touch up. As she pursed her lips and tousled her hair one final time, she caught a glimmer of movement in her reflection. She turned and focused on the moonlit skyline. A cable hanging down from the Embassy's roof. A body descending the building. A metallic glint. *An automatic rifle?* Whatever it was, the body was heading towards the lit floor of the gala. Tierney's gut knotted up. *Norah!*

Tierney flipped open the clutch and swiped around for her mobile phone. No phone to warn her. Her mind flitted to where she had left it on her vanity. How could she have forgotten it?

She dropped the clutch and ran towards the guardhouse. *The closest radio.* The heels went next. As her hose-covered feet sliced against asphalt debris, she grimaced but doubled her speed.

Reaching the rear of the structure, she banged her fists on the bulletproof window. "Jeffrey!" He was sitting at his computer, back to her, headset in place.

No response.

"Jeffrey!" She banged louder.

No time. Scale the gate.

She climbed the gate's iron bars without effort, reaching the top and passing over, when the hem of her dress caught on a finial. She lost her balance and fell as it tore. Shoulder first, her body slammed down to the cold pavement. Jeffrey turned towards the commotion—Tierney, a mound of emerald satin laying outside the gate. He ripped off his headset and stumbled towards her.

"Alert them," she cried, her words coming in uneven gasps. "Security, inside! Intruder cabling down building. Rifle! The gala!" She held her shoulder, feeling the pain intensify.

He grabbed the radio from his belt. "Code red. Repeat, code red. Armed suspect attempting external entry. Grand Briefing Room."

The moment of silence that hung in the air was suffocating.

"Copy that. Code red," a garbled voice responded, and the building's alarms blared.

Jeffrey bent down to Tierney. "Don't move. I'll get you help," he said, as an armed Embassy guard stormed up to secure the entrance, machine gun drawn.

Before Tierney could form another word, the three instinctively covered their heads to the sound of shattering glass from above.

WEDNESDAY, NOVEMBER 14, 2007

Park View, CA, USA

Silicon Valley

Nothing bad can happen when you're a stay-at-home mom. Tierney's mantra played on repeat in her head as she drove Finn to kindergarten. She had never needed a mantra at their preschool in Queen Anne, Washington. There she had been able to volunteer alongside Finn as much as she wanted. The co-op, in fact, coveted her time. That wasn't the case here in California.

Ever since Finn started at Apricot Grove School, Tierney had found herself with four idle hours she hadn't had in six years. And it wasn't good for her. She knew other parents who dreamed of the extra time that came with their kids starting school, but no thank you. Tierney needed the constant distraction, and knowing what he was up to.

The plan after walking Finn to his classroom: find Mara. Something so simple shouldn't be so difficult. Was the room parent avoiding her on purpose? No, that would be weird.

Tierney wasn't a typical mom at the private school. She was the one who'd show up with chlorine-damp hair, wearing faded jeans and a T-shirt, unlike most others whose styled hair and manicured nails made them look as if they had somewhere to be (some did). But new families in town should be considered an asset—a fresh well to draw from, both financially and for volunteer hours. She and Sean had already made their annual donation, over the requested amount. Plus, she would make a useful addition as a classroom helper—she'd spent years at Finn's preschool honing those skills. But two months and two weeks into the school year she'd yet to break into the tight-knit room parent community.

The logistics and settling in that come with any move had been enough diversion, for a while. The idle time now between drop off and pick up was making her hands tingle. If she could somehow lock Mara inside a windowless room until they could agree on a—

"The light isn't getting any greener, Mom," Finn said from the back seat, as an impatient horn blared from behind. He was sounding more like his college-age cousin, Ryan, every day. *His idol.*

"Thanks, Buddy." Tierney refocused on the intersection near the school and smiled at her son's precociousness.

She made the left turn onto Slate Lane, sitting in determination to check things off the Park View Bucket List tacked to the cork board above her nightstand. The only volunteering she'd uncovered so far was assisting the PTA with updating emergency supplies on campus. Safety was in her wheelhouse, but she didn't want more random tasks.

She had hoped to be Finn's room parent, but Mara seemingly secured that role before the first day of school. Tierney still couldn't get a job helping with craft hour, or even reading time. Heck, she'd be fine with math centers, and she despised math. She even put her name on a sub list for volunteers, but had yet to be called. That would make anyone feel as if they were being shunned. But the mom cliques at the school were intense, and Tierney learned early on that navigating them with care was critical. She shook her head at what used to require her careful navigating. This was all she had now, though, and she was on a mission.

"Talk to Mara" was the blanket response when speaking with other parents about their volunteering efforts; Mara's name had been ricocheting around her head for weeks. The problem was, Mara was never alone. Tierney just needed to get the damn room parent alone for an entourage-free conversation.

"You'll find your opportunity soon enough," said BB, her former roommate and best friend since Trinity College, during their last Skype. "You don't want to jump into the first opening anyway and get stuck volunteering with a bunch of bananas."

Her unfiltered way with words was usually right. And she had the professional credentials to cite bananas, being a successful psychologist. But Tierney would accept anything in the classroom at this point.

She pulled into a parking space between an Audi wagon and a Lexus SUV, and parked Betty, their white Subaru Outback. She opened the door, being mindful not to hit the Audi. It was the same model Sean had her test drive last month, but she still didn't feel the need to upgrade just because his compensation had tripled this year.

She stepped out of the car and zipped up her sweatshirt. She felt the familiar tightness in her right shoulder as she twisted her long hair into a messy bun.

Tierney helped Finn unbuckle himself from the five-point-harness booster seat, and attempted to make small talk with the moms and the few dads gathered at the crosswalk. As the pack advanced, the crossing guard's backwards Oakland Raiders cap, frayed neon vest, and duct-taped *Josh* name tag grabbed her attention, but not for what she saw. Was it weed she smelled? The low cloud cover must be messing with her nose. Administration would never allow a stoner crossing guard a foot near campus. Maybe it was one of the passers-by.

The school was abuzz as it was every morning five minutes before the bell.

"Are you serious?" a mom lamented on the walk up. "Our orthodontist recommended the same thing last week," she continued, telling an eager-faced listener while trying to control her purebred-something on a leash with one hand and a fussing baby in a jogger with the other. "We'll have to grab lattes soon to compare notes. Braces in first grade seem too young."

Pumpkin-spiced, no doubt. Does anyone drink black coffee around here? She was missing her early morning lap swim lane by the minute but needed to keep focus.

"Pick up the pace, Mom," Finn said, a few feet ahead. He looked so much like her, with sparkly green eyes, fair skin, and jet-black hair.

"Maybe if you held my hand, it would be easier for me to keep up with you and those fast sneakers." She could easily outrun him but didn't dare. Not here.

Finn smirked and darted ahead even faster at the sight of friends near the kindergarten wing.

Tierney was happy for her son, and knew it had been the right decision to send him here instead of homeschooling, her initial idea. "He's too outgoing for that," Sean had said. "It wouldn't be in his best interest, socially or academically," the preschool director had advised. All true. But as she continued down the path, little things still disquieted her, like how the school's property wasn't fenced in. Her childhood public schools in New York City could lock kids safely in and threats out; they frequently did. Here, the openness continued for miles, with mountain vistas from every vantage point.

At she pondered the disturbingly trusting community, an image of Norah flashed behind her eyes, but Tierney blinked it aside. What would've been her partner's fiftieth birthday was now only two days away. *The deadline.* She sighed and continued on.

Tierney reached Finn and the row of backpacks hung low and neat along the wall on equidistant pegs. Mrs. Ferber opened the door to welcome her kiddos, as she called them, dressed in their tidy red and navy plaid uniforms. Tierney planted a kiss on Finn's forehead before he squirmed away, and she went to look for Mara.

Tierney headed towards the main corridor and opened the double doors. She found herself witness to a heated discussion—something about cookies—among a large group of coiffed women. Mara, with her ombré-shaded hair, stood in the center like a queen.

The sight of the nicely-dressed lot took hold of Tierney. She could feel her throat tightening, and the whine of radio interference began buzzing in her head. *Not again.* She slid her palms, now slick with sweat, into her pockets and bypassed the group, giving her walk a look of great purpose.

Tierney returned to the comforting embrace of Betty. She sat for a few minutes to stabilize her breathing, rubbing the braided nylon band on the watch BB had selected for her during their Nantucket trip two years ago.

"The grounding benefit of feeling nearby fabrics," she had shared that afternoon in the gift shop after one of Tierney's episodes. The watch had been on her wrist ever since. A bit of therapy. Real therapy was for others, not an O'Shaughnessy.

As she headed out on errands and approached the stop sign, she was surprised to see Mara's black Mercedes-Benz G-Class SUV already backing out. Tierney knew the car well—always parked near the office in the "Reserved for Wright Family" spot they had "won" last year at the school auction. Tierney envisioned four-wheeling over the sidewalk to barricade her in for a quick discussion. Or maybe a tail would be more appropriate, then run into her by accident? *Stalking—now that would be weird.* No, she could remain patient a bit longer.

Tierney adjusted her sweatshirt bunching underneath the seat belt. She couldn't imagine wearing the designer get-ups that Mara and her pals wore. But she'd always been a tomboy, having grown up around three older brothers and their buddies. Regardless, she learned long ago it was dangerous to care how she looked.

—

Two hours later, Tierney had one remaining item on her to-do list. She removed the lightweight package from her passenger seat and entered the post office's lobby. The line was at least ten people deep. She fished out the new iPhone Sean had ordered for her when his entire office upgraded their standard-issue BlackBerrys, thanks to having Apple as a client. No text updates on how his day was going in San Francisco. Sean had never had to prep for a day like this. Meetings with the SEC, yes. But not the FBI. No news was good news, she hoped.

"Nice to see a familiar face in this hellish line."

Tierney turned to see her sunny next-door neighbor approaching at a quick clip, dressed in yoga attire. Gemma had stopped by the first day of their move-in with a gift of artisanal coffee beans and one of the friendliest smiles Tierney had ever encountered. They'd hit it off and she insisted on being called Gem. Although her kids were a few years older than Finn, the women always found something to talk about.

"You, too. It hasn't moved an inch."

"I used to stop in quickly and get on with my day. That new development in town is making Park View feel so 'big city' now. I told Rob I'd send this off to his parents before class," Gem said, holding up a padded envelope addressed to Mumbai, "and now look at this."

"Oh, jump in front of me. No worries. I already got in my thirty minutes at the pool this morning."

She smiled and traded places with Tierney. "Remember, if you ever want to join me at the studio, say the word. You'd love Marc's Hatha class. There's been more moms from school, too, so it would be another fun way for you to meet people."

"There's something about a swim that works for me, but I promise to reach out if I change my mind." The thought of a group exercise class made Tierney uneasy. She had grown accustomed to her shared lane where swimmers typically kept to themselves.

"Sounds good. How's everything going? Almost done with unpacking?"

"Doing a little each day. I'll get there. It would be great to park the cars in the garage for a change."

"Wouldn't that be nice. My minivan has never enjoyed the same privilege as our BMW."

Tierney laughed. "You know, I'm still trying to find a way to volunteer in Finn's classroom. I submitted my name as a helper for the party after the Kindergarten Sing, so we'll see."

"I remember wanting in the classroom. Some years were great with a room parent—they welcomed offers for extra help. But others, real control freaks. Something will work out, though. My world now is so different—middle schoolers have no interest in mommy showing up on campus," she giggled. "And look at this cute box of yours."

The line nudged forward with the opening of a second service window.

"Care package for our nephew at San Diego State." Tierney smiled at its exterior, adorned with superhero stickers and marker drawings. "Ryan's been homesick so I made a batch of his favorite last night. Then Finn decided it needed pizzazz."

"Lucky guy to get treats from his fancy baking aunt. What kind?"

"Irish shortbread, his favorite. I love having a reason to bake when I can."

"Maybe we can bake together sometime. I know I'd learn a thing or two from a professional."

"Former professional." Gem was one of the few people who knew part of Tierney's backstory—the one as a baker.

Tierney turned into the cul-de-sac and their garage door was wide open. *Second time this week!* Her foggy brain was getting tiresome. Sean told her last time not to worry about the door; they lived in one of the safest towns in the area. But still, it was unsettling to have left the house like that.

Before going inside through the laundry room, she watched the garage door tick down, wondering if something had blocked its path earlier. Nope. She did a quick sweep of the house to rule out intruders or anything off kilter (more nope), then checked email, texts, and the house phone in the kitchen for any replies about volunteering. They were probably the only family in Silicon Valley to still have a landline.

"Always be reachable and able to call out for help," her police officer dad would say. Her brothers still had the antiquated technology, too.

No messages. Just more alone time with her thoughts. She sighed and started in on the foyer, straightening upended shoes and putting away toys, all the while listening for odd sounds. The house was always in some kind of disarray due to their move in June, although, truly more of a reflection of her internal state.

As she passed the office, she recalled how early Sean had to catch the train for his long day in the city. She wondered if he was still happy to have made the jump a few years back from the tax side of accounting to the forensic side. She looked at her watch. In a matter of minutes, he would be sitting in on FBI depositions alongside high-profile Silicon Valley clients and their lawyers.

Still an hour before pick-up, she retreated to the couch and opened the neighborhood's book club selection: *Eat, Pray, Love* by Elizabeth Gilbert. She had one chapter left and could understand why BB said the book was trending to be her 2007 favorite.

Tierney had originally declined Gem's invite to join the book club, knowing how debilitating it could be for her to approach large groups of well-dressed women, especially when solo. The mistake she had made of looking at case file photos from the Grand Briefing Room scene after the gala had resulted in years of nightmares, and difficulty around female groups at all. The brain was weird that way. But she had made some progress with the passing of time.

When Gem explained that the book club was a casual, come-as-you-are kind of gathering, Tierney agreed to go with her at least once. But after this morning, she wondered if that had been smart. She hadn't factored in how Norah's birthday milestone might complicate her healing progress.

—

"Where are my hugs?" Sean walked through the front door, right on time for dinner.

Finn, wearing his Superman cape from Halloween, raced to greet him and flew up into his arms. Her boys looked adorable together with the same short haircut (and barber), although Sean's shade was a sandy brown. Tierney followed with a tentative smile, scanning for clues on how her husband's day had gone. Stressful. She could hear it in his voice, a skill she had picked up after a few hostage negotiations as well as seven years of marriage.

Tierney and Sean kissed, and Louie slipped inside before the door shut. She adored their little Lynx Point cat, and the way he'd always pass by her with a reassuring cheek rub against the leg.

Sean had brought him home a few months after their wedding as a therapy pet. The rescue kitten, a runt, with the big task of rescuing her—via kneading paws and purrs—on those days she could only find energy to tuck the quilt up under her chin.

Later that evening and with Finn in bed, Tierney and Sean could catch up. Knowing whiskey was in order without asking, she poured him a glass of Macallan 18 from the bottle her youngest brother had sent Sean earlier that year as congratulations for promotion to partner at Camp & Giffin. She took a quick nip herself before handing over the green crystal lowball tumbler. The glasses were a favorite from the bar set she'd inherited from her parents. It had been years since they'd passed—her dad from cancer and her mom a month later, from grief. But Tierney was thankful to have reminders around her home from a happy childhood, like the festive gatherings with family and friends when the glasses were used.

Tierney clicked on the TV and lowered the volume as Louie jumped on the couch, curling into his favorite spot, Tierney's lap.

"It's looking bleak," Sean began as they settled in to watch local news—their evening routine. Sean took a long swig. "Clients are panicking. No one thought the stock-option backdating scandal would reach their companies."

"The office environment must feel so tense." The firm Sean worked for was based in Seattle, but he had been tapped to manage their California office, which specialized in equity accounting.

"They're deposing entire teams and recording sessions. One of the HR managers was even called in to meet with the FBI after the first round. I'm guessing she might have known about the inconsistencies but didn't want to be the whistleblower."

Tierney ran her hand across Louie's dappled grey fur and thought of the families. It's one thing to have goings-on at the office, but investigations eventually trickled into home life. The law didn't wait for an ideal time or place to unfold. She recalled an afternoon during her foundation training with the Garda, Ireland's national police and security service, witnessing a father's arrest for insider trading in the middle of school pickup on the playground. Despite the man's wrongdoings, a pit had settled in Tierney's stomach over the team not waiting a few extra moments for the child to hug his father goodbye. She made the mistake of sharing her empathy with a male trainee, who told her to not be "such a girl about it."

Tierney's attention returned to Sean. "I assumed investigations would've focused on CFOs and their direct reports."

Sean nodded and swirled the ice in his glass. "But enough about me. How did things go with this Mara? Get a chance to ask about volunteering?"

"Oh, that." Tierney gave a little shake of her head. "Today didn't go the way I'd hoped. I know my situation is silly compared to what you're dealing with."

"Nonsense. Social communities and your time with Finn are important."

Sean always knew the right thing to say. She leaned on his shoulder, taking in the warmth of his skin through the starched oxford.

"Don't worry." He kissed the top of her head. "These things take time. I remember my sister telling mom how the PTA at their elementary school was a nightmare at the beginning. The established friendships from preschool years made it difficult."

"Great. If someone with Lily's charisma had trouble with cliques, I'm doomed."

"You'll get there."

The two watched the broadcast of a live protest taking place a mile from their home, demanding safety on busy roads.

Another cyclist had been hit by a car. At least this one was going to be okay, not like the guy a few months back that was hit in front of the community center and still in a coma. Drivers vs. cyclists. One protester held a sign that read, "DRIVE LIKE YOUR KIDS LIVE HERE." Another sign read, "MORE TRAILS AND BIKE LANES."

"I've seen these protesters on my way to the train, ironically disrupting traffic while advocating for safety."

"They've been profiled in the *Daily Gazette*, too. I hope safety issues improve by the time Finn rides to school."

Sean yawned and downed the last few drops. "I should get to bed. Taking Caltrain's early bullet tomorrow." He gave her knee a gentle squeeze and stood. "Love you."

"Love you more. I'll be back from the pool before you need to leave."

"You've been so dedicated about swimming every morning."

"Trying." Tierney gave a cheerful thumbs-up. What other choice did she have? The pool was her only reliable outlet. "I'll join you soon. Just need a few more minutes to tidy."

Sean put his glass in the sink and quietly made his way down the hallway.

Who was Tierney kidding? A few more minutes wasn't going to help anything. She despised bedtime, and needed to calm her mind before facing the pillow—and the insomnia. At least the nightmares about Norah had subsided, but the 5-0 milestone was eating away at her.

THURSDAY, NOVEMBER 15

Tierney activated her fog lights and drove out of the cul-de-sac. She wanted to arrive at Schick Pool before it opened at 6:00 a.m. It was either that or stare at the ceiling for another hour.

Their family had spent hours swimming this summer at the outdoor pool, and Finn had made many friends from the surrounding public schools. Tons of families, au pairs, nannies, and lifeguards enjoyed the space, which was open year-round. She hoped to soon feel the same sense of community at Apricot Grove.

While parking, Tierney noted the best part of fall swimming: it wasn't as crowded with the darker mornings and colder weather. And it felt much less frenzied with school in session. Bell was the exception.

Bell is what Tierney named the older woman whose weathered white VW Scirocco was always nearby. Its windows were covered from the inside with crumpled Taco Bell wrappers, stacks of disintegrating cardboard and grocery bags, and a collection of once-colorful stuffed animals across the back window. It was hard to imagine that it was safe to drive yet had up-to-date registration on its plates.

Today, Bell's VW was in a space near the end of the lot. *Did she park overnight?* Cops were known to turn a blind eye to the unhoused; she certainly hadn't always enforced the rules. But maybe Bell was simply a hoarder. Tierney initially thought she might be onsite to use the locker room, but noticed her out on occasion in the shallow lanes. The woman only did backstroke, though, never sharing a lane due to what Tierney assumed to be an inability to swim in a straight line. Those familiar would keep away, but for a newcomer—so bold as to slip into the lane without the standard courtesy wave—Bell would bound out and exit the facility like an overflowing fountain soda, dripping wet. Nonetheless, she seemed harmless.

Tierney headed towards the pool lobby's glass doors. She was fond of the lemon-yellow paint of the facility's interior as well as the multimedia sea mural that greeted patrons—both more welcoming than Brad, the gruff head lifeguard-manager who was manning the front desk today.

"Card." He extended his hand to Tierney when it was her turn at check-in.

"Hi there." She passed it over and wrote her name on the sign-in sheet neatly.

Brad looked more disheveled than usual, with bloodshot eyes, his dirty-blond hair rakishly sticking out in all directions, and coffee stains on his sweatshirt. He attempted to punch the card a few times. In frustration, he slammed down the tool on his desk, causing Tierney and the woman behind her to lurch back, before walking over to a filing cabinet by a futon. He yanked open and slammed shut two metal drawers before retrieving a replacement, but not before Tierney saw a near-empty bottle of vodka clanking around the bottom drawer. *Nice.*

Brad returned her card, punched in a random place.

Tierney smiled her thank you and returned it to her wallet. She entered the women's locker room and recognized some faces, including a lifeguard restocking toilet paper, and a few au pairs—probably cramming in a quick swim before returning home to help get kids dressed, fed, and off to school.

Tierney hung up her things in an available locker and spun the dial of her combination lock. She made her way towards the door leading outside and noticed a new sign taped to the large mirror above the sinks:

Reminder
Limit showers to 5 minutes | No overnight locker storage

The drought in this state didn't look to be ending anytime soon. There was never such a sign at their last community pool. Tierney pushed open the door and headed into the chill of autumn. She placed her towel on a picnic table and—

Dammit to hell. Her heart skittered. On the grass nearby, Dummy was lying motionless. Finn thought it was the coolest thing, with its big sneakers and featureless face. For her it was a reminder of hours spent waiting for the coroner to take over a vic. Young swimmers would play with the manikin until reprimanded by Brad's whistle and subsequent yell from the office doorway, "Dummy is for lifeguard training only!" They must be setting up for a CPR course or new lifeguard training later today.

Tierney walked around Dummy toward an open lane. She adjusted her goggles over her swim cap, pulled on her fins, and slid into the chlorinated water—a balmy seventy-nine degrees. After a few laps, she found her hypnotic flow. The water helped wash away her worries, at least for a while. Swimming had become the best activity to provide any relief from her racing thoughts, which now fixated on Norah's birthday and what it represented. She swam faster.

BB had been recommending a meditation practice for years. And a gratitude journal. But "woo-woo" activities like that weren't of interest.

After a five-minute warm up, she paused at the wall to remove her fins and switched to breaststroke. *Didn't Melville write something about meditation and water being wedded forever?* She'd need to remind BB of that salient tidbit. "Traditional therapy isn't for me" was her blanket response whenever BB (or Sean) proposed THAT idea.

"Join you?" A late arrival called out to Tierney from the pool's edge as she neared. It looked like a guy named Dean who had shared her lane a few times, but she couldn't be sure; goggled faces were a challenge.

Tierney raised a thumbs-up and reversed course with a flip turn. With busy hands, she was better able to relax and cope with whatever unsettling memory her past threw out since walking away from her career in Dublin eight years ago. Baking projects used to hold that honor until she had Finn, and being a stay-at-home parent became all consuming. But how she had thrived at Dublin's Baking Academy six months after resigning from the Crisis Intervention Squad. And baking for a catering event is how she'd met Sean.

Tierney switched to backstroke and her focus turned to the four designated Masters lanes at the deepest end of the pool. The Master's group warmups had commenced, but two blond lifeguards were running drills instead of Brad, who was typically outside by now. *What would he do without his team to bail him out?*

Tierney had noticed the Master's membership fliers in the lobby a few months ago, but wasn't interested. She was content with swimming at her own pace to the white noise of splashes, and observing. It was intriguing to see what toys the group used for workouts. Some days involved waist belts, enabling swimmers to slow-motion "run" down lanes. Then there were the weights for dry land practice. Those were Tierney's favorite, especially the large black rubber-looking barbells that made her think of ancient Popeye cartoons she had watched with her brothers. Seeing those swimmers spring out of the deep end to pump a few sets and jump back in was entertaining. The woman with a snake tattoo on her neck was especially skillful with the kettlebells.

Tierney reached the wall and paused for a breath. The man sharing her lane finished his lap and stopped beside her, pulling up his goggles. *Dean.* "Working on your time? You've been whizzing by."

"Not as fast as I'd like. Those jerks are at it again," he said, out of breath, and rubbed his droopy eyelids. "I swear, I could throttle them. They are such a distraction."

Tierney wasn't a fan of their antics, either. Those swimmers from Masters, whom Tierney called the Stingrays, were known to deep-dive the full distance of the pool, passing underneath lap swimmers across all lanes, and always wore black swimsuits. The production made her feel as if she was swimming in a fever of stingrays. "I asked my husband about their workout style. He thinks they might be brushing up on their scuba skills, or training for an event like that Alcatraz swim?"

"Perhaps, but it's annoying for everyone else. They'd better be done soon."

Tierney could see the two practicing this morning had reached the end. "Appear to be."

"Great." Dean pulled down his goggles and reset his watch. "Let's see if I can get back in the zone. Enjoy your swim," he said, and pushed off the wall.

Tierney empathized with his frustration. It was hard to have one's flow interrupted. The sole Stingray she had an issue with was the one who swam face up. So creepy to see someone looking at you while swimming. But she didn't ID him this morning, unlike the swimmer two lanes over who swam like a perp at gunpoint, treading water while dolphin-kicking in place with palms raised. He looked ridiculous.

Aside from the random behaviors, Tierney enjoyed the eclectic nature of the pool's clientele. These were more her people than the cookie-cutter crew at Finn's school would ever be, especially the ones onsite for the sheer joy of swimming.

Tierney returned to her stomach for another batch of breast-stroke and took in a whiff of something dissolving around her—sunscreen or perfume today. At times, the experience was a pleasant surprise, like a coconut scent that would take her back to the Maui vacation in eighth grade with her family. But more often than not it was an overripe smell, like BO or a strong men's cologne. A woodsy one always reminded her of a guy BB had dated in college before she came out.

She recognized a few more regulars, including Craig, whom she had learned was Mara's husband after seeing them together at Back to School Night. He was easy to spot: Hollywood handsome, the tallest of all the men (about six-foot-four like Sean), flaxen hair, and shoulders that jutted out in a wide V. He was always chummy with the lifeguards and other swimmers. *Like husband, like wife.* Tierney wondered, though, why he swam at the public pool. Gem had mentioned before that Mara's family belonged to the Park View Country Club.

Seeing Craig reminded her of today's primary yet recurring task: talk to Mara. The gatekeeper who couldn't be bothered with replying to her messages. She'd try again to catch a moment with her at school and finally secure something tangible.

—

The best laid plans. Tierney missed Mara at morning drop-off thanks to circling back home for Finn's backpack, so wanted to stay on task with errands and not be late for pick-up. She entered the pet store and hoped they had re-stocked Louie's favorite kibble. Such a fussy palate he had, considering his litter had been rescued from a dumpster.

En route to the cat food section, she observed two white-haired women at the pet-tag-engraving kiosk with a chihuahua in tow. *The cute grandmas from water fitness?* Those women were easy to spot at the pool with their retro, plastic daisy-covered swim caps—one white, one yellow—but it was harder without those markers. Regardless, the swimmers reminded Tierney of her Grandma Molly, who'd also worn her swim cap on the way to the pool instead of waiting to put it on poolside like most swimmers.

At the thought of elderly women, a sadness swept over Tierney; Norah would never get to be fifty or their age either. Tierney took in a deep breath, refocused, and asked a salesperson for assistance in retrieving a fifteen-pound bag of kibble from inventory while she perused the cat toys. Nothing of interest; her Louie preferred real lizards and mice from the yard.

When she finally got in line, the two elderly women were checking out. As one presented her cash to the clerk and suppressed a cough, the other smiled. *Definitely them.* White Daisy's raspy cough, and Yellow Daisy's sweet expression. Plus, the comfortable way they stood together—a familiarity she had seen time and again at the pool, no doubt resulting from years together. And how nice they had a dog.

Tierney often wondered what the two talked about, especially while hanging onto lane lines during class and sunning themselves. Probably best friend things, like she and BB. Tierney missed having BB nearby. They had been inseparable since college. And when BB decided to make the move from Ireland to Queen Anne with her once Sean proposed, happy for a change of her own and away from an increasingly unaccepting work environment, Tierney was elated to still have her pal around. But the texts, phone calls, and Skypes would have to be it for now.

—

"Sorry, Louie. I'm in a rush." Tierney scooped aside his malleable body from the Subaru's trunk where he'd just jumped in, and continued unloading grocery bags. But Louie loved his groceries, and returned to stick his entire head into each bag with intrigue. As Tierney reached for the last bag, his pupils grew large, ears went back, and he crouched low, growling, in the corner. "What the heck?"

Tierney was moving so quickly that she hadn't registered approaching footsteps. She nearly launched from her Adidas when she turned to find Mildred standing a few inches away—the smell of mixed nuts hot on her nosy neighbor's breath.

Wearing an orange, long-sleeved Clemson polo, the woman with a thin smile peered over Tierney's shoulder into the Subaru, with her border collie, Snickers, nervously in tow.

Louie hissed, preparing his attack. Tierney intervened and put him inside the house. Cat scratch fever was not something she wanted to add to this neighbor's list of complaints.

"Hear the Davis's house went for two hundred thousand over asking?" Mildred said when Tierney returned.

"Sounds great for the neighborhood." Tierney forced a smile, trying to be polite so Mildred wouldn't start profiling her as the "not so nice new woman."

"It should've gotten more. I never would've chosen their realtor."

"I'm not that savvy about the realtor community here. Seems many people decide to remodel instead of sell, based on all the construction projects around town."

"There are indeed a lot of remodels. Don't you hate when crews speed through? My biggest pet peeve, though, is when they park their big trucks in front of my home."

Tierney's middle brother was a contractor. She was now kicking herself for bringing up the local construction scene and having to listen to gibberish instead of getting cold stuff in the fridge. But she did her best to make courteous conversation while Mildred's eyes darted between hers and the garage's interior. There wasn't much to see except tons of moving boxes still awaiting the daunting task of a sort-through—number two on her bucket list.

"And that landlord of yours—" Mildred interrupted herself and walked a few paces into the garage. "Is that a spear up there? I've been wondering about the shape." Mildred repositioned her turned-up collar.

"Oh, it's an old harpoon. Just some of Sean's game-fishing equipment. Hasn't gone in years, but wants to venture out when his workload lightens."

"Hmm. Good thing it's up high. I'd hate for Finn to get hurt."

Mildred's stance reflected more interest in the garage's inventory than genuine concern for her son. "He'd know better. And speaking of Finn, I need to finish a few things before pick-up." Tierney balanced the last bag on her hip and shut the hatchback. "Nice chatting."

"Yes, well, I'm off to golf. See you at book club? Heard you were added to the invite list. I've already finished the memoir."

"I'll be there." *Only if Gem was going.* Tierney passed through the garage and the sight of the box labeled "T's stuff: Crisis Intervention Squad," in BB's handwriting, stung like a blast of pepper spray. She didn't dare pause, though, and risk drawing attention from Mildred, so she continued her pace inside. The thought of having to discuss the Squad reference was, well, unimaginable. She dropped the groceries on the counter and returned outside.

Orange-clad Mildred was thankfully down a house, busy analyzing a newly planted shrub. Tierney slowly exhaled the breath she'd been holding, and leaned on Sean's workbench. Survivor's guilt, that's what BB called this. Seeing the box was always a trigger. Sean must've been looking for something and accidentally pulled it forward. It hadn't been opened since BB went into headquarters on her behalf to collect personal effects and labeled it.

Tierney seized the opportunity to rotate the box, label out of sight, and push it back deeper. As the box jettisoned forward, though, she winced and jerked back her right arm, holding the shoulder she had just hyperextended. "That was dumb."

The old tape on top was beginning to lose its stick. It had lasted two moves, but re-taping it would have to wait. She needed to get back in the pool for a reset.

—

Tierney was on her third coffee by the time she parked for an 11:30 a.m. swim. She'd be in and out in twenty this time, although the check-in line was already wrapped around the star jasmine bushes that edged the pool and surrounded Park View Community Center. She shut off the engine and realized why it had been so easy to park at the popular swim time. Her spot was next to the VW along with Bell, who was busy talking to herself on the small section of grass in front of their cars. Tierney smiled, but Bell didn't break from her private conversation with an imaginary something in hand.

Tierney once made eye contact, noticing her piercing amber eyes, but Bell had quickly glanced back at her feet. The two would occasionally cross paths in the locker room, but Bell kept to herself. Tierney typically did, too.

From the back of the line, Tierney recognized some water fitness participants looking just as anxious to get into the pool. The grandmas were easy to spot, already donning their plastic daisy-covered swim caps. Tierney wasn't sure where they were from by their accents, as they spoke infrequently and, when they did, their English wasn't strong. But she once overheard another swimmer say they were Hungarian, which was one of the greatest things about Silicon Valley—such a melting pot and so accepting. *Apricot Grove should follow that lead.*

Two of the pregnant ladies, first-time moms, recognized Tierney and waved. Such a joyful time that period in her own life had been, yet sprinkled with blue moments in knowing that Norah would never meet her child.

After three minutes in line, a dog year for a swimmer eager to get in the pool, Tierney bypassed the locker room and headed outside. Sunshine flooded the pool deck, a brightness needed on this birthday eve.

Tierney found an available lane and dove in. The water soothingly enveloped her as she found her pace. She forced her regrets to the surface as best as she could, and focused on her to-dos with the school's emergency supplies project. Her body relaxed at the thought of doing something to keep everyone safe at Apricot Grove.

After a few more laps, Tierney's shoulder ache intensified so she reverted to a kick board session. She looked over to the nearby shallow pool and it was nice to see that not much had changed with the water fitness class since summer.

The group consisted of about fifteen elderly women, the pregnant ladies, and one male spectator—the husband who'd sit on the side after helping his wife enter the water, with assistance from a lifeguard and the ADA-compliant pool lift. The woman had been in a car accident earlier that year and the pool was prescribed to advance her recovery. But now the chair sat unused and covered as she entered via steps using a waterproof cane. *Lovely progress.*

Then there was the water fitness instructor, Joan, whose name Tierney knew from participants yelling it out to whichever lifeguard was manning the chair on days she had been running late.

"Where's Joan?"

"Should we start without Joan?"

Lifeguards weren't supposed to allow distraction while on duty, but their lack of response was probably more because they knew Joan would eventually turn up. She was a tall, large-busted woman and as tan as dark toast, smothered in what must either be baby oil or sunscreen with zero SPF.

Tierney had once described her to BB. "Think elderly Jane Fonda, in a hot pink one-piece and a big sun hat, who never gets in the water." But such energy. Her music, too, especially when Michael Jackson's *Thriller* blasted. Tierney enjoyed when the group was instructed to tread water, since the entire pool was a shallow end. Many would cheat and stand on the plaster while appearing to tread.

Tierney's attention returned to her lap pool. Two Stingrays and the dolphin-kicker guy were surprisingly there again, too, along with that woodsy-scented cologne in the water, making its way over. *Drakkar Noir?* The sight of the men made Tierney wonder what the Masters did for a living to have so much available pool time. *Ouch.* She was one to talk.

—

Laura was the first parent Tierney noticed waiting outside Mrs. Ferber's classroom for pick-up. Another stay-at-home mom who didn't have an au pair or nanny, she was easy to recognize with her cropped hair.

"The kids made a cute craft today," she said to Tierney, pointing to the windows alongside the classroom where students could be seen putting on paper pilgrim hats as they lined up for departure. One child had his on upside down.

"Very creative," Tierney said and glanced around. "Hey, any chance you've seen Mara? Was hoping to catch her and ask if anyone needs a sub for their volunteer spot."

"Still? Mara does run a tight ship. Max is her only one, so she's pretty immersed in his world here. She was that way at preschool, too."

"I can understand that." *All too well.*

"You do know she arranged for the room parent gig with Mrs. Ferber last year? Max is repeating kindergarten."

Tierney nodded in response to her suspicion being confirmed.

Laura proceeded to share her own assignment yesterday with the Kindergarten Sing rehearsal, which hadn't been a volunteer role she'd requested, but was better than her time-suck committee last year of securing donations for the spring silent auction. "So, we don't always get the volunteer activities we want anyway."

"That's fine, but something in the classroom on occasion would be nice."

"My husband keeps nudging me to find part-time work and not waste time with this school stuff, that our little Laurel and Mason will be fine here without me. But what he doesn't get is that I don't want a random job between school runs. I'm a dermatologist by trade, so my career interests don't easily sync with part-time work."

The bell rang and Laura's first grader ran up from his classroom to ask for playground time.

"Only a few minutes until Laurel and I come find you," Laura said, and returned to her conversation with Tierney. "Plus, I know myself. If I try to do it all, I could very well implode. I already attempted part-time at the medical office when Mason started preschool, and that's exactly what happened. Volunteering here just feels more logical while I figure it all out." Laura drew in a deep breath. "Sorry, I'm dumping. It's hard to explain."

"No, I get it. You love being a mom but feel kinda stuck." *Shut up, Tierney.* Her stomach roiled at the conversation floodgates she might have just opened about past careers.

"Exactly. You can relate?"

Their discussion thankfully halted when up walked Regina—Mara's bestie, neighbor, and the parent Tierney was helping with emergency supplies.

"How's the day treating you ladies?" Regina said, brushing away a long lock of hair from her shoulder.

"I was just wondering about Mara," Tierney interjected, intent on moving along the chat. "Think she's the one picking up Max today?"

"I am. He and Derek are having a playdate," Regina said with a braggish smile that elevated her already high cheekbones. "Mara has some party prep. Another fancy dinner tonight for Craig's business prospects."

"Sounds exciting," Laura said.

"He's still looking for the next cutting-edge technology to capture his interest," Regina said with jazz hands. "It's going on eight months since his last company went public and Mara said he's getting antsy."

"Got it. I wonder what their menu will be," said Laura. "French?"

"It's Greek tonight. She's been anti-French cuisine ever since their family returned from that summer in Provence a while back. Think they over indulged."

"Mara is so creative, and her parties are amazing," Laura said to Tierney. "She goes all-out for events, especially her holiday cookie exchange."

Gem had mentioned the great Wright parties—home decked out in a way that would turn Martha Stewart sage green with envy. At least the cookie part sounded fun.

"It's a memorable event. Probably the only time of year I'm okay with treats," Regina said. "By the way, not sure if you heard, but Mara is on a no nut campaign for snacks on campus after the incident with Max the other day. Some absurd mom sent her kid to school with peanut butter birthday treats in her backpack to distribute at lunch instead of going through the teacher. Can you imagine?" Regina's mascara-fringed eyes bulged.

Tierney hadn't heard about the incident, but she could understand how frightening it must have been for Max. "My cousin had a nut allergy and my aunt was super protective until he outgrew it."

"It's not to be taken lightly," Regina said. "Mr. Tsai had to race into the office for an EpiPen. It was scary but Max is fine. Many of us think treats should be done away with at school. I mean, have you seen the garbage parents send in? All that sugar and food coloring?"

"Totally. I'd love to join that campaign," Laura said.

"More support would be great." Regina ignored Laura and kept her focus on Tierney. "Since you can understand the seriousness. I'll let Mara know. We could use extra hands."

"Oh sure." Tierney wasn't sure, but now wasn't the time to decline a role when she was trying to secure one.

Laura's lips pressed tight at the exclusion, but the mood lightened with the release of Finn's class.

Regina corralled Max and Derek and returned her focus to Laura. "Almost forgot. Would you mind posting this volunteer list on Mrs. Ferber's door? She looks busy with another parent." Regina pulled out a tan sheet of paper with a turkey design from her Chanel bag. "Mara asked me to but I need to scoot if I'm going to make it home in time to meet the landscaper."

"Of course," Laura said, with enthusiasm.

Regina and the boys headed off campus and Laura held out the sheet for review. It was the volunteer list for the Kindergarten Sing classroom party. Tierney's heart plunged at the sight of not being one of the names. *What the utter hell.*

Tierney opened her mouth to comment, point out another exclusion, or scream—she wasn't sure which—but shut it. The last thing she should be was catty where Mara and her pals were concerned. She was horrible with cliques, but at least knew that much. She'd stay the course and find another way in. Although, maybe that optimism should now include looking into something part time—with baking projects, of course, not perps.

—

After school, Tierney followed Finn inside when something looked off in the laundry room. Her fins weren't in her mesh swim bag hanging on the hook. She went back outside to see if they'd fallen out somewhere inside Betty. No luck. She must've left them at the pool. *What a scattered day.* The fins were nice ones, too, a thirty-ninth birthday gift this year from her eldest brother, the police officer. She could wait until tomorrow morning's swim to look but would hate for someone to walk off with them. The lost and found bin wasn't exactly secure.

"Schick Pool, this is Riley, may I help you?"

"Oh, hi Riley. I might have left my fins at the pool today, or maybe they blew into the gutter? Gillespie is written on the bottom in Sharpie, although pretty faded. Anyone turn them in?"

"Hold a sec?"

"Sure." The line went quiet. The lifeguards didn't wear name tags, but Tierney knew Riley as Finn's favorite, the one with tight brown curls who ran the swim relay at Schick's Olympics and Field Day. Such an exciting event it had been for her son—complete with a water balloon toss, melon relay, and a "push your favorite lifeguard into the pool" activity.

"Found 'em," Riley said cheerily upon return. "We open again at six for evening swimmers."

Three times to the pool? A personal record.

—

In the parking lot, families were taking time saying their goodbyes from what looked to have been a party at the adjacent community center. Minutes passed as Tierney waited for a spot. Through Betty's windshield, she was surprised to see Josh, Apricot Grove's crossing guard. He was walking his bike alongside a tall blonde in lifeguard attire, glamorous-looking sunglasses and hair swept into a high ponytail. Something about her was familiar.

Sitting up straighter in her seat, Tierney caught sight of Brad passing through the lobby as the couple neared the doors. Josh waved to him from outside but Brad halted in place, gave the two a hard stare, and continued on through the lobby. The young woman kissed Josh and headed in before he rode away.

Tierney became distracted by a car finally backing out of its spot. Now in a rush to get home and finish making dinner, she double-timed it into the lobby. From behind the customer service desk, there was no Brad or support staff. Instead, Dummy had been propped up in the chair. *The things that go on around here.* Tierney signed in anyway.

She approached the overflowing lost and found bin and saw that Riley had left her fins on top. Tierney looked out across the pool deck and saw her relieving the guard up in the high chair by the deep end. She made eye contact once Riley took her seat, and waved thank you with her fins.

The air had grown damp as Tierney returned out front. Driving across town in rush hour traffic wasn't something she'd factored, which she could see already forming a block away. She called Sean to share her ETA, and asked him to start the wild rice side dish. What she'd thought would be a quick excursion had already taken too long.

As she approached the intersection, a group of bike safety protesters on the sidewalk, waving vibrant-colored picket signs, had begun flowing down into the lane opposite her and halting traffic, including a classic Porsche 911 that Tierney recognized as Craig's. Tierney passed on through before protesters reached her lane, happy to have avoided the looming chaos. She hoped nothing else was going to derail her schedule.

* * *

It was almost 9:30 p.m. when Detective Sergeant Howard Sutton received the call and made the twenty-minute drive to Schick Pool. As he stood near a body floating in the shallow end, area lights illuminating the crime scene, he habitually ran a hand through his thinning hair. "What do you mean she has no fingerprints? Everyone has fingerprints."

"True, some identifiable markers. But look." The County Medical Examiner lifted the victim's right hand. "No original fingerprints. I'd say four, five years ago—all fingers were burned at some point, based on the scarring here. The thumbs and a few fingers have even more recent cuts."

"Do you find that odd?" Sutton's new partner, Detective Antonio Ayala, stood peering over Sutton's shoulder.

"I no longer find anything odd."

Sutton sighed at Ayala's presence. "Where's that manager/ head lifeguard who runs this place? Surely, he can help with an ID while we secure dental records."

"Over there," said the police officer first on scene after the cleaning crew's 911 call.

Sutton and the rookie detective turned in the direction of the lit office to see an unshaven, haggard man through the windows. "Doesn't quite match the David Hasselhoff image I was expecting," Sutton said.

"Who?" Ayala asked.

A pause.

"His name is Brad Madrone," the officer continued. "One of the cleaners found him passed out in the office after she'd already called in the body. He's been sitting on the futon like that, just staring off. Hungover, or, make that, smells hungover."

"This should be interesting," Ayala said, but instantly shut his mouth at Sutton's glare, and took a big gulp from his large McDonald's soda.

"Get rid of that," Sutton barked, and shook his head. "No eating or drinking at a crime scene." He returned his attention to the victim. "Any idea what caused that gash on her head?"

"Not yet," the medical examiner said. "Something metallic, though. The team already started the weapon search, and Forensics found blood splatter on the cement by the ADA pool lift."

Sutton approached the cordoned-off area where the photographer was taking pictures.

Ayala stood frozen for a moment before handing his soda to a nearby officer, and scurried behind Sutton. The two partners stood in silence while observing the space, then headed towards the office.

The door was propped open and Sutton tapped his latex-gloved knuckles as he entered. A few framed photos of swim teams labeled with past years hung on a wall next to a tall metal filing cabinet.

"I already told the cop," Brad said while remaining seated on the futon that looked more like a lumpy bed. "She needed a job and I needed the extra help. We were short-staffed."

"Greetings," Sutton said, making the requisite introductions for himself and Ayala before flipping open his notepad and turning on the recording device he'd placed where Brad could see it. He lowered his readers and shared the few details already provided by responding officers. "Anything you'd like to modify?"

"That all sounds right. I fell asleep in here after locking the lobby doors, and one of the cleaners woke me. Within minutes, the place was crawling with cops."

Sutton glanced around. Heaps of paperwork were stacked haphazardly on the reception counter near an older model IBM desktop computer, and the sliding glass window to interact with patrons out in the lobby was open. "I understand you have no employee file on the deceased. You're legally required to check employment eligibility documents before hiring someone," Sutton said, clicking his pen open and shut.

Brad shrugged his shoulders. "Um, sorry? Write me up at my next review." He turned to look outside as the victim's body was being zipped into a bag. His cocky air diminished, along with all color in his face.

"Your next review is the least of your worries." A multi-media mural on the far wall caught Sutton's eye, along with the CCTV camera placed high up near a large plastic swordfish like the one at his favorite Chinese restaurant in San Jose. He approached the wall and traced a finger along a sun-faded outline of what appeared to have been made from some kind of fishing harpoon or deep-sea spear. "What used to be here?"

Ayala came to his side and pointed to a display hook loosely hanging from the sheetrock, along with unswept dust from the space on the floor directly below.

"No idea. Never really noticed. I'm not much into art," Brad replied, and swallowed hard.

"I see. And how's the quality of these cameras around the property?" Sutton pointed his pen up.

Brad shrugged again. "How should I know? Nothing's ever happened around here."

"Until now." Sutton looked at Ayala. "Put in a request with Facilities for the CCTV footage."

Beads of sweat started forming on Brad's forehead. He wiped his brow with the back of his hand and glanced outside the window again. "Uh, I think I'm going to be sick," he said, and covered his mouth. He jumped up, ran out the door and into the men's locker room. Two uniforms followed him inside.

Sutton sighed, stated the time aloud, and hit stop on the recording. He closed his notebook. "This could take a while." Not only was he referring to the wait time on Brad, but the case itself. He had never handled a murder case without his former partner.

FRIDAY, NOVEMBER 16

Happy Birthday, Norah.

Tierney tiptoed down the hallway, avoiding the creaky floorboards with precision on her way to the kitchen. She filled her travel mug from the carafe Sean had left on warm before starting his 5:00 a.m. call with the East Coast team, and stood for a moment to savor a sip of black magic. Norah would've loved the blend, too. Tierney raised the mug in a heavenly toast.

Slipping into her flip-flops near the front door, she swung the faded swim bag over her shoulder and headed outside into the dawn air. Success. She'd made it without waking Finn.

Tierney zipped up her fleece-lined parka and continued down the steps, following the paved path towards the *Daily Gazette* near the edge of the driveway. The paper was quaint, jammed with high school football scores, articles about new local businesses, recipes, and a police blotter section recounting incidents of mysteriously-tipped garbage bins, driving violations, and illegally picked fruit from trees on properties. She always skimmed it in her warm car before driving to the public pool.

The squirrels were up and out early as well this morning, chattering loudly and playing chase across their expansive, lush lawn. A bit too lush, she worried, now that the drought dictated water-saving measures. She'd never been concerned about a drought before.

As she neared the paper, a blinding circular light bounced around the corner, making its way towards her in the cul-de-sac.

She squinted and registered four brown and white dog paws pattering against the sidewalk. *Snickers.* Mildred was out earlier than usual for her neighborhood watch.

"You aren't going to the pool, are you?" Mildred dimmed the headlamp wrapped around her orange Clemson beanie.

"Same as every morning. Why?" Tierney reached down for the paper and hoped to make the conversation quick. The early lap swim was her sacred time, an hour round-trip that cleared away the cobwebs and helped prepare for the day—especially today. Swims made her a better mom. That's what she had time for now, not catching up with Mildred. Plus, her toes were chilly; she should be driving away by now with the heater on high.

Mildred scoffed. "What would you all do around here without me?" She flung her leash-free arm in an outward direction, referencing her fiefdom.

"Pardon? I'm still waking up, apparently."

"Well, you won't be swimming today. Pool's closed." She tapped the paper in Tierney's hand. "I'll bet that head lifeguard is somehow involved. My friend who takes water fitness always said he ran with a bad crowd."

Confused, Tierney asked, "You mean Brad?"

"Don't recall the name. And the paper doesn't offer much detail," she tsk-tsked. "But let me know what the scuttlebutt is at school drop-off this morning."

Tierney watched as the empty-nester turned on her heels and crossed over to her house.

"Baby needs his breakfast, don't you sugar?" Mildred cooed, patting Snickers's side.

Tierney walked back to the front porch where the light was better. She slid off the rubber band around the newspaper and stopped abruptly at the sight of the headline:

Lifeguard Found Dead at Schick Pool

Her breath caught. *Dead? Which lifeguard? Who was working yesterday? Think, Think.* Her lap swims bubbled together in her head.

She read the article quickly, trying to make sense of it all. Beyond a death due to "suspicious circumstances" and the pool being closed, there wasn't much—no name of the victim, no leads. The reporter must've learned of the incident close to deadline.

The idea of a murderer on the loose in this idyllic community was unbelievable. She had seen her share of murders in Ireland—but thought all of that was behind her. And of all days for this to be happening.

Tierney shut her eyes and inhaled deeply through her nose. The French roast now tasted bitter in the back of her throat as it threatened to reverse course with each acidic stomach churn. After her best attempt at a slow exhale, she directed her eyes to the handle a few inches from reach. Her hand managed to grab hold and she clumsily pushed open the door, causing it to clank against the stopper. She needed Sean but he was still on his call behind the office door.

The sound of Finn's sheets rustled as he began to stir.

She leaned back against the closed front door, hand gripped around her watchband, and slid down to the floor.

Pull it together. Just breathe.

Tierney counted her breaths for a minute until she reduced the frequency. Glancing at the *Daily Gazette* on the hardwood floor where she'd dropped it, her thoughts pivoted. Was Finn ever unsafe at the pool? No, he was never out of her sight. He loved the pool, but how would she share the lifeguard news with him? *Was it one he'd met over summer? Riley, his favorite? How could a murder happen in this peaceful town? Is someone still on the loose with intent to kill?* Her stomach lurched with each passing question.

She heard Finn enter the bathroom, so steeled herself and bypassed the door to find her game face. To pretend once again in her life that nothing was out of the ordinary when things couldn't be further from ordinary.

Tierney wanted to call BB for advice but knew her friend's early routine—already preparing for a group session. Regardless, Finn would soon realize she was at home instead of the pool, so she'd have to go it alone. He knew to play with his tractors and dump trucks in the family room whenever he rose before she'd returned from the pool, and not interrupt Sean unless the house was burning down, so she still had time to think.

Tierney remembered how she'd prefer to hear bad things from her dad first about happenings in their community so she wasn't blindsided at school, even as a youngster. Yes, that was it—she'd simply share the facts she knew, which weren't many, and get Finn to class. Then determine what to do next.

Tierney waited for waffles to be on Finn's plate, along with an extra dousing of maple syrup, before starting in.

"Do you think it could be Riley?" he asked.

"The paper didn't give a name, bud. Sorry I don't know more. But I'll let you know what I know when I know it."

He nodded and took another bite. Overall, Finn seemed surprised but okay with the news. Children were so resilient. But she still wanted to talk to BB, to make sure she got the communication as right as possible after he'd spent a day with other kids—marinating in each other's thoughts and questions. Death could be so scarring.

Finn had experienced the loss of something before—his pre-school's Guinea pig, which he'd handled okay. But murder was a different beast. She didn't want to sound too knowledgeable about the topic, though. She'd never talked with Finn about her Squad job.

After muddling through her own breakfast, Tierney went into the garage to leave a message for BB while Finn got dressed in the clean uniform she'd set out on his bed.

"It's me," Tierney spoke quietly to BB's voicemail. "Sorry, I know you're swamped, but you're not going to believe this. There's been a death in town, actually a murder. And on Norah's birthday of all days. I'm concerned it could be a lifeguard Finn knows. Would love your advice on how to talk with him? Murder, we know, being my least favorite subject, and I don't want to transfer my worries onto him. Anyway, if you can, please call or text before he gets home with more questions? Thanks."

Sean was still on his call by the time they needed to leave for school, but Tierney left him a sticky note on top of the newspaper at his place setting. She couldn't interrupt his flow today, even with a text. His biggest client meeting yet was scheduled later that afternoon with a judge in San Francisco.

On the drive to school, Tierney glanced a few times at Finn in the rear-view mirror for signs of distress, but he was acting normal and crashing Hot Wheels together midair. Tierney could see the school looked off, though, as she approached the main intersection. Parents and their kids were walking haphazardly across the street to reach campus. There was no Josh to be found, and traffic was backing up. *Where was he? Hopefully being questioned by police.* She had seen him in front of the pool lobby last night.

Some parents and au pairs were holding the newspaper. Others were showing it to those who possibly hadn't yet seen, heard, or fully processed the news. Some parents were crying. Tierney doubted many had ever experienced such a thing in their community. It never gets easier, she wanted to tell them.

Tierney and Finn reached the kindergarten wing. She spotted Laura, as well as Regina with both Derek and Max, but no sign of Mara.

"Stuff like this never happens in Park View," Laura said softly. "I couldn't sleep after seeing the late-night news."

"Sean and I went to bed early. I just found out this morning from the paper."

Mrs. Ferber opened her classroom door and the kids filtered inside. Tierney hugged Finn before he entered. *He'll be safe in class.* She looked around campus and saw that Laura had walked off to a group of gathered parents continuing their loud, speculative conversation about potential murder victims; a few lifeguards had apparently babysat for families on the side. Tierney wasn't in a chatty mood nor ready to return home. She also wouldn't have the pool as an outlet, and not for some time. Her shoulders slumped.

She returned to Betty and flipped through the stash of Celtic music CDs she kept in the door's side pocket. She decided on *Celtic Symphony*, which always took her to a happier place—that first time meeting her dad's big Irish Catholic family in Galway and baking with Grandma Molly at the family cottage. She hit play.

Her thoughts whooshed back to elementary school when her family of six had flown from New York to Ireland for a two-week extended family reunion at Christmastime. Tierney knew it would warm Molly's heart to see her listening to it now, even if it was while driving to a crime scene. Tierney needed to see Schick Pool with her own eyes.

She parallel parked along the street next to the swim facility and turned off the ignition. Her pool really was closed off. Police cruisers and news crews thronged the lot, but not as many as she was used to seeing in Dublin. Park View's team was obviously smaller, but should be savvy enough to engage other jurisdictions for help. And she hoped she wasn't the only one to notice Bell's car was gone. Tierney had never not seen it there. *Bell must've witnessed something.*

It was a chaotic scene as she watched two men in forensics attire slowly traipsing through the flourishing jasmine. What had been a fragrant greeting on her family's first visit to the pool could now be housing evidence.

Community members had begun leaving flowers and memorial candles in front of the neon yellow *Crime Scene Do Not Cross* tape, and loitered around the neighboring park. Many were blatantly gawking or out for an ill-timed stroll. She felt the urge to hop out and interview them, to assist staff with the investigation. To tell onlookers to take some steps back. But she wasn't in the right frame of mind nor with clearance to do so.

A few of the pregnant ladies were near the playground, including one she hadn't seen in a while no longer looking pregnant and cooing into a stroller.

An elderly man with a deep tan rattled by on a bike. Plastic garbage bags hung from both sides, and a wire basket behind his seat was partially filled with empty cans and bottles for recycling. He slowed near one of the trash cans, but continued past at the flurry of officers nearby.

Tierney also noticed the Daisy Caps slowly walking their chihuahua, pausing by the jasmine at the park's entrance to let their pup lift his leg before crossing the street and into the neighboring apartment complex. Tierney recalled how thankful her mom had been for their favorite places to be within walking distance from home once Dad retired. But now the elderly swimmers were without a favorite outlet, like her. The community pool in the nearest town was closed for restructuring.

Tierney's body deflated like a punctured pool float. She grew more exhausted at the sight of the crime scene. It had been a while since she had driven by one; Norah's had been the last. Back then, there had been hundreds of flowers, candles, cards, stuffed animals and . . . She hadn't been able to get out of her car back then either. What she needed was a nap before dozing off in the car. Anxiety was exhausting. She turned on the Subaru and headed home.

* * *

Detective Sutton yawned and returned his coffee mug to the worn leather coaster on his desk, covering the embossed "25 Years on the Force" imprint. Over half of his twenty-eight-year career had been spent in this hoity-toity town.

He was still processing the details Brad had shared after sobering up, and hit play on the recording again.

BRAD: Here's the deal. Tatyana came to the US to be an au pair and we dated for a while. Things didn't work out with her host family and I eventually offered her a job during the evening lap session. On the down-low.

SUTTON: Okay, so it's Tatyana. Last name?

BRAD: Her last name? Umm . . .

Sound of Ayala scoffing

SUTTON: You said you two were dating?

BRAD: Maltov, maybe?

SUTTON: So, we just have Tatyana. Did you ever notice any scarring on her hands?

BRAD: What scarring? I never did anything to hurt her!

SUTTON: Settle down. Tell me more about this host family and why things didn't work out.

BRAD: No clue. She never wanted to talk about it. And she'd never let me pick her up from there. Said it wasn't professional, so we'd meet at my place.

SUTTON: How did you two first meet?

BRAD: At Bob's Bar. It was one of her hangouts.

SUTTON: So, her au pair job was ending. And the lifeguarding job was enough income for her after she was officially let go?

BRAD: The lifeguarding came later. She first got a gig with some Russian math tutoring company, so she was making bills that way once she learned the agency would be unable to re-match her with another family.

SUTTON: I see. And she was living with you?

BRAD: For a while.

SUTTON: But she wasn't living with you at the time of her death?

BRAD: We kinda broke up a few weeks ago.

SUTTON: Did she leave any belongings at your place?

BRAD: No. But she didn't have much to begin with. Sold most of her stuff on Craigslist after her au pair job. Everything fit in a big duffle, now that I think of it. Had it on the day she moved out and in with someone else.

SUTTON: And who was that?

BRAD: This guy from, well, I, I'm actually not sure.

Sutton rewound the recording to that last remark, noting Brad's hesitation at sharing a name.

BRAD: Can I go now? I need something to eat. And unless you're gonna arrest me for incomplete employment records, I think you have to let me go?

SUTTON: Fine. We know where to find you. But don't go far. And maybe toss in a shower while you're at it.

Sutton drained his coffee mug and leaned back in his chair.

"Just made a new pot if you want to beat everyone to it," said Joelle, his favorite dispatcher, as she passed through the bullpen.

He smiled and tipped his head towards her. The station had only two dispatchers. Sutton didn't know the other one well; that one had young kids and was always calling in sick.

The station, with its utilitarian carpet, drop-tile ceiling, and beige walls, felt electric this morning. Fellow officers in-the-know were sharing what they'd seen at the crime scene with any colleague who hadn't yet heard. The Records Supervisor was intrigued with the minutiae.

Just yesterday, Sutton was wondering what was keeping him in Park View. Irene had moved on. And his new partner would be arriving in a few hours. He had zero desire to train some wannabe detective in his late twenties, yet here he was.

"I've called a few au pair placement agencies so far, like you asked, but nothing yet on who the victim could be," Ayala said, and sat on the corner of Sutton's desk.

"Get your ass off my desk."

Ayala jumped to a standing position. "Uh, so, I'll keep at it and let you know."

"You do that."

Ayala slurped his soda.

"Can't you drink coffee like a normal cop?" Sutton said, and turned away. He picked up the list of lap swimmers and lifeguards who had signed in at the pool last night and flipped through the pages. There were a lot. He wanted to start reaching people before the upcoming weekend made that more challenging.

* * *

"Norah!" Tierney jolted awake from her nap into a seated position, the Embassy night never more vivid. Her heart was pounding, and it took a few minutes to collect herself while she remained motionless on the bed, clenching her pillow. When she finally reached over to check her cell, she saw she had missed a text from Gem about the murder, a text from Sean about the newspaper article, and a returned call from BB. Tierney pulled the phone to her ear and hit play.

"Hey, so sorry to hear the news."

BB's voice wrapped around Tierney like a hug.

"Horrible that a murder has hit this close to home. I can talk after nine tonight if that's not too late? Swamped with the group now and then individual appointments. You know the drill. Call back if you need me and I'll pick up. But continue to answer all of Finn's questions truthfully and make him feel safe, that nothing is being hidden from him. That school is keeping him safe, and his friends. He is safe at home with his family, and that the local police are on it. And most importantly? He has a badass for a mother. Let's try not to forget that part."

Badass? Too long ago. But she would try her best to avoid calling back. She'd already imposed on BB enough over the years.

It was still two hours before pick-up. She texted BB, saying she was fine for now, then called both Gem and Sean to discuss the lifeguard's death in private before Finn was home.

Tierney returned her cell to its charger and stared down at her hands. She needed her pool. She couldn't recall the last time she hadn't had a day of swimming. Everything ached.

She flipped on the bathroom light and blasted the tub faucet. She stepped out of her clothes and into the rising water, closing her eyes as she sunk in. She tipped her sore shoulder deeper, just as the Squad's physical therapist had demonstrated eight years ago at the Dublin Aquatic Center.

Tierney recalled how that first thirty-minute session, part of her post-surgery rotator cuff rehabilitation, had gotten her out of her flat—something she hadn't done since Norah's funeral. By then, though, she had grown increasingly frustrated at being unable to fully use her right arm, so did her best to follow along. And it had been a relief to feel weightless for a while.

By her third PT session, she had begun to feel the positive effects while away from the pool, with less pain when helping BB make meals, and the desire to add in some baking projects while BB was at work. She had even asked the physical therapist if it would be okay for her to practice in the pool on her own in between sessions—a resounding yes. He'd ultimately recommended she try easy laps once the pain lessened, something she'd never done before, and build a practice.

It had been months since Tierney thought of doing the routine, but how that physical therapist had been right about the value of lap swimming. She had swum her way though many guilt-stricken days in that Dublin pool, and into her final decision to move on from the Squad and apply to the baking academy.

Tierney's logical brain knew she was safe at home now, but her racing thoughts and heart, still beating loudly and with great force, indicated otherwise. Knowing she couldn't stay in the tub all day, though, she toweled off. The hum of the hairdryer was soothing, but hair dried fast. She had no choice but to dress and face the rest of the day—a day Norah had planned to announce her retirement from the Squad, keeping a promise to her husband for a calmer future, and step aside for Tierney to lead. *Hadn't that plan gone well.*

—

While slicing carrots and celery for dinner's minestrone soup, Tierney recognized the Five O'Clock News theme music from the TV she'd left on in the other room. She tossed the veggies into the pot, turned the knob to simmer, and sat on the couch as the headlines began—the lead story being the Schick Pool investigation. The in-studio broadcast cut to a live press conference on City Hall steps. She watched as the Park View Police Chief took the podium with the mayor at his side.

The mayor stood tall, while the chief struggled to close the middle button on his dress coat. Tierney wondered if the latter had ever worked outside of Park View.

The chief cleared his throat and began, stating he would only be sharing basic information, and would be taking no questions, as not to compromise the investigation.

Great. They have nothing.

"A lifeguard's body was found on the property of Schick Pool yesterday after swim hours by the evening janitorial crew," he continued. "The cause of death is currently under investigation by the County's Office of the Medical Examiner-Coroner, but we have ruled this case a homicide. The pool has been closed off until further notice, as the crime scene is processed."

Tierney's heart sank. She couldn't believe tragedy had followed her to Park View. She thought she was away from this sort of thing, but here it was again, and at her favorite place. Louie jumped up on the couch and began a batch of biscuits in her lap.

"We will be reaching out to staff and patrons, and expect full cooperation with our investigation as we bring justice to this individual," he continued.

"Chief!" a reporter yelled. "Can you share the victim's name?"

The chief opened his mouth to reply but the mayor moved in front of him to speak into the microphone. "To reiterate, we will not be taking questions."

Strange. Why taking so long with a name?

"And should anyone have information relevant to the case," the chief said after reclaiming the microphone, "please contact the anonymous tip line we have established for such calls, which can be found here." The chief pointed to a large poster held up by a nearby staffer, which featured a phone number in bold letters. "Or on the Park View Police Department's website."

Finn came into the family room as the press conference wrapped and Tierney finished writing down the phone number on a sticky note. She'd be contacted soon so wanted to start thinking through what she'd say. She didn't know what might be helpful, but would want to share her account of the evening.

The news switched to a weather report as Finn joined her on the couch and pet a purring Louie. Tierney noticed Finn was holding his cape.

"Is Riley okay?"

The hitch in his voice tugged at her heartstrings, and she put an arm around him. "They still haven't announced a name. But hey, how about we play Hot Wheels? I have time before finishing dinner."

"Okay," he said with a little smile. "I'll set them up."

Tierney placed the sticky note on the wall by the kitchen phone. She had information to share, didn't she? She had been at the pool that evening, albeit briefly. Detectives would want her details, and she'd be ready.

After dinner, Tierney was reminded of the evening's neighborhood book club. She had intended to pass after such a crappy day, but Gem encouraged her to walk over together for "just an hour," and Sean thought it would be a healthy change of scenery. So she rallied. Maybe she'd even have a beer there to toast Norah, which was her birthday tradition.

"Black knit, or black with white flowers?" Tierney asked Louie while holding up two tops on hangers—options to accompany her dressier dark jeans. Picking something for a book club shouldn't be this hard.

Tierney typically wore her brothers' hand-me-downs when she was younger, unless there was a special occasion, which wasn't often. She never got much into fashion until college. But still, even post-graduation, joining the Squad and then catering, there was typically a uniform.

It had been a long time since she cared much about her appearance. Not even on her wedding day, with the simple white satin maxi she had chosen for the civil ceremony. The night Norah died had been the last time she had allowed herself to really care how she looked.

"Hon?"

Tierney startled out of her thoughts as she realized Sean had walked in and said something. "Sorry?"

"Gem will be here soon. Can I help you pick a top?" Sean asked.

"Oh, let's see—"

"Definitely the more fitted one. To highlight that gorgeous figure."

Tierney smiled, and was glad Sean had interrupted her before she began to spiral over thoughts of the gala. "Knit it is."

Tierney caught Sean's gaze in the mirror as she put on the top and bent down to grab her loafers. "My Irish supermodel" is what he called her, and frequently pointed out that with her porcelain-smooth skin and striking features, she should value her beauty. She paid no mind to his compliments, though, nor to his colleagues' double-takes when she'd accompany him to work functions.

"I'll finish the dishes while you get ready," Sean said.

"My sweetheart." She gave him a quick kiss for understanding her nervousness about the event. Tierney was a bit excited, though, to have something scheduled with Gem, whom she was enjoying getting to know. And someone might have something solid to share about the investigation by now.

—

The two ladies walked the three blocks to Simone's home and the book club was in full swing by the time they arrived. The event looked more like a party through the front window. Tierney's breath quickened at the number of nicely dressed women she saw, and a faint buzz began humming in her ear. But Gem's presence helped her feel grounded and she was able to shake it off.

Gem introduced Tierney to Simone first, an older mom with her youngest in high school. It was interesting to see a total range of guests fill the space—women whom Tierney profiled as being in their early thirties, all the way up to the group's founders who Gem had shared were predominantly in their fifties, including Mildred.

The book was already being discussed by a few guests before the formal discussion was set to take place over dessert. There was the camp that raved about the read, and the camp that apparently never read a word. The latter simply attended for a night out with a side of gossip.

"I felt so empowered by the end," one woman was sharing with a small group. "Like I should get out there and search for my own best self."

"It made me want to pack up and go to Tuscany for a culinary adventure," another woman said, before Gem introduced Tierney.

"Nice to meet you. Actually, do you swim at Schick?" asked a woman named Lisa. "I mean, did you?"

"I did. Loved it there. Did you go often? So tragic what's happened."

"I used to, but it grew more difficult after my third. And yes, so horrible. I saw Brad driving out of the gas station downtown this morning, though. Looking as terrible as ever, but at least we know he's not the victim."

"Oh, that is good to know. Hopefully we'll see others around town, too." Tierney was pleased to hear Brad was safe, but the datapoint made Riley's odds worse.

"Well, I've called the tip line with my thoughts," said another. "There's always this leathery guy riding his bike around the community center when I'm there with my kids—rummaging through garbage cans for bottles and such. Looks totally sketch and I wouldn't be surprised to learn he's somehow involved."

"I've called in details, too," said another woman. "My eldest used to lifeguard at the pool. He said it was a popular spot to buy weed so thinks it must've been a drug deal gone bad."

Great. The police department must be inundated with speculative calls from residents. Hope they contact me soon.

"I never noticed anything like that going on during my swims," Lisa said. "Let's just hope detectives figure it out soon and the pool reopens."

"Why don't you swim at the Redwood Club?" a woman with bobbed blonde hair and too much bronzer asked while sipping her wine. "The pool is prettier and the atmosphere isn't as scrappy. Or dangerous, for that matter."

"I don't have a membership, Gretchen. Plus, the community pool is closer—which is more important when exercise is my goal, not trying to impress anyone."

"Well, it might be worth considering now with Schick closed." Gretchen punctuated her point with a polished fingernail.

Tierney didn't know if she should respond to the snarky exchange but felt the need to support her pool. "I'm not sure what I'll do without Schick as an outlet."

"You're going to join me at yoga, that's what," Gem said, her mouth curving into a smile.

"Yoga is a great outlet, but my entire family is a bunch of fish," Lisa said. "We started heating our pool. Can't exactly do laps as I'd like, but at least it's something."

"It may be a while before you swim at Schick again. I hear they had to drain the pool—sanitation reasons." Gretchen faked heebie-jeebies. "And good luck getting it refilled anytime soon with this drought. Some of our City Council members are serious environmentalists. My sister's pool remodel permit has been held up for months."

Gretchen's words felt like a punch to the gut as Gem pulled Tierney through, literally by the arm, to the next group.

"Sorry, gals," Gem said. "Need to keep Tierney's introductions moving before book discussion."

Tierney was stunned to hear her pool may never reopen. She considered that the lifeguard's body might have been found in the water, but hoped it was somewhere else on the property. The drought factor, though? Nonetheless, she forced a sympathetic smile at Lisa as she passed. She agreed with her about swimming at the Redwood Club. Tierney and Sean had attended a client social there in August where she had observed the pool scene from the dining room's balcony. The thought of swimming at a fancy club where she couldn't relax didn't appeal, even if it meant no swimming at all.

"Hey, ladies," Laura chirped as Gem and Tierney entered the living room.

Gem had mentioned on the walk over that Laura used to live in the neighborhood before moving near Mara, so she was grandfathered into book club. "But heads-up that she's always proposing books from the self-help genre, so feel free to think of any books you'd like for our next gathering or hers could be it."

The three spoke mostly about drought-tolerant plants Laura had discovered, but when the conversation turned to her gopher problem, Tierney excused herself for that beer. She found a makeshift bar on the kitchen island and bumped into Mildred, who was wearing a bright orange silk scarf.

"Like some chardonnay?" Mildred said, handing a glass to Tierney before she could decline.

Tierney accepted the heavy pour, noting there actually were no other choices, besides Pellegrino and red wine. Disappointing. She preferred beer or distilled options to help relax. If BB had been there, she would've handed her the flask tucked inside her blazer pocket. She smiled at that thought, but then swallowed hard. If Norah had been there, she would've found a polite way to get something more to her liking from the husband's bar.

Tierney sampled her wine as Mildred ranted about the neighborhood's online community page she moderated, and how she prayed someone would post something meaty about the investigation. When Tierney had heard enough, she changed the subject by mentioning her assignment to update emergency supplies on campus.

"It's really important to have safety protocols in place," Gem said as she and another woman joined the conversation.

"Wholeheartedly agree," said the other woman. "Our schools should do a better job there. I'm Franny, by the way. Don't think we've met."

"Tierney."

"Franny is the librarian at Apricot Grove," Gem said.

Tierney hadn't yet visited the school's library, so she didn't recognize Franny. "My son loves library time. He's in Mrs. Ferber's class."

"That's nice to hear. And she's great fun. A rowdy bunch she has this year, though." Franny laughed sweetly. "Now that I think about it, I could use another helper on her class's library day. I mentioned it to Mara a while back but she must've forgotten. If you have time next week, stop by my desk and I'll show you the ropes?"

"That would be wonderful!"

Simone rang a bell so the ladies headed over to the living room where a few platters of assorted cookies, blondies, and brownies were set out on the coffee and end tables. Tierney had volunteered to bring treats but Gem recommended she not for her first event.

"Hosts can sometimes be competitive with what they serve," Gem had advised.

Simone was a known fan of Bonnie's Bakery, a cute spot on Main Street with a periwinkle-and-white-striped awning which Tierney had only driven past. She glanced at Simone's desserts and thought the bakery had done a nice job, but her own frosted cookies in the shape of books, bookmarks, and bookworms would've been a perfect addition, and free.

—

"Isn't it funny how things work out?" Tierney said on the walk home with Gem. "To think I've been passed over for so many things with Finn's class and tonight an opportunity just presented itself."

"Sorry I didn't think about Franny sooner as a resource. And that Mara, she really is a control freak to have ignored a librarian's request for extra support."

"I really don't understand it."

"Now if Franny could just have a job for Rob, all would be well."

Tierney heard the despondent shift in Gem's tone and slowed their pace. She recalled the news about Rob's layoff from a data storage company, the week after school began, but was never sure if Gem wanted to discuss it. "A job search around the holidays must be challenging, and for you to keep him upbeat."

Gem's eyes got teary. "It's been over three months now, and so tough seeing him stressed, especially with the next Apricot Grove bill due soon."

Tierney continued to listen as tears now streamed down Gem's face.

"I mean, he has a master's degree, for goodness' sake. And is the smartest guy I know. Just because management wanted to take the company in a new direction—it's all so frustrating." Gem pulled a tissue from her purse. "He can't even cash out his stock options because there's this back-dating investigation going on. Can you imagine?"

Tierney unfortunately could, from what Sean had shared about the industry-wide scandal.

"The company's stock plan is frozen while executives are being investigated. It's scary. And now he's worried they'll never pay out."

"Don't write off those assets yet. It's too early to know how they'll be handled."

"I'm doing my best to stay positive." Gem looked at Tierney. "Rob did have a third-round interview yesterday with a start-up, though."

"There you go." Tierney playfully smacked Gem's arm. "That sounds super positive."

"And I still have yoga to help calm my mind. But even that's been tough, and staying focused is supposed to be my thing."

"I know how hard it can be to concentrate while exercising, but I think it's great you're sticking with a practice," Tierney said as the two reached Gem's driveway.

"Our back-up plan is that I return to my elementary school teaching gig. My pay used to be a wash with childcare costs, but the kids are older now, and at least we'd have insurance."

"It's nice to have that in your back pocket. But Rob will most likely land something soon so you're not forced into a decision. My youngest brother is in tech and has been out of work a few times, but something always works out. And usually for the better."

"You're a wonderful listener," Gem said through sniffles. "Thanks for being my confidant." She hugged Tierney.

"My pleasure. Honestly, I just try to channel my friend BB. She's this sensational psychologist with a private practice in Seattle and has been trying to get me into a meditation practice for years. She'd think it's great you're doing yoga."

A broad smile broke across Gem's face. "Sounds like a caring friend. Are the Bs short for something?"

"Her name is Belinda, which she hates. Her family gave her a nickname at age eight while vacationing at a dude ranch. On the first try, she hit a perfect shot with a BB gun."

"Impressive. Did you grow up together?"

"She was my roommate at Trinity College. She's always telling me—"

"I thought you went to a baking academy in Ireland?"

"Yes, um, well, both actually." Tierney could feel her face flushing over her fumbled words. "Trinity is where I went for undergrad. But my criminology degree didn't turn out to be my thing, so I changed gears quickly. Decided to explore the baking route instead."

"Wow, that would be a change. But more fun than criminology."

"Yes, although much to the initial disappointment of my police officer brother, and father, if he'd been alive." Tierney was now eager to change the subject. "But if I hadn't pivoted to baking, I never would've met Sean, or moved here and met you."

"Yay for pivots."

"Well, I should go. I'll keep you posted on the Franny thing, and best wishes to Rob." Tierney gave Gem a parting hug and headed up her driveway. She registered the dull ache in her chest from talking about criminology. She was usually guarded about sharing her first career path; it must've been the wine. She could handle her whiskey and beer, but wine was a newer thing, and one she should get a handle on to remain in control.

Finn would already be in bed so she turned the key with care, but her evening wasn't over. She went inside to find Sean—to have that proper toast for Norah, and reveal that she finally had a volunteer role with Finn's class. A positive thing to mark a difficult day.

Sutton and Ayala were working around the clock, but they were going on day two and had barely scratched the surface. To say Sutton disliked weekends was an understatement; they always impeded progress on cases. And this wasn't like that murder case in town a few years back. He and Irene had cracked that one wide open in two days. Well, Irene had. She'd sensed something was off about the husband's story that his wife had fallen down the basement stairs. *But isn't it always the significant other?*

Sutton finally succumbed to Ayala's requests to assist, engaged his new partner with the sign-in sheets and speaking to witnesses, and the two had made a dent. But what could they really get done on days when people weren't as accessible? The lull was getting to him, and the "helpful details" being called in by concerned citizens, predominantly busybody moms from local schools, were muddying the waters.

While waiting for his phone to ring with something, callbacks, anything of value, he lowered his readers, slouched over his office keyboard, and scrolled through recent Park View happenings. He registered a trend—a few drug-related incidents and sightings. One involved a history teacher at the high school reported by students as being "out of it" during class. The guy was suspended without pay after found to be high on cocaine—giving new meaning to the "High" in Park View High School. *This perfect little town looks less perfect each day.*

He leaned back in his chair and his thoughts went to an open case he was privy to, being managed by the DEA. A bike messenger hit by a car a few months ago right in front of the Park View Community Center, and still in a coma. "A brick of cocaine found in his possession," which they've been able to keep from the press. Having an officer stationed outside his hospital room door 24/7 since September was getting expensive, though, and gave the chief one more thing to be pissed about.

Sutton used to complain about his short case stack of uninspiring stuff. A multi-city rash of car break-ins, a jewelry store robbery downtown, a restaurant fire under investigation by the insurance company—but his arson inspector colleague had gotten that one. *Lucky guy.* Or so he had thought. He had a murder investigation to focus on now, and he wasn't going to blow it.

* * *

Tierney's morning schedule was highlighted by Finn's last soccer game of the season. Sean would have to miss it in order to meet a work deadline, though, so she'd have to go it alone.

Finn hopped out of the car and Tierney helped tuck in his Pythons jersey.

"Ready for the game?"

"I've been ready my whole life." Finn bounded off at the sight of his teammates gathering around the coach to start warm-up drills.

Tierney smiled at his remark and energy. He was carrying himself just as Ryan had two weekends ago when they watched his Aztecs team play against Cal and Stanford during their Bay Area games. Such an impressive striker her nephew was for a freshman. Finn loved soccer and his new friends, too. Although Finn was the smallest male player on the team, he was fast and had "such power," as Sean frequently boasted.

The group of parents at the public elementary school's field was sparser than usual, but it was their earliest game yet, and definitely a busier time of year. Plus, there was the team's end-of-season party scheduled for later that afternoon at a park, so perhaps some decided to attend it instead?

Tierney approached a few parents who had set up chairs near the center of the field, and spread out her blanket on the grass nearby, placing it a careful distance from the freshly painted field lines. She plopped down and pulled out her coffee mug along with the day's *Daily Gazette*. She looked around the field and found it bizarre to be one of the only moms. And it wasn't because the others all held full-time jobs and were playing catch up from a busy work week. The Junior League philanthropy organization was the alleged draw. *To each her own.* Tierney felt lucky to be able to show up for Finn.

Tierney unfolded the newspaper and the front-page article was about the investigation. It included a photo of the case's lead detective, a fiftyish man named Howard Sutton, who shared that the city was actively pursuing all leads. *Why haven't I received a call?* She skimmed through, more nothing, when cheerful hollering from the field drew her attention.

Tierney spotted Finn passing the ball with Max, Mara's son. She still didn't understand how the boy was able to join their team mid-season from another. Rumor had it that Mara requested a transfer due to coaching conflicts, whatever that meant in kindergarten. But as for Max's family this morning, it was just Natalia, their au pair from Poland, and Craig, who was watching the game from under an oak tree with some dads. Was Mara really so busy to miss her only child's last game? The Junior League's requirement couldn't be that much of a time suck; it wasn't for Gem. Tierney had never seen Mara at a game.

The Pythons coach had introduced himself and his rambunctious twin boys at the September parent meeting. He was an artist with a deep love of soccer from his Italian roots. Colorful paint remnants could always be seen under his fingernails and speckled in his dark brown hair. With Justine, a Biotech executive, as his wife, he was seemingly able to pursue his own interests. Their family was one she knew of with a live-in nanny.

Tierney was reminded of a conversation she overheard with Justine at Back to School Night about a presentation she had recently given in Munich. How passionately she had spoken of her job. Tierney used to feel that way about her career. To know the work she did kept people safe. She was envious of someone whose professional path had been the right choice. The right fit. Where the work you did mattered but nothing bad happened. Helping people was what she missed most about her Squad work.

During halftime, she tossed the newspaper in her bag and headed to the restroom while the kids enjoyed sliced oranges. The first girls' bathroom she checked was locked. Availability was always unpredictable on weekends but Tierney lucked out on her second attempt. A mom wearing the opposing Grizzly team's colors exited and the two exchanged smiles. Tierney noticed the woman must've sat too close to the field lines based on the white powder smudge on her jeans.

Tierney hung up her purse on the hook in the only working stall and noticed powder residue on top of the toilet paper holder. Intuitively, she touched her fingertip to the substance and raised it to her nose.

"Oh my God," she whispered. The metallic smell she'd know anywhere. *Coke on an elementary school campus? And at nine in the morning?* She dug for a tissue in her purse and cleared away the cocaine residue, flushing it to avoid any potential transfer to children. She quickly peed, washed her hands, and exited.

Tierney spotted the woman making her way back to the opposing team's side. Tierney didn't recognize her. No surprise; she barely knew parents on Finn's team. She noted the time and would get her license plate number after the game to call the police department's non-emergency line. Although, she'd first call the hotline with her details about the investigation. She wasn't going to wait any longer for them to reach out.

The second half started and Finn was first to dribble towards the goal. "Go Finn!" Tierney moved with him down field, but his kick was blocked by the goalie. Although this half wasn't as high scoring as the first, the Pythons won.

Tierney and Finn headed to the car and she looked for the mom in the parking lot but instead saw her walking off the field with her son. She asked Finn if he knew the boy and he shook his head no. They must live nearby because they appeared to be walking home. *Thankfully, not driving.*

Tierney enjoyed her car time with Finn. There was something about the back seat, with him talking to her hair, that invited more open conversation.

"A nice win for the last game," Tierney said. "Coach's drills are working well, and Kyle's goal at the end was exciting."

Finn drove his Matchbox Lamborghini Countach up his arm and parked it on his shoulder. "Max should've taken the first two goals instead of passing to Derek. He's a bully. Always bringing peanuts to school and waving them at Max. Asking if peanuts scare him."

"That's terrible! Next time you see something like that, please tell Mrs. Ferber." Tierney glanced in the rearview mirror for a response.

"Okay."

"Thanks, buddy. We don't want anyone getting sick." Tierney was surprised by Derek's dangerous behavior, especially after his mother's recent rant about a parent bringing in peanut butter treats to school. And what of the seemingly tight relationship between the boy's moms, Mara and Regina, as well as being neighbors? One more thing about Mara she couldn't make sense of. "As for soccer, though, you're right. Max gave him great assists. Maybe he's trying to be nice to get Derek to stop the teasing."

"Maybe. Derek bullies me, too, about being short. I'm gonna get the first goal next season and show him."

"That's the attitude. Keep practicing and you will." Tierney knew there was always a bigger story behind a bully's home life.

Tierney thought more about Derek as she set eyes on his dad, Ian, in her sideview mirror—approaching quickly in his silver Tesla Roadster prototype. He flew past going double the speed limit.

She had noticed a few of those "marketing cars" around town, but couldn't understand the appeal of driving something all electric that might run out of juice. Ian's car had a CHP 11-99 Foundation license plate frame, which was obtained via a hefty donation to support California Highway Patrol heroes. Tierney wasn't a Californian, but had heard that some wealthy types would donate to the fund with primary intent of avoiding speeding tickets via the display frame. But Ian could have law enforcement roots. Regardless, he should slow the hell down.

When they returned home, Tierney headed inside to tell Sean about the drugs but he was on a call. She went to help Finn reach a snack from a high shelf in the pantry, but he had already pulled over a chair from the breakfast table. She returned it to the set and, after seeing her son was occupied, researched the city's non-emergency dispatch center on her laptop. She jotted it down on a sticky note and placed her calls from the garage where Finn would be out of earshot.

She found it odd how the dispatcher, Joelle, who'd agreed to intake both the non-emergency and tip line details, didn't act surprised by the coke incident, nor that Tierney hadn't been called yet to discuss her evening visit at Schick. Well, nothing should surprise Tierney anymore. She couldn't help but think, though, that investigations moved more quickly in Dublin. Regardless, she returned both sticky note numbers to the wall by the kitchen phone.

The early morning activity had caught up with her so she decided to take a quick nap while Finn played Minecraft, and before she'd need to plate up the brownies they'd signed up to bring to the team party. She kicked off her sneakers and made her way down the hall. Not paying attention, she stepped on something and winced. She bent down to find a Hot Wheels patrol car. Ironically, it was one of her favorites, with the colored emergency lights on top. She returned it to Finn's toy basket and sighed; a sense of longing stirred in her core as she headed into her bedroom. She closed her eyes but, instead of dozing off, her thoughts ticked back to that afternoon in New York City so long ago.

~ ~ ~

Tierney did as her dad instructed. *Sit tight.* It wouldn't be long. She wasn't locked in, but safe. Safe within the heavy confines of steel, and behind the bullet proof partition she always found so intriguing. She could get out if she needed to, but why? The lemony scent of Clorox was exhilarating, a fresh reminder of the bad guy scene cleaned up a short time ago in the spot she now occupied. Perched on the hard plastic. Quietly observing, waiting. She could wait forever.

She was used to playing in the back seat, but this was the first time she got to ride on official business. She sat up straighter and looked outside through the car's cloudy window, watching her dad and his partner walking in stride up the tidy steps of the last brown house on the block. Bright green plants flowed out of their pots. A nice neighborhood. Nicer than hers.

Her dad and his partner, Jacob, were laughing about something. She wouldn't be laughing. She would have her hands in her pockets to absorb the sweat. But they were adults. Adults weren't scared of things. Plus, they had done this a zillion times. She had heard the stories around the dinner table for years.

That time the guy lunged at them with a samurai sword in an alley but dropped it the second he faced two guns drawn. Or when the wife came to the door with blood all over her mink coat and handed over her pearl-handled purse gun, sobbing on Jacob and getting her husband's blood all over his new uniform. Or the guy fighting with his girlfriend outside Tavern on the Green after she'd declined his marriage proposal. He shot her just as Dad and Jacob pulled up. That guy got off when the "quacks" convinced the judge he wasn't in his right mind. That was the first time she'd seen her dad really mad about work stuff.

"Domestic disturbance" is what Mary had dispatched a few minutes ago, along with the address. Tierney wondered what cookies were on her desk today. Or maybe they were brownies. That's when it dawned on her—she had the new girl at school to thank for today. A day that began with tears but ended with her being here. She didn't need that girl's party anyway. Spaghetti at Patsy's Italian Restaurant and a sleepover. What kind of friend birthday celebration was that? Food and sleep. Hers were way better. Bowling, mini golf, going to the movies. Like her three brothers' parties.

The new girl wasn't a nice girl, but she had nice friends—they were Tierney's friends. She knew them first.

"Why are twelve-year-old girls so mean?" her mom had said while hugging her in the kitchen. Tierney's disappointments were hard on her mom. She almost didn't tell her she hadn't been invited to another birthday party, but she couldn't hide the tears this time. She wasn't good at hiding her emotions. Not yet.

Her mom didn't know how to help. She hadn't been twelve in a hundred years and Tierney's brothers never experienced this stuff at school. Drama, her dad called it. Mean-spiritedness, her mom clarified. But a broken bone? Now that was something her parents could fix in a jiffy with a quick trip to the doctor. The mental stuff was a tougher beast to slay.

It was her dad who had the idea.

"Grab your sweater, Teeny. You have plans tonight, too. We're going out on the town."

She had been begging for years to go on a ride-along. Her brothers got to go whenever they asked, but she was always "too young." Until now.

A guy answered the door. Nicely dressed in a shirt with a pointy collar like her dad wore to Mass. Didn't look to have a knife, or one she could see yet. The three men were busy talking calmly outside on the landing when a side window on the second floor popped open. A tie-dyed pillowcase stuffed full flew out and landed on the shrub below. Two thin arms appeared from the window, followed by a head of tight curls, and then a boy, who pulled himself to a seated position. He perched on the window ledge, looking at the ground, calculating the distance to his pillowcase.

Tierney, wide-eyed, stared at him. Younger than her, like fourth grade? She glanced over to her dad and Jacob, now inside the foyer and speaking to the guy with a woman next to him—long, curly hair. The couple was smiling.

Tierney turned back to the boy who was now looking directly at her. She couldn't break the stare. She couldn't interrupt her dad while he was working. She didn't know how to use the radio and call Mary for backup. What if he jumps? Right in front of her and she did nothing.

Sit tight. She couldn't.

She pulled her eyes away and quietly opened the patrol car's door on the street side so as not to interfere with her dad's questioning. The hum of distant city noise—honking cars and wailing sirens—was a helpful distraction, along with her vast experience of stealthily-played hide and seek. She crouched behind the car and maneuvered toward the boy in the window. His eyes tracked her every move.

"What did you do?" the boy said quietly as she approached.

"Huh?" she gestured.

"What did you do to get arrested?"

"No," she said, matching his volume. "I'm on a ride-along with my dad. He's the one talking to your dad now."

"That jerk isn't my dad."

"Oh, sorry. I assumed."

"Yeah, everyone does. My real dad isn't a jerk, except when he sends me here for a month. He doesn't want to, but the judge says he has to."

"To stay with your mom?"

"Yeah, and stepdad. He hates me as much as I hate him."

Tierney noticed a red mark under his eye. A mark she'd seen on her brothers numerous times after a rough game on the field.

"You aren't going to jump, are you?"

"I've done it before. Better than going back in there."

"You could tell my dad what happened. He can help you. Arrest the guy for hitting your face."

"He'd just talk his way out of it and do it again. Or hit my mom."

"Does he do that, too?"

"Sometimes," he said, finally looking away, down at his feet. "She has bruises all over her arm. She doesn't think I know."

"If the judge knows that, he can keep him away from her. And you."

"Really, how?"

"I don't know how it works, but my dad does. You should go back inside and tell him. Let him see your face. It's evidence."

"I can't. I'll mess up her life."

"She's your mom. She loves you."

"Not always. She married him, didn't she? He's rich. She loves this house more than me."

"Well, if that's true you should be with your real dad all the time."

He continued to look down. Tears now fell from his eyes. "I just, I just, feel so sad."

Tierney sighed. She knew what being sad felt like, at school anyway. "Well, you're not alone now. I'm Tierney. What's your name?"

"Simon," he said, wiping his eyes along his sleeve.

"Nice to meet you, Simon. Please go back inside, and downstairs to see my dad before he leaves. He's the one with black hair like me." She crossed the fingers on her left hand and hoped he took her advice. And that she was saying the right thing. Her dad had never mentioned how he handled a situation like this.

No reply.

"You won't be alone. I'll watch you from the car, okay?" Tierney continued. "You can do this. Just tell him what you've told me. He can call Mary in dispatch on his radio and they'll send a nice person over to talk with you and your mom while they take your stepdad to the station."

He didn't say no, so Tierney seized another moment and picked up his pillowcase.

"Go back inside. I'll throw this up to you."

"You sure it will be okay?" he said, sniffing.

"Yes. Because if you don't do something it could be worse next time. I know it doesn't feel like it now, but you're helping your mom." She thought about her words and knew she was right.

"Okay. I'll be down in a minute."

"Great. It will take me a sec to get back in the car anyway. You don't want me to get in trouble either, right?" Tierney smiled.

"No, I don't. I'll go inside."

"Okay, I'll see you soon. Look for me."

Simon swung his legs around and hopped back inside. Tierney threw up the pillowcase. He caught it and, eyes still damp, returned her smile.

"See you soon," he said softly, and closed the window.

Tierney made her way back to the patrol car like that gazelle she saw on *Wild Kingdom* last Sunday, masterfully crossing the open field unnoticed by the distracted lioness. She re-settled inside and fixed her eyes on the front door. Prepared to exit and help Simon at any moment, she held the door handle. Her palms surprisingly weren't sweaty.

"Where is he?" she whispered. She was beginning to worry he had changed his mind when she saw him stand by his mom's side. He looked out at the patrol car and Tierney gave him a thumbs-up through the window. She watched as he started to talk with her dad, who nodded and put his hand briefly on Simon's shoulder. Simon kept talking as the stepdad became more animated with his hands. Jacob took a step toward him.

"Good, keep going Simon," Tierney whispered.

Simon reached out for his mom's hand but then pushed up her sleeve with his other, showing her skin for a brief moment until she pulled her arm tightly against her chest. The stepdad's face looked defiant now, his body agitated and hands moving in all directions as his voice grew loud enough for Tierney to hear from inside the car.

Jacob moved toward him again and the man shoved him away. The mom cowered into the house, pulling Simon closely against her. As the man became enraged, Jacob pulled out his cuffs and swung him around by the arm, pushing his face against the door frame. He cuffed his right hand behind his back and then his left as Simon and his mom looked on fearfully, both now crying.

It was up to her dad now. Tierney could see him tip his head towards the radio on his shoulder as he called for backup. He walked down the stoop while Jacob had the man under control and gathering neighbors gawked. Her dad approached the patrol car. Tierney leaned back into her seat, attempting to look as if nothing out of the ordinary was happening. He opened the passenger side door up front to grab his clipboard and called for another patrol car to transport the perp. Then he looked squarely at Tierney with pride.

"Mary in dispatch, eh?"

~ ~ ~

Tierney laid in bed, her island of safety, as the ride-along replayed in her mind. The old question remained: How could her chosen career path have been such the wrong trajectory? The Squad work had always been stressful, which she could handle up until Norah's death. She knew in her heart that she'd still be there if Norah hadn't died. But how could she have predicted any of that?

"You made the best career decision you could've with the information you had at the time," BB often reminded her. And it had been the right decision to join the Garda after graduation—their elite, fast-tracker program that her valedictorian status helped secure, which ultimately led her to remain in Ireland and join the Squad. Such an opportunity it had been. But as she looked back on her life, she wondered how she had come to this point.

What would her younger self think? She had no career now, and until recently had been at the mercy of cliquey women gatekeeping the daily routine she wanted. Maybe she should've taken her mom's advice and majored in English.

Tierney went to find Sean in the office. She could see in his expression that he registered her teetering on the edge, and he offered to take Finn to the team party.

"Happy to," he said as he hugged her. "I feel badly for missing his last game and could use some fresh air myself."

Once her boys departed, Tierney texted BB to see if they could move up their talk today while the house was quiet. She needed her friend's ear.

Five minutes later, BB replied.

Keats! So good to see a text from you instead of a patient. Give me 20 <3

Tierney smiled at the sight of her nickname. The freshman lit class where the two met, the only Irish Americans in class, seemed a lifetime ago.

She set up her laptop for the Skype on the kitchen counter and sat on a barstool. While waiting, she doodled on the latest realtor's freebie notepad sent in the mail.

The call came through and BB burst onto the screen—donning a mini red cheese wax circle attached to her nose like a clown. "Just wrapping up a snack," she said, unable to contain her signature chuckle. BB's laugh was contagious.

"Oh, how I've missed you, you goof."

BB tossed the red wax onto a plate at her desk. "You know I can't help myself when it comes to making you laugh."

"Sure this earlier time works?"

"You are the best distraction from more casework."

"Funny. Sean tells me the same thing. You're welcome."

BB pushed up her glasses on the bridge of her nose. "So, what the heck is going on? Should I assume from your demeanor that the lifeguard murder is making your PTSD worse?"

Tierney squirmed under her friend's keen eye. "The police are on it, I think. But having this murder happen is disturbing. I thought being in a safe, new town would help me further escape all those parts of my past, but everything is bubbling up again. Plus, the fiftieth birthday thing."

BB nodded. "I know you had set that date as a deadline for having your life all back on track, but it was just a goal, not an imperative. So, timing has shifted a bit?"

"It's more than a shift; it's being late again. And God, I've had eight years! All this free time now, too. I can't be with Finn on campus, I can't swim, and I've checked everything off our move-in list. A vet for Louie was the last item. And this new school? Man, it's the pits."

"Sounds like a slogan for Apricot Grove." BB chuckled. "Well, you're a public-school kid at heart, but it has been a nice place for Finn. Do you think you could somehow assert yourself?"

"You mean like just bring cookies to yet another class party I've been excluded from?"

"Great idea. A small platter of your finest? Just in case they 'didn't have enough.'" BB made quotation marks with her fingers.

"I guess I could."

"I know you could. Once they see your work, this Mara chick will want you at every school function. At minimum, do it for Finn. I can already see his sweet freckled face beaming with pride over his mom's creations."

"Maybe you're right."

"I'm rarely wrong."

"Ha. It's just so . . . not fun." Tierney sighed.

BB paused. "Yes, about that. I'm not feeling your excitement. And you do seem unusually melancholy. You know, sometimes the thing we think we want isn't what we want at all? Perhaps getting involved at the school isn't—"

"But it should be. Finn spends so much time there."

"I hear you. But perhaps doing something more meaningful to you would feel more rewarding. Have you given thought to my idea of teaching a corporate negotiation class at the community college instead of trying to break into the coven? Let's not forget that impressive skill set of yours."

"I know I could look into other things. I've thought about popping by the local bakery for project work. But I really want to be where Finn is—and give this stay-at-home mom thing a solid go."

"Understood."

"Although maybe if I ever do come to terms with . . . *Norah's* . . . her death I could share my insights with college students about the field. I mean, as they relate to business negotiation, not hostage. But until then, I'd just be showing them what a total mess of a human looks like as a result of the field."

"That would not make for a marketable syllabus. Okay, let's table the idea for now. I know the pool is closed, but how about other exercise? Still finding things to help with the anxiety?"

"Funny you should ask. I hurt my shoulder again. You know my Squad box?"

"How could I forget?"

"Right. I moved it so my nosy neighbor wouldn't see it, and I hurt my shoulder."

"Sorry, Keats. The irony—opening up old wounds literally and figuratively? Perhaps it's a sign. That you should sit down with the box and—"

"I just need a little more time."

"You will be ready one day. I have great faith. But just remember, to pass through guilt, grief, and all those uncomfortable emotions, you must confront them. Feel your feelings."

"I know, I know."

"Staying busy and pushing away your past with Norah only serves as a Band-Aid. And an eight-year-old Band-Aid gets p—"

Tierney flinched at hearing Norah's name aloud. "We don't have to talk about that now. You have enough patients. You certainly don't need another."

"You are my best friend, not my patient. Don't ever forget that."

"I know, I didn't mean it that way."

"Besides, Mosely is your guy. And he's ready to discuss Norah and that night at the embassy whenever you are. Norah would want that for you. I ran into him at a conference just last month at Harvard. It's a sign."

Tierney appreciated BB's efforts to discuss Norah, to keep her name out in the universe. But that didn't make it easier to hear. Maybe BB was right, though. With the politics of Apricot Grove's parent community, Norah's fiftieth, and not even a call back from the police station to feel as if she was contributing in some small way to her community, she had reached an all-time low. "Well, I guess I could give him a call."

BB straightened in her chair and her eyes gleamed. "Excellent. The profession has made inroads into survivor's guilt since your time in Dublin. And one bad therapy experience does not them all make. Mosely will be a great fit. I can feel it in my bones."

"I still have his number."

"Double excellent."

"It's just been hard. And I'm so tired." Tierney's head drooped forward into her hands, feeling defeated.

"Well, you've taken a huge step in agreeing to call. And soon, okay?"

Tierney nodded while still holding her head.

"Now, tell me something you're looking forward to."

Tierney thought for a moment and looked up. "Seeing the guys at Christmas. The Tahoe cabin we've rented looks amazing." The mere mention of her three brothers and their families lightened her mood.

"Sounds magnificent. I'll be enjoying the fine company of Sue's relatives."

"How is Sue?" Tierney loved hearing BB's life updates. How far her best friend had come in her relationships since college. From that teary night BB opened up to her that she had been questioning her sexuality, to finally, after graduation, coming out to her parents. Oh, how poorly that heart-wrenching experience had gone. Although they had disowned her, BB would always be family to her.

"Still the love of my life. She's been frustrated with my workload lately. And I get it. With her teaching schedule, she'd prefer I be home earlier."

"That's hard. And the holidays won't ease things up."

"How does our dream husband juggle work-life balance?"

Tierney smiled at how thoughtful Sean had been just an hour ago. "He is amazing. But work is picking up for him, too. The number of clients he's now juggling—it's a matter of time before he won't be home to join us for dinner. But we still find moments to be together."

"It must be tough being head man now. The news up here has been profiling more execs indicted for illegal stock-option backdating. And it's not isolated to high tech anymore."

"I imagine financial crime could happen in any industry that offers stock option grants."

"I've been trying to explain it to Sue. So, the problem is when CEOs or other top executives somehow set official grant dates retroactively to make them more valuable?"

"That's how Sean put it. He said there's different accounting methods and ways data can be reported. The serious problem is when the 'bad execs' grant 'in-the-money' options to both new and current employees, while backdating documents so it appears the options were at-the-money when granted, thus making them more valuable."

"Listen to you sounding so mathy."

"Funny. I think I have all that right. I just know it's gotten serious. The US Attorney's Office, the SEC, the FBI, and the IRS are all involved."

"Wouldn't want to be an invited guest at that party of four."

"Me neither. Sean said it's intimidating at times. It's the most stressful position he's ever had, but he's my rock. Nothing gets him. Lord knows I'm handful enough."

BB chuckled again. "But always remember how much we adore you."

—

"Mom, Mom, I got a hat trick at the party during our scrimmage! Coach said that's what three goals is called." Finn flew into her arms.

"Nice job, bud." Tierney gave him a bear hug.

"And I scored, too." Sean held up a six-pack of beer. "Max's dad, Craig, is a home brewer."

"That's fun," Tierney said. "Hey, Finn, why don't you wash your hands and go change. And leave your cleats in the laundry room."

He kicked off his shoes in the kitchen and ran down the hall. Sean put the beer in the fridge, tossed Finn's cleats in the laundry room, and pulled up a stool next to Tierney.

"Derek's dad is Ian, right? I think he was on something today at the park."

"What makes you say that?"

"There was a group of us watching the scrimmage and whenever he'd share something, he spoke in rapid-fire, and his pupils were dilated. I'm only saying because I've seen it before, with that new hire in the Seattle office. Remember the junior accountant we had to let go when clients reported his odd behavior? He was a mess."

"Oh, that's right." And Tierney recalled all too well what it was like to have a perp on something during a hostage situation, adding an entire level of complexity.

"Anyway, wanted to mention it after your story about the mom in the restroom."

"Weird coincidence?"

"Super weird. But also, in case Finn ever ends up having an option to carpool with Derek's family. His au pair was at the party, too, though. At least she was smart enough to drive separately, and get Derek home in one piece."

"That's good to hear. And noted. Although, I don't see much carpooling in our future. Something tells me their family and the Gillespies are like oil and water."

Sutton appreciated the lighter traffic that came with his weekend commute from San Jose, especially when he got an early start and a first crack at making the communal coffee in the break room—with double grounds. After pressing the brew button, he took a seat at his desk and had barely opened his attaché case when the sound of Ayala's voice surprised him.

He turned to see his partner finishing a conversation with a new records specialist, and take a seat at his desk across from Sutton's—laptop already up and running. Sutton wasn't sure if he was impressed, annoyed, or both.

"Morning. Au Pair Match in San Mateo finally called back and has a Tatyana on file from Moscow," Ayala said. "Her supervisor will be driving down to the morgue later this morning. If the victim is a match, her name is Tatyana Popov. Twenty-two, and would've been in the States for around nine months."

"Continue," Sutton replied, and clicked his pen.

"If it is her, the supervisor confirmed that Tatyana was let go by her original host family in April when the mom filed for divorce and moved out of the area, taking the kids to live with her parents in Chicago."

"Back in April? Was Tatyana set up with another family?" Sutton was pleased to hear progress had potentially been made, but knew not to get too excited in case it wasn't the same person.

"Au Pair Match tried to re-match her with a new family, unsuccessfully. But, get this. Her work visa was terminated months ago, and the company assumed she'd returned to Moscow as instructed during her exit interview. They'd even arranged and paid for her flight home. Plus, an au pair visa doesn't allow employment outside of the host family, so any job, lifeguard or otherwise, would've been illegal."

"Great. Let's hope she's our girl." Sutton walked out with his empty coffee mug.

* * *

Tierney had enjoyed her morning with Finn playing dump trucks on the family room floor, but BB was right—she needed more physical activity. She was going stir crazy without the pool. She knew Gem typically went to yoga on Sundays, and Sean was home, so she could steal away for an hour and give it a try. But yoga? Is that even exercise? So much time steeped in one's thoughts. *God help me.*

"What'd you think?" Gem asked jovially after class. "Love it or hate it?"

"Challenging," Tierney said. "I used to think yoga was mostly stretching, but it was a tough workout. I can already feel it in my muscles. And Marc gave me pointers while walking around so I didn't strain my shoulder. I can see why he's popular."

"Join me anytime."

They reached the cubbies where Laura was leaning down to collect her belongings. As she shoved her yoga mat into an over-loaded bag, out fell a book, *Holiday Survival 101.*

Gem slipped it back into Laura's bag. "Isn't that the one you recommended as our next book club pick?" Gem asked.

"It is." Laura said. "Did you vote for it on Simone's clipboard?"

"I haven't voted yet. But I've heard it's an insightful read."

"I'm almost through it a second time," Laura continued. "You're welcome to borrow it when I'm done. I get so stressed around the holidays."

"Me, too. My parents will be arriving soon from India and I still have so much to do." Gem returned Laura's smile and turned to Tierney. "Hey, before we go, I need to reload my membership card."

"Okay. Think I'll just pay as I go until I really know what's going on with my shoulder," Tierney replied.

"I'll let the front desk know."

Tierney nodded. "I'm going to visit the restroom."

"Down there to the left," Gem said over her shoulder as she and Laura walked off.

Tierney approached the single restroom but it was occupied. While waiting, she was distracted by Regina and the snarky blonde-bobbed woman from book club—Gretchen something. They were by the side wall whispering loudly. Something about Ian staying late at work more frequently.

Regina sat down to put on her shoes and Gretchen walked over to the purified water cooler near the restroom.

"Jennie just went in," Gretchen said to Tierney. "She's preggers so will be a while. Usually takes our class but is trying out the less intense one today. She's far along."

"No worries. I don't mind waiting."

"I saw you arrive with Gem. Your kids go to Apricot Grove?" She brought the water cup to her lips.

"Yes, my son does. I'm Tierney."

"Gretchen. I remember you from book club." She smiled, showing a lipstick smudge on her front incisor. "My niece is in Ms. Stuart's kindergarten class. I occasionally help my sister with pick-up. I think I've seen you dropping off in the other kindergarten room?"

"Yes, Finn adores Mrs. Ferber."

"Not many parents say that. Everyone wants Ms. Stuart. She's so young and energetic, filled with great ideas and innovative programs. A recent USC grad, too. Come to think of it, I don't know where Mrs. Ferber went to college."

Tierney was taken aback by the negative comments after the positive class they had just completed. "Well, Finn is excited to go to school each morning, so no complaints here." Tierney glanced towards the front desk to see if Gem would be throwing her a lifeline anytime soon.

"Enjoying your new home?"

"Very much, especially with Gem and Rob next door. We're renting for now. Wanted to make sure things were a good fit before buying our forever home, but we couldn't be happier with the neighborhood."

"What made you pick Silicon Valley?"

"My husband was transferred here to run his company's San Francisco office, but we wanted a house in the suburbs."

"Makes sense. Is he in VC?"

"No, although venture capital is big around here. He works for Camp & Giffin in the financial district."

"Isn't that the accounting firm all the high tech companies are hiring to help with litigation? The whole options backdating scandal?"

"I wouldn't say all of them, but yes, they—"

"Your husband works for Camp & Giffin?" Regina asked with a scowl upon joining the line.

"Yes, heard of them?" Tierney wondered why the look.

"No," Regina responded coolly. "Just joining the conversation."

The bathroom door opened to save Tierney from further interaction with the intense women, but as she turned, her breath skipped.

"It's about time, Missy," Gretchen said to Jennie while pointing to the small line that had formed. Gretchen's remark had been enough to divert Jennie's eyes away from Tierney's startled expression.

Jennie looked like Norah—vibrant blue eyes, red hair, and a broad smile that could warm a soul. Jennie laughed at Gretchen's remark while holding the door open for Tierney, who had composed herself—on the outside—to pass.

"Sorry for being slow, ladies," Jennie said as Tierney entered the bathroom.

Tierney quickly shut the flimsy door. Her close-fitting yoga top was the only thing holding her thudding heart in place. She steadied herself against the bathroom sink and tried to slow her breathing as outside chatter turned to the town's investigation. She splashed cold water on her face and looked up in the mirror. *For God's sake, Tierney.*

After what felt like an eternity, but only two minutes per the time, she couldn't hold up the restroom any longer. She peed as fast as she could and readied her exit.

"All yours," Tierney said to Regina, next in line, in her best casual voice.

"Jennie, have you met Tierney?" Gretchen said, and Tierney stopped in place.

"Not yet." Jennie politely extended her hand. "My kids go to Johnson Academy across town."

"Oh, nice," Tierney said, and they shook hands.

"Actually, speaking of Johnson," Jennie said, "a mom from school is saving a spot for me. I'd better claim it before I end up shoved in the corner." She began waddling her way over to the instruction room. "Wish me luck, ladies," she said. "I may be back at Marc's next week."

Tierney was thankful her interaction with Jennie had been brief.

"I really should throw her a baby shower," Regina said.

"I love baby showers," Gretchen crooned.

Feeling the conversation didn't involve her, Tierney wanted to go find Gem, but she could see her neighbor through the front glass door now talking on her cell.

"Me, too." Regina continued and turned her back to Tierney. "Jennie mentioned a few weeks ago that Mara had offered to throw one. I guess since Jennie had thrown one for Max? They've known each other since Junior League. Anyway, Mara hasn't mentioned any plans so I think I'll just jump in."

Tierney took Regina's blatant cue and walked over to the water cooler.

Regina finally entered the restroom, and Gretchen grew distracted by a new rack of clothing the receptionist was rolling into the boutique area. Off she went, just as Gem returned inside.

"Sorry about that," Gem said as she reached Tierney. "That was Rob on the phone. He just got an offer for a job he interviewed for weeks ago! He's friends with the recruiter and she told him to expect a written letter first thing tomorrow."

"How nice of her to call on a weekend. I'm so happy for you guys." Tierney embraced Gem and the two proceeded to the parking lot.

"We're thrilled. Next time you and I should drive together so we can chat more after class."

"Sounds good. Actually, any chance you guys are free tonight after dinner to pop over for a quick toast? Sean and I would love to celebrate."

"How sweet. We'd love that."

"Great. And thanks again for my guest pass."

"Anytime. What a perfect day for you to have been here with me—when Rob gets an offer. You're my lucky charm."

"Not sure about that. It's more the other way around."

"Don't be silly. Actually, I'm going to the mall this afternoon and could use some more luck in finding a dress for my niece's wedding. Wanna come?" asked Gem as they reached their cars.

"Oh, I'm not—" Tierney's knee-jerk response was tempered by BB's standing advice to be more open with female friends. "I mean, sure. I could use a new date night outfit."

"Fab. Makeovers, too? You really should highlight those beautiful green eyes."

Tierney smiled, wondering what she had just gotten herself into. But she'd have more hang out time with Gem, which she was enjoying. Besides, she couldn't remember the last time she bought new clothes. And she hadn't worn a full face of makeup in . . . well . . . eight years.

"I'll pick you up in an hour," Gem said.

Tierney's thoughts returned to Jennie on the drive home. A Norah lookalike. *Unbelievable.*

Tierney placed her yoga bag and mat on the floor near her untouched swim gear in the laundry room. She missed her swim lane. Yoga had been a nice distraction, until it wasn't. But at least it had been something to do. And so was shopping with Gem.

———

Gem planned what turned out to be a full afternoon at the mall. They started with Gem's dress for the wedding, but then the focus turned to Tierney.

"We have to get you out of that uniform and into something new."

Tierney looked down at her jeans and black tee. Maybe she did wear the same thing a lot.

They headed to Gem's favorite shop for a stylish night-on-the-town outfit. Tierney was open to recommendations but passed on the tank dresses. She wasn't ready to let Gem see her shoulder scars.

"You and that great figure. You are the easiest friend to shop for." Gem and the salesgirl assisted with the selection of a few new tops, a sweater, slacks, and a dress. Tierney blushed her way through all of the attention. Shopping was not her realm of expertise, but it reminded her of the outings she and Norah had enjoyed along Grafton Street.

After lunch, they went to Nordstrom for makeovers, although Tierney had just agreed to mascara and a tinted sunscreen. On their way to another boutique for shoes, they came upon the mall's hair salon.

"Let's just see if they have availability." Gem opened the salon's door, and Tierney prayed they were booked. She waited nervously outside while checking for any texts from Sean, but knew as soon as Gem returned with a radiant smile that her friend had scored.

"You did tell me last month you were looking for a new salon," Gem said coyly. "Just a little trim with a few layers for movement?" Gem shook her dark chocolate-brown hair for effect, and coerced Tierney and her long, straight hair inside.

—

It was dark by the time the women returned home.

"Wowza! Look at my hot wife." Sean beamed at the sight of Tierney and twirled her around the kitchen. "And love the hair."

"Oh, yes, that." She tucked some stray strands behind her ear. "It hadn't been on the agenda, but Gem is persuasive. I guess I like the layers."

Tierney unpacked her purchases after dinner, laying everything out on the bed. She hadn't noticed that her makeup purchase included a free lipstick. Tierney never used to be superstitious about wearing lipstick, but for years, Chapstick had been the closest thing she used. She tossed the sample in her vanity's bottom drawer.

All in all, Tierney had a lovely day. She felt pampered and excited for her upcoming date night, play, or whatever it would be with Sean. But still, she couldn't help but feel guilty for indulging herself.

Tierney and Sean hadn't hung out with Rob and Gem together since Halloween—for their Park View tradition of pulling a wagon full of adult beverages and red Solo cups from house to house while socializing among parents. It had been an opportunity to see their new neighborhood, and the full-size candy bars every house seemed to dole out, come alive for an evening.

In preparation for tonight's gathering, Tierney sliced up the extra batch of brownies she'd baked along with the soccer teams'. Sean opened a bottle of wine and prepared a bucket of assorted beers, and root beer for Finn and Gem's son who would be joining, too, for a promised hour of Xbox.

"Don't mind the clutter," Tierney said to her neighbors. "Still getting settled from the move."

"I was actually eyeing the brownies. They're gorgeous," Gem said, and helped the boys to a treat before they sped off to the family room.

"They're scrumptious, too," Sean said, accepting a brownie for himself. "Tierney and I actually met over a dessert platter."

"Do tell," Gem said, and took a bite.

"It was in Dublin," Tierney said. "I was working one of the Baking Academy's catering gigs for Sean's big-wig employer, Arthur Andersen. He asked if I had any chocolate eclairs in back after evaluating the dessert options."

"To which she replied, at the sight of Gillespie on my lanyard, that my request was shamefully neither a dessert native to Ireland nor my heritage."

"That's endearing," Gem said.

"And so was he," Tierney said, and playfully kissed him on the cheek. "Having a long-distance relationship was exciting, too. But I was ready to get out of Dublin and join him in Seattle when he proposed."

"Well, cheers to that love story," said Rob as he raised his beer bottle. "Hey, this is Craig's beer." He popped off his bottle's beer top. "He subbed in a few times on the Vibora basketball team we'd play against."

Sean paused for a moment at Rob's comment before replying. "Didn't know he worked at Vibora. He's a dad on Finn's soccer team."

"Craig doesn't actually work at Vibora," Rob clarified. "He'd just sub for Ian when he couldn't make it. Which was often, actually. Vibora was my former company's biggest rival. The games would get pretty heated, so we got to know their players well."

"Wait, Regina's husband, Ian?" Tierney asked, wondering if that explained Regina's odd response at yoga after the mention of Sean's company name. Vibora was one of the client companies taking up much of Sean's headspace.

"Yeah. Ian works at Vibora. Regina told everyone about his huge compensation package when he started there earlier this year. So annoying," Gem said.

"He and Craig are buds," Rob continued. "We were always happy to have Craig sub, though, and bring his brew. Still run into him occasionally over at Bob's Bar."

"Well, here's to joining a new company's basketball team." Sean clinked his beer against Rob's.

"Hear, hear. And to the police making progress on the lifeguard case," Gem said.

"And to the pool reopening," added Tierney.

MONDAY, NOVEMBER 19

Traffic around campus was less chaotic this morning, but the anxious atmosphere remained. As Tierney and Finn approached the crosswalk, Josh was wearing dark sunglasses and had signs of a black eye behind the frames. It was a few days old, being more faded and yellowish in tone than dark—a sight she knew all too well from her own healing history.

She started to wonder what he did in his free time. And hadn't he missed his shift the morning after the lifeguard murder? *Stop it, Tierney. Police are handling things.*

Tierney didn't care for rumors about the case, so maneuvered around the speculative lifeguard discussions yet again after drop-off, signed in at the office for a volunteer sticker, and entered the library. She breathed in the comforting scent of books. She had spent hours alone in the stacks at lunch and recess during her own school days, far away from catty girl cliques.

She was pleased to find Franny reading at her desk. Such an inviting space she had with Scholastic posters and prima-ry-colored decor.

"Nice to see you." Franny smiled as she looked over her readers, attached to a puka-shell eyeglass chain.

"Book club was wonderful. I still can't believe you're a neigh-bor," said Tierney.

"I know, right? Simone always does a lovely job. And, yes, I had asked you to stop in." Franny's expression turned sheepish.

Tierney tried to play it cool as she braced for unfortunate news. "How does it look for me to help out on Mrs. Ferber's library day?"

"I'm so sorry, Tierney." She pulled off her readers and they fell a few inches below her collarbone. "Mara emailed and apologized for not getting back to me sooner. Said she confirmed the open spot with Stevie's mom. She thought she had hit send on an earlier message but caught her oversight."

Why is Mara blocking me? "Oh, that's fine. Things happen." Tierney wondered if she was kidding herself about ever getting time with Finn on campus.

Franny's eyes perked up. "But you know, the Spring Book Faire will be here before we know it. My committee lead could always use more help with that?"

"That would be great."

"I'll add you to the list right now." She retrieved her glasses and faced the computer. "We'll gear up once the book shipment date is set."

Tierney confirmed the spelling of Gillespie and, although frustrated, appreciated Franny's kindness.

Franny hit the return key. "You're all set."

Tierney turned to leave.

"And Tierney?"

Tierney glanced back.

"I've seen stuff like this a handful of times." She spoke softly and looked over to the door before continuing. "Mara has a reputation of being quite unpleasant when she senses things aren't in her control. And with their family being a big donor, the staff doesn't have much leverage."

"Appreciate the warning. I've seen the parking spot out front." Tierney smiled and continued outside. Maybe she would never be the right fit for this school. Not stylish enough? Not social enough? The self-deprecating thoughts whisked around her head. She could almost hear Mara saying to consider herself lucky for having gotten the emergency supply kit project.

Tierney needed the pool to swim off her disappointment. Sadly, not an option.

Back at home, she tossed her keys onto the kitchen counter. Her anxiety was draining. It was hours until pick-up and she felt as if she'd already run a marathon. But she couldn't nap. If she crawled into bed now, she might never leave. And as she stood in the middle of her home, alone with nothing that required her attention, she could feel the buzzing inside her body intensify.

Why couldn't she have somewhere to go, some center to help out with this afternoon to sequester her thoughts? Daytime was becoming a nightmare. She needed her lane. Somewhere she didn't feel like a fish out of water. Or something, anything of interest, to occupy her time.

Tomorrow was the Kindergarten Sing—an exciting day for Finn. Wait, that's it. That's where her focus should be.

She headed into the kitchen for some home therapy—the kind she'd enjoyed regularly before Finn was born. Baking. She was reminded of her plan to call Dr. Mosely, too, but tabled it. She'd call soon.

"Put all that energy to use," Tierney's mom would say when she and her brothers were younger. *Good idea, Mom.* She pressed play on the stereo in the family room where *Gaelic Rhapsody* could always be found at the ready.

Sounds of a favorite melody permeated the room, transporting her back to the Connemara Coast—a happier place before any tragic memories had indelibly marked her life.

Grandma Molly had been Tierney's first female role model; she idolized her. Molly not only juggled a large family but was famous in town for baking the "best shepherd's pies for miles," which she sold out of the Dutch-style door on the side of the family cottage. She was an independent lady for her time, and the one who encouraged Tierney to apply to Trinity.

Tierney preheated the oven and opened the pantry door to commence her ingredient search: pastry flour, sugar, salt, baking powder, and vanilla extract. *God, the creamy and comforting fragrance of vanilla.* She pulled eggs from the fridge, along with unsalted butter to soften on the counter. Electric mixer? No. Today she'd do it all by hand.

She tied on her apron, washed her hands, each finger methodically, and got to work. Today's project would be what she planned to bring to Finn's party after the Kindergarten Sing—iced vanilla sugar cookies. If she still found courage to bring them. She knew the recipe by heart, having perfected it over the years. Today she would plan for three different shapes, including Finn's favorite, "chunky turkey."

She greased the pan and hummed along to the music filling the room. She sifted the flour three times, beat the eggs in their own separate glass bowl, creamed the unsalted butter and sugar together before adding them into the batter, then stirred the batter slowly until perfectly combined.

The scent of a warming oven. The light and familiar feel of working dough beneath her palms. Finally—transported back to a peaceful state. Before she knew it, the cookie sheets were in the oven and she was preparing the icing. Her heart rate had dropped to a normal level.

—

"Can I have three?" Finn was thrilled upon arrival home, and never the wiser for how his mom's mental state had been taxed over the past few hours.

"Just two," Tierney said. "You don't want to wreck dinner. I'll be making your favorite, lemony shrimp with white beans and couscous."

"Awesome sauce!"

"And please help me remember to clear away the plates quickly when we're done, okay? You know how sneaky Louie gets with snatching shrimp tails off plates before I've loaded the dishwasher."

"I will. Does helping mean I can have another cookie after dinner?"

Tierney smiled wide. "Yes, it does, my little negotiator. Avoiding a shrimp tail choking hazard most definitely warrants another cookie."

As she plated up cookies for the class party, she no longer gave a damn about what the snack police at school might say about her sweet cookie recipe or, for that matter, not having a formal sign-up spot.

Yes, BB, I can assert myself.

TUESDAY, NOVEMBER 20

Sutton was pacing the station's hallway. He had been feeling confident, pleased with the weekend's win—an official victim ID. But his confidence was short-lived once they'd hit a wall with notifying next of kin and being authorized to release information to the public.

He and Ayala had each called the number Au Pair Match provided as Tatyana's emergency contact, but when they got the victim's mother on the line, neither could understand a lick with the language barrier. Sutton wasn't a patient person, but began wondering why everything was taking so damn long with this case. TV detectives had their man within 48 hours, although those cases were typically in big cities like LA and New York with huge staff. *And experience.*

"There you are. I've got news," Ayala said, as he caught up with Sutton on the walk back to his desk. "Finally got the vic's mother on the line again with a Russian interpreter. Sorry that took a decade. We really should have better access to interpreters for situations like—"

"Tell me something I don't know."

"Right. So, the mother said she wasn't aware that her daughter was in America. Seemed out of it, too. And that part wasn't the language barrier."

"That's odd."

"And sad. She said we could keep the body when I asked for an address on where to ship remains. And then hung up." Ayala shook his head. "The home address Tatyana had in her Au Pair Match file turns out to be a Moscow post office."

"Christ. That is sad. Any other relatives we can talk with? A sibling, or someone she might've confided in?" Sutton sat down at his desk and reached for a pen.

"Only the mother. Said it was just the two of them."

"Let's change gears, then." Sutton clicked his pen rapidly. "Track down the host parents, for anything out of the ordinary while she was their au pair. I'll do a sweep of Tatyana's bank statements to see if there are indeed deposits from a Russian math tutoring company as Brad suggested, and will check in with tech. I know her cell was found at the bottom of the pool, but there's no reason why her phone records haven't been pulled by now."

* * *

Tierney parked in her usual spot, and Sean pulled up nearby in his Audi TT. Although Sean couldn't stay long for the Kindergarten Sing after the starting bell, she was glad he could make it at all. On their walk down to the multipurpose room, they greeted a few parents they had met during family swims and at recent soccer games. *If he could just be here every morning.*

The parent herd gathered around the auditorium's entrance. Sean met Justine for the first time and shared his admiration for her husband's coaching prowess. Tierney felt proud as he continued to greet and exchange handshakes with other dads, including Craig and Ian. The local murder was at the forefront of minds, with brief discussions here and there, but most kept conversations to a minimum—except for Lisa, the fellow swimmer Tierney had met during book club who was now standing next to her, along with an arriving group of friends.

"Hey, you. Seen any other lifeguards around town?" Lisa asked.

"Not yet, unfortunately. But I'm actively scanning whenever I'm out." Tierney reached for her watchband, beginning to feel buzzy with the large group of women cascading around her.

"I've checked in with every swimmer I know but no one has anything new. Let's hope they solve the case soon. I know I'd sleep better," Lisa said.

"No offense, ladies, but Park View is better off without the pool," said one of Lisa's pals. "My darling au pair found their clientele to be quite unsavory. She speaks six languages and once tried befriending an elderly woman she thought to be Russian but was rebuffed. I could never convince her to take my son to open swim again, which was probably for the best."

"Sorry she experienced that," Tierney said, wondering which elderly woman. "Although, people can be sensitive about their nationalities."

"Good point," Lisa said.

"I'm hoping the police will announce progress soon, though," Tierney continued. "It doesn't usually take so long to notify next of kin, which I assume is the hold-up at this stage of the investigation." She was as surprised as Lisa and her friends looked by the words she'd just uttered. *Shut up, Tierney.* No wine to blame this time, just nervous energy.

"Didn't realize we had a law enforcement expert at Apricot Grove," another woman said with a raised brow.

"Oh, I just assume that's what's happening." Tierney laughed and slipped her damp hands into her jacket pockets. "I mean, based on all those cop movies I've seen."

"Of course. That is what typically happens next," Lisa said and nodded at her friends.

"Looks as if the kids are lining up," Tierney said. "Excuse me a sec while I grab a few photos of my son." She walked off to an open space and pulled out her camera. Thrilled to have created distance from the women and an activity to focus on, she waved at Finn to get his attention while he stood cheerfully among classmates.

Tierney took a few shots, occasionally checking a frame, and glanced back at the spot she'd recently occupied. The sight of Sean looking so at ease, engaging with other parents, made her heart overflow. She also saw that Craig was deep in conversation with Justine, talking loudly about a new position she had at an innovative start-up with faster-acting and more portable EpiPens, while Ian was chatting up all the women around him—except his wife, Regina.

Tierney took a few more photos and caught a glimpse of Mara walking up from the parking lot to join Regina. It looked as if Mara's right hand was wrapped in a large bandage like the kind Tierney had put across Finn's skinned knee last month. Tierney wondered what happened, and why she joined Regina instead of Craig.

Parents were invited to take their seats inside so Tierney made her way back to Sean. The group had grown larger, with both kindergarten classes participating in the Sing. She sat down and saw Regina ask Laura to take a quick posed picture of her with Mara in their complementing Burberry sweaters. Laura had mentioned a while back that the two women would frequently ask her to take photos of them, yet never include her in one. It was tacky; Tierney gave her that. Come to think of it, the women's au pairs were wearing similar tops today, too. Tierney was reminded of the annoying Stingrays and their matching black swimsuits.

The lights dimmed and the children commenced with their program. During the first number, Tierney noticed how enthusiastically Finn was singing. She couldn't help herself from smiling. Her eyes soon floated away from Finn, though, and over to a student at the end of a row holding onto the velvet stage curtain as he sang. The heavy fabric flowed with each movement and, before Mrs. Ferber coaxed him into releasing it, Tierney's skin grew prickly. Her mind flashed to a cold room with thick burgundy velvet curtains—the afternoon at Trinity that had catapulted her from youngest in the Squad to Norah's protégé.

~ ~ ~

"Listen up, team," Norah began. "The situation is as follows. We have a distraught wife. Learned that her shite husband, a popular professor here at uni, has been cavorting with a student. Students, actually, as one of the latecomers revealed to us a few minutes ago. The wife entered the lecture hall towards the end of class armed with a pistol, apparently the husband's favorite from his prized gun collection. Twenty-eight junior freshes remain inside, one's been shot that we know of, in the foot. Weapon currently in view near the podium, held firmly against the husband's temple and intermittently waved towards anyone else who dares to move.

"Easy peasy," Ronan piped in and started to stand.

Norah's jaw clenched. "Sit your ass down," she said to her partner, who had arrived drunk and useless to work again, and shoved him back into his chair—too intoxicated to retaliate.

Tierney was standing off to the side of the room, trying her best to ignore snickers from male colleagues over the Norah-Ronan exchange and focus on the hostages. The tech team had just activated a live feed of the classroom via CCTV, and Tierney recognized the space instantly. It was the lecture hall from her Intro to Criminology class years ago, as well as a handful of other courses she'd taken. She remembered it well.

"The floor plan should be available from Campus Security within twenty but we'll work to engage the wife beforehand,"

Norah said while adjusting her headset. "Get her on the phone," she said to a tech, who dialed the number.

The team looked on as the wife let the call go to voicemail.

"We'll try again in two," Norah said and raised her finger for the tech to end the call.

Tierney took in a deep breath and walked around the others to reach Norah. "We don't need a floor plan. I recall the layout of the lecture hall, and there's a pass-through to another classroom hidden behind those burgundy velvet drapes," Tierney said, and pointed to the side of the CCTV screen. "Officers can hole up in that space until timing is right."

"You sure about that?" Norah said with a curious grin.

"I say we wait for the floor plan," Ronan said with a slur from his chair.

"That would be best," agreed the lead agent standing to his right, as others in the room mumbled support of Ronan's more cautious proposal.

"I'm positive," said Tierney as adrenaline began pulsing through her body. "We shouldn't waste time. One hostage has already been shot."

Norah gave Tierney a hard stare before picking up Ronan's headset and handing it to her. "Walk the team through the path."

Tierney recalled the feeling—simultaneously calm and energized as she instructed the Garda officers into position. Her intel enabled the team to deescalate the scene quickly, while Norah talked down the wife via phone. All hostages were brought to safety unharmed—including the dog of a husband.

By the end of the day, Ronan had been removed from active duty and Norah had secured Tierney as her new partner, thanks to a direct appointment from the Squad's Chief Inspector himself.

The situation room had been so cold that afternoon at Trinity, but not as cold as the following months would prove to be from male counterparts who believed the promotion should've been one of theirs. Tierney eventually found her footing within the Squad, though, and could handle any negativity directed her way.

~ ~ ~

Tierney shivered out of the memory and refocused on Finn at stage left.

Sean took her hand. "Okay?" he mouthed.

"Just a chill," she whispered.

Sean returned his gaze to the performance, and she gave a long steady exhale, scanning the auditorium for secondary exits.

Sean was able to see the first two numbers before departing. Tierney wished he could've stayed longer.

As students took their final bow and the audience thinned, Tierney began worrying about the "unauthorized" sugar cookies in her trunk. *Assert yourself. Just walk the snacks in and leave. You can do this.* The absurdity of the self-talk wasn't lost on her, in light of the memory she'd just processed.

She retrieved her masterpieces from Betty and prepared entry into the classroom. At least the recipe supported the no-nut rule.

Justine was the first volunteer she saw inside. The woman looked uncomfortable, shifting her balance from leg to leg. *Way more at home in a boardroom, no doubt.* Her son, though, was all smiles—possibly at the rare sight of his volunteering mom. Coach was no doubt volunteering next door in Ms. Stuart's class for the twin brother.

Tierney stood up taller, walked her tray through the room, which was wriggling with student excitement, and placed the cookies on the back counter among other snacks. Unnoticed. That is, except by Regina, whose stare was searing a crater into Tierney's torso.

Tierney completed her mission and exited the room with an audible exhale. She had left her mark and a win to celebrate.

There were still a few hours before returning for pick-up, so she decided to swing by Peet's. Maybe she'd even try one of those trendy new pumpkin-spiced lattes? *When in Rome.*

—

Tierney entered the coffee shop and her eyes went immediately to the two police officers ordering ahead in line. She wondered if they had experienced dark things in their career before the town's lifeguard murder. *Probably just parking tickets.*

"I don't know what got into those kids yesterday, thinking they could turn the bathroom into drug central," said the barista while preparing their drinks.

What?

"Teens will be teens," said the first officer.

"I've smelled weed around here before, out back when tossing trash," the barista continued, moving her hand in a half circle, "or when I'm gassing up over at the station. But lines of coke residue on our Koala Kare baby changing station here in the restroom? Never would've imagined."

"Lots of wealthy kids in the area with their parents' funny money, but I'm sure a lesson was learned by those three. We're keeping a close eye on the schools," the second officer said in between tastes while Tierney placed her order with another barista.

"And why high school kids think elementary school campuses are a great distribution channel is beyond me," said a patron standing off to the side.

Tierney had noticed her earlier, too, awaiting a baked item in the warmer.

"School moms are notoriously observant around a campus," she continued. "My friend's husband is the principal at Johnson

Academy and got a call just the other day from a parent reporting suspicious behavior on school property before pick-up."

"Doesn't surprise me. It's like those police procedurals I'm addicted to on TV," the barista said. "The bad guys keeping it right out in the open so no one suspects a thing." She waved her hands again theatrically. "By the way, how are things going with the lifeguard murder investigation?"

"Tyranny?"

Dammit. Tierney thought her beverage would've taken longer. She walked over to the napkins after securing the lid, hoping officers would continue being careless and share something— especially about a victim.

"Afraid we can't discuss the case," the first officer said.

"Of course not, apologies. Let's just hope things are sorted soon."

The men nodded and found a table in the back of the shop.

Tierney headed outside and tasted her coffee. She gagged, having forgotten what she'd ordered. *Lord.* The garbage can was nearby, but she didn't want to be seen as insulting or wasteful. She'd have to endure the pumpkin scent on the short ride home before pouring it in the sink.

—

Tierney spent the next hour at her laptop working on the emergency supplies project for Regina and her PTA committee. She itemized the shopping list as well as the budget figure needed for approval. Although Tierney hadn't been given much to do at Apricot Grove, she'd at least do a stellar job with what she had.

She emailed Regina with the details and went into the kitchen to make lunch. When she returned, she was surprised to already see a reply:

Tierney,

Thanks for the details. This all looks great and falls within budget. Please proceed with the purchases and deliver them, along with receipts, to Mara's home (address in directory) by Sunday. The new rolling backpacks for each classroom's supplies were mistakenly delivered to her home instead of school, so we're just planning an assembly event there at some point. ~Regina

P.S. Please note we are trying to educate parents about not bringing unauthorized sugar on campus, like the cookies you made for Mrs. Ferber's class.

Was she seriously being reprimanded for the cookies? *Please.* Regardless, she now looked forward to having a reason to stop by Mara's home and potentially getting some one-on-one time.

She closed her email and wasn't sure what to work on next. She pulled out her cell phone and scrolled through contacts. She hovered over Dr. Mosely's name and noticed the time at the top of the screen. Today's minimum day schedule. *Finn!*

She raced over to school and was five minutes late by the time she parked. In front of Finn's classroom, she was relieved to see a small group of student stragglers outside the door. One of the girls was helping Finn tie on his cape, which her son now insisted on bringing daily in his backpack. She made a mental note to ask BB about childhood anxiety.

"Sorry I'm late, bud. The early pick-up totally slipped my mind."

"Glad you were running late." Mrs. Ferber appeared in the doorway. "I've been wanting to speak with you. Have a moment?"

"Oh, sure." Tierney asked Finn to wait at the picnic table outside the classroom. "Where I can see you, okay? I'll just be a bit."

Mrs. Ferber motioned to the two chairs at a small table near her whiteboard. "I wanted to discuss Finn's recent behavior in class." She shared that Finn had been unusually fractious lately, and asked Tierney if she knew of anything that might be niggling at him.

The first thing that came to mind was that Tierney needed a dictionary, but she gathered from Mrs. Ferber's tone that Finn's recent bullying comments about Derek was where she should start. She considered sharing the peanut comments directed at Max, too, but decided it might be overstepping to fight another child's battle.

"Let's just say you're not the first to mention Derek," Mrs. Ferber said, and thanked her for being candid. "I'll certainly keep my eye on it."

Max was the only name Finn had specifically mentioned being teased so she wondered if Mara had complained as well. *And about her bestie's child?* But to be honest, there could be a handful of affected students.

"I'd appreciate that," Tierney replied. "I should also mention he's been concerned about the local investigation. I've been worried we might know the lifeguard who was killed and, well, my nervous tendencies may be rubbing off on him."

"The kiddos have been talking about the investigation quite a bit during class. But we've been following district protocol—to answer questions to the best of our ability while squelching the rumor mill. We still don't know much yet, though, do we?"

"The investigation has been moving slowly, but more details must be forthcoming." Why the heck Park View didn't seem to be roping in assistance from the sheriff's office and other jurisdictions was baffling. *And still no call back from the station.*

"Indeed. But I'll keep a watch on the prattle. I really enjoy having Finn in class and find his precociousness refreshing. I've even added him to the list as a student to watch for Apricot Grove's GATE program come fourth grade."

"That's so nice to hear." Tierney was thankful, since she was still bothered by a babysitter's remark last year that Finn's precociousness was concerning. "Oh, and speaking of class, I still haven't been able to snag a volunteer role. Any ideas?"

"Just stay on Mara. I give her full rein to fill volunteering spots so I can focus on teaching."

"Of course. Yes, I'll do that."

Tierney rose to leave when Mrs. Ferber interjected, "My, I almost forgot. I wanted to tell you that the cookies you brought in earlier today for the class party were outstanding. Finn told everyone that his mom is a professional baker. It was charming to see how proud he is of you."

"Oh, wonderful. I was worried they might've been too sugary, with the healthier snack rule on the rise?"

"The recipe didn't have nuts which is my only rule. Besides, everyone enjoyed them. Mara even asked if she could take the extras home."

"That is a surprise!" *Bite me, Regina.*

Tierney headed outside to meet Finn. She couldn't believe what she'd just learned but her focus changed to concern when she didn't see him at the picnic table. "Finn?" She called out, looking around the campus with, oddly, no sign of children. A panic began to brew inside of her. She was about to scream his name when she heard his voice off in the distance.

"Mom, you missed it," Finn yelled from the edge of campus near the grass. "Josh almost got hit by a car in the crosswalk!"

Thank God Finn's safe. She was elated at the sight of her son, but then registered his comment. "Wait, is Josh okay?" Tierney reached Finn and could see a few kids and their parents talking with Josh as he brushed his grass-stained jeans and picked up his Oakland Raiders cap.

"Sure you're okay?" a dad asked as Tierney and Finn approached the crosswalk.

"All good. All in the line of duty."

Josh was clearly trying to move on from the incident, but Tierney sensed he was still shaken.

"Well, it's outrageous," said a mother. "And thank God there were no children with you in the crosswalk when the car sped through."

"I think I got the license plate," another parent said. "I'll call it in to the police station. As well as to that organization protesting road safety. They need to hear about this incident. People or bikes, it doesn't matter. We need changes around town before someone else ends up in a coma like that poor bike messenger."

"Really, all good. No need," Josh said, pulling himself together, and peddled off.

Tierney and Finn continued over to Betty. "It would've been much safer to have waited for me at the picnic table than on the grass with the other kids near the crosswalk."

"Sorry. I'll listen next time."

She hugged him tightly and unlocked his door. "I'm just glad you're safe."

"But I did see the car," Finn said. "It looked kinda like that one parked at the pool this summer."

"You mean the old white VW?" Tierney thought of Bell's parked car in the pool lot.

"Yeah, I think so. It was white for sure, and small," Finn said.

"Well, if that mom did get the license plate, the police will uncover the make and model. I should call them too, just in case, and share your feedback. Small white VW like the one always parked at Schick?"

"Yep, that's what I'd tell them." Finn flipped around his cape before sliding into his car seat, smiling from ear to ear.

"Gotcha," Tierney said. *Bell's Scirocco.* "They'll investigate so nothing dangerous happens around school again."

—

Tierney put down the new novel she had been reading on the couch and held her breath. The broadcaster had just shared the latest happenings with the investigation, including the victim—female. *Oh God, please not Riley.*

"She has been identified as twenty-two-year-old Tatyana Popov."

Tierney didn't recognize the lifeguard's name. Her shoulders came down a millimeter, but still. Any murder is tragic. She ran her hand nervously across Louie's fur as the broadcast continued.

"Schick Pool will remain closed to the public until further notice, as City Council evaluates options due to current drought restrictions and conflicting opinions on refilling. In the meantime, should anyone have information surrounding this case or details about Ms. Popov that might prove relevant, please contact the anonymous tip line established by the Park View Police Department on your screen."

As the number aired, so did a passport photo of the victim. Tierney's heart sank at the sight of the familiar face. She had met her back in February on an Alaska Airlines flight to San Jose.

~ ~ ~

Tierney checked the flight path on the seat-back screen in front of her, for the seventh time. Or eighth? The airplane icon's location indicated thirty more minutes. A good thing, since the screaming toddler in the row across the aisle from her wanted off the plane and was making sure all passengers knew it.

She refocused on the final list of executive rentals the realtor had emailed. Tierney and Sean had narrowed it down to three and she was flying out to meet him for the tours. Sean had originally intended to make the selection during one of his now bi-monthly trips to Silicon Valley, but at Lily's encouragement and offer to watch Finn, who adored his aunt and uncle, Tierney booked a last-minute flight to join Sean for a three-day weekend. She was growing more excited about exploring what would soon be their new hometown as she clicked through the listings.

By the time she'd finally bought her ticket, there were only middle seats available. Not her first choice, but the flight was a fairly quick one—although it now felt otherwise. The AC was on blizzard mode and, after at least ten minutes of what had morphed into shrieks, Tierney couldn't help but empathize with the toddler's mother. She had been in that position before with Finn on flights to the East Coast. The drained woman looked distraught, having seemingly removed every toy and snack from her oversized purse.

The brunette seated next to Tierney unplugged her earphones and stood to open an overhead bin. With her height close to six feet, she had no trouble retrieving a duffle bag with her mitten-covered hands that was shoved behind a roller bag, and returned to her seat. Her long hair fell around her slouched shoulders—a visual reminder for Tierney to sit up straighter herself—as the young woman shuffled through the duffle's contents to reveal what looked to be a large ball of tinfoil. She then turned to the frazzled mom across the aisle and presented the ball in her palm. "Was wondering if someone could help me with this?" she said in what sounded like a slight Russian accent.

The mother looked at her with a confused expression that quickly evolved into one of gratitude. She leaned back in her seat so her son could see the shimmery silver, about the size of a tennis ball. "Davey, do you think we could help this nice lady unwrap something?"

The boy quieted and a look of intrigue settled across his teary, snot-streaked face. He reached across his mother to grab it but she intervened.

"Sit back nicely and I'll hand it to you."

Davey did as his mother asked and she pulled down his tray table. She placed the ball in his hands and showed him how to carefully remove the first layer of foil, which revealed a bright colored sticker placed neatly within the first layer. The boy held up the sticker in awe and his mother helped peel away the backing and affix it to his shirt. After touching and gazing at the sticker for a while, he started in on the next layer to reveal another colorful sticker. Based on the size of the ball, passengers had been saved for the remainder of the flight.

"That was brilliant," Tierney whispered to the young woman. "You must have younger siblings."

"Thanks, but no. I always wanted a younger brother or sister. Just lots of cousins for me."

"Oh, well that works, too. Are you flying out to see them?"

"No, I'm here to start a new job. This is the last leg of my trip from Moscow."

"That's quite a distance. You must be tired."

"A bit. These help me sleep," she said, and wiggled her earphones. "I'm going to be an au pair for a family with four kids. I packed my bag with a few things ready to go just in case. Wanted to make a good impression on the car ride home with them." She smiled.

"You're certainly off to an impressive start. Have you been an au pair before?"

"This will be my first time. First time to America, too. I'm excited to be here. Everything feels so open and rich. I thought the program would be a good way to make a fresh start. Reinvent myself like you see in the movies?"

Tierney nodded. She, of all people, understood the desire to start a new life.

"There's not much for me back in Moscow—" She paused an extra beat. "Being an au pair sounded like a great opportunity. What about you? Live in San Jose?"

"No. We're in Seattle, but planning a move to the Silicon Valley area for my husband's job. I'm flying out to look at rental properties with him in Park View, and we'll most likely relocate this summer once my son finishes preschool."

"That's nice. I've heard it's a great area to live. Low crime. Lots of culture and things to do on weekends, with San Francisco to the north and San Jose to the south."

"Sounds like a great area for a young person as well."

"I hope so," she said, and yawned. "Well, I'll let you get back to your laptop. Nice talking with you."

"You as well. And cheers to a fresh start." Tierney raised her Alaska coffee cup for a mock toast.

"Yes. May it be everything we wish." The young woman inserted her earphones and closed her eyes, a hopeful expression settled across her face.

~ ~ ~

A lifeguard? What happened to her au pair placement? Tierney scooped up Louie from her lap and held him close. She wondered why she'd never noticed the young woman at the pool. But surely their airline interaction would be important to the investigation. And the tone Tierney had registered when Tatyana spoke of leaving Moscow. A sadness. *Reinvent herself. From what?*

Tierney had the sudden urge to buy flowers downtown and deliver them to the pool, in tribute to Tatyana. But that feeling soon faded; flowers weren't going to change anything. Something more helpful was needed, something that might break open the investigation. Her intel would be of interest to that detective. The Garda would've wanted any details about a victim. Plus, how could she not call in what she knew? The two women had made a connection on that plane. She owed it to her—another woman who never fully had a chance to live. *Just like Norah.*

Tierney made her way into the kitchen and dialed the tip line number on the sticky note. Joelle answered again. Was she the town's only dispatcher?

WEDNESDAY, NOVEMBER 21

Over morning coffee, Tierney was still processing her conversation with Joelle. The dispatcher hadn't seemed surprised by this call-in of hers either, nor with the mention of the Josh crosswalk incident. Maybe Tierney needed to give the small-town police department more credit, now that they'd already learned of the au pair piece and gotten a complete picture of her world back in Moscow. Still, Tierney had had a tough time falling asleep last night at the memory of Tatyana.

It had been a long time since she'd had any interaction with a murder victim, and it was disturbing to learn what a horrible turn the young woman's American experience had taken. She wished there was some way she could help.

—

On approach to the classroom, Tierney spotted Natalia talking with Regina's au pair by the windows. She hung back near an open picnic table, but could still hear their loud conversation.

"I can't shake that first time I met Tatyana at Au Pair Match's bonding bonfire at Poplar Beach," said Regina's au pair in her German accent. "She was so excited to be in America. Said she wanted to start a new life and find a handsome husband like Ian or Craig. And don't forget DJ."

"How could I forget DJ. But Craig? Really? She'd mentioned Ian before, but never Craig."

"She first noticed Craig at a birthday party pick-up one afternoon, and occasionally asked after him. Like where he worked, how many kids he had, and what Mara was like."

"Weird. He's married."

"Well, so are the other men. Technically."

Tierney shook her head at what she was hearing—recalling Grandma Molly reciting Edgar Allan Poe whenever Tierney had mentioned school gossip to her. "Believe nothing you hear, and only one half that you see." Park View residents could use a little Molly in their lives.

—

Later that morning, Gem called Tierney to share some "exciting" news. "I know you've only met Jennie once, but I added your name to Regina's baby shower invite list. It's Jennie's third, but it's her first boy. And who doesn't love a shower and chance to celebrate? Regina emailed our yoga group this morning asking for guest names. She's throwing together something at her home on Sunday afternoon before Jennie pops."

"Oh, that is—"

"I'm so happy you joined me in class the other day so I had a solid reason to add your name."

Tierney could feel Gem's smile through the line, but that didn't stop the discomfort from weaving its way through her limbs. She responded with all the excitement she could muster. Tierney did appreciate the inclusion, but *dammit*. She had no desire to face Jennie's Norah-ness a second time, much less attend another event with a large group of decked-out women.

—

After school, Finn went outside to kick around his soccer ball with neighbor boys who had gathered in the cul-de-sac while Tierney tackled decorations. Sean had pulled down the Thanksgiving box front and center. Unfortunately, the Squad box had made its way forward again, too. She sighed and shoved it further back with her foot. "Out of sight, out of mind." But as she pushed it away, the top flap wavered. She was reminded of the need to re-tape it just as the dryer beeped.

Once done with the load of clothes, she returned to her prior intention—*boxes*. She went outside to search for packing tape and saw that Finn was returning, juggling the soccer ball on his knee. He shared that Mildred had reprimanded the boys for doing tricks on persimmons that had fallen from her tree out front. "She told us to go home immediately or she'd call our parents."

"What tricks?" Tierney asked as her eyes fixed on the packing tape she had spotted on the top shelf of Sean's workbench.

"To see whose scooter jump made the biggest splat."

Tierney laughed; she couldn't fault Mildred there. She wouldn't want a gooey mess in front of her home, either.

"I'm hungry. Gonna get a snack," he said as Tierney heard the soccer ball bounce away from him. "Cool. Is this yours?"

Tierney turned to see him holding up the top of her old uniform, his soccer ball now resting on the half-open Squad box. A wave of nausea washed over her as she came face to face with the red-trimmed, black fabric uniform and shiny shield.

Her son was admiring the old uniform and her photo on the affixed security badge, his finger tracking across the metal shield. She couldn't let Finn see her crumbling from within, so she forced composure before his eyes glanced up for her response.

"Yep, a long time ago," she said, as coolly as she could, and turned her body back towards the workbench to hide her controlled exhale.

"Were you in the FBI?"

"Sort of." She focused on her watchband, feeling queasy about discussing what she used to do for a living with him but knowing she needed to be truthful.

"Did you carry a gun?"

"Sometimes that was necessary."

"Cool. Can I have the star?"

"Oh, I should polish it up first. Stuff in that box is dusty. How about you leave it there and I'll see what I can do?"

"Okay," he said, leaving the shirt on top of the box and heading inside for his snack. "I hope we have rainbow Goldfish."

As the door shut behind him, Tierney breathed out with force. Why hadn't she taken care of the damn box sooner? She picked up the roll of packing tape and approached the uniform with caution, as if it would bite. Her damp hands pushed the fabric back down into the box. Being careful to not make eye contact with any other contents, she closed the flap quickly and sectioned off a long piece of tape with a rip. She sealed the box with three more long pieces and placed the Thanksgiving box on top. That box she could handle.

Tierney soon headed inside with her chosen decorations and a few cookbooks, but hesitated on the top step. She leaned back to observe the space above. *Sean's harpoon—gone.*

She put down the items she was holding and looked in spots where the harpoon could've fallen. No sign of it. She shuffled around a few other boxes in the vicinity but still nothing. It was gone.

She found Finn and asked if any of the boys had been playing inside the garage. *But wouldn't it have been up too high?* Plus, she would've heard any activity. He shook his head no and continued crunching. She went outside to search again, but there was no sign of it.

"Sweetheart, did you move the harpoon?" Tierney asked Sean when he got home.

"No, why?"

"I think someone took it."

"You mean stole it?"

They walked into the garage.

"Should we file a police report?" He stared at the open wall space.

"We don't know what day it was taken so I don't think we have much to go on." Tierney felt embarrassed at the thought of being unable to provide Joelle with a date or details.

"Are you sure?"

"I'm sure."

"Okay, but is anything else missing?" He looked around where the harpoon had been, and in between various nooks.

"Hard to say with all the boxes, but I don't think so. I checked around, too, and asked Finn about it, but he said no one had been playing in here. To be honest, though, I have accidentally left the garage door open a few times." Her shoulders slackened with the confession.

"It's okay hon, we've both been at fault there." He put his arm around her. "But man, this was supposed to be a safe town."

"Seriously?" She turned to face him. "Have we not been watching the same evening news?"

* * *

Ayala leaned into the staffroom doorway from the hall. "Nothing out of the ordinary with Tatyana according to the host mom. Said she was an absolute doll, great with the kids, and never a problem. Did you find anything in Tatyana's checking account since Au Pair Match let her go?"

Sutton was filling his mug while listening to the end of a voice message on his cell. "Good to hear," he replied, and slipped the phone into his back pocket. "And no large deposits or anything off, but there were consistent bi-monthly deposits from the Russian Math School through September. Looked like a real job. Grab a cup for yourself."

"I'm set, thanks. Hit the drive-thru earlier." Ayala walked in and opened the fridge door to reveal his enormous chilling soda.

"Disappointing. Have you spoken with the math school yet?"

"Still on my list. Their HR manager has been on vacation."

"See if you can get them on the line from wherever they're vacationing. I have a few leads to pursue from Tatyana's cell phone records."

"Calls to Moscow?"

"No, frequent calls to a hair salon called Treat. Actually, you take that one," he said, and handed Ayala the details, "and I'll focus on what seems to be a friend—a fellow au pair named Natalia. As soon as Au Pair Match provides her address, we'll head over." Sutton looked down at his watch and noticed the late hour. "Crap. I'm starting to hate holidays. It's almost after hours. If we don't hear back soon, we may have to wait until after Thanksgiving."

* * *

Once dinner was cleared away, Tierney needed something to fend off the brewing anxiety from having seen her uniform, so settled on what she knew best. She pulled ingredients from the pantry. She'd already decided on Porter Cake for their Thanksgiving dessert, so that would be her focus once Sean retired to the office. Its baked aroma alone would be a comfort. Even though her parents had typically served it at Christmas, she didn't want to wait.

"I'm all done with the math matching game," Finn said as he entered the kitchen. "It was fun."

Math and fun? So Sean's child. "Wonderful. How about using those math skills to help measure ingredients for a special O'Shaughnessy dessert? We'll be serving it tomorrow night for Thanksgiving with Auntie Lily and Uncle Hugh." Tierney smiled at the thought of seeing Sean's sister and brother-in-law soon.

"Cool. I wish Ryan was coming with them."

"Me, too, bud. It gets harder to fly home for every holiday once you're in college."

"I guess."

"Hey, why don't you grab that measuring cup and we'll start with the—Oh wait." Tierney approached the family room bookshelf and returned with an Irish cookbook she had brought inside from the Thanksgiving box. "It's a family heirloom." She handed it to Finn, excited at the opportunity to show him.

Finn flipped through the pages. "I don't know any of these words except the 'Molly O'Shaughnessy' on the first page. Is it a different language?"

A warmth crept over Tierney at the aged scent and sight of the book in her son's hands. She hadn't looked through it in years, the last time being when she started using it in her Dublin flat after Norah's murder. "It's in Irish, and my first cookbook. Molly was my grandmother. So, your great grandmother. I inherited it and it's super special." Tierney helped him find the Porter Cake page and the English notes Molly had transcribed for her in the margins.

Tierney's memories of her grandmother's kitchen flooded in; it was as if Molly were there, too, showing Finn the measurements alongside. She pulled up a stool for Finn near the counter and the mother-son team began. As the cake neared completion, though, the cookbook had become a visible reminder of much more than baking with Molly. Tierney's memories of the last time she used it began to grab hold.

She went to put away the brown sugar, but it passed through her damp grip and dropped to the floor. As she bent down, her thoughts deposited her right back to her Dublin flat. She could see herself on that floor, mid-panic attack, sobbing uncontrollably and unable to move.

In the kitchen here with Finn, Tierney's heart began to race. She squeezed her fists and tried to will it away, but there would be no stopping it this time.

Sean walked into the kitchen to refill his water, rubbing his eyes from having stared at a screen the past few hours. He noticed the baking project and smiled. As he turned to head back out, though, he hesitated at the sight of the cookbook in Finn's hands and looked at Tierney.

She could feel the color draining from her face as he held her gaze, with tears welling up.

"That cake looks awesome," Sean said, taking charge. "But hey, mom's had a long day. How about we start the clean-up?"

"I don't want to clean up yet." Finn glanced to Tierney for support, but his feisty expression changed to one of concern.

"It's okay, bud. Just feeling a bit tired," Tierney said, kissing Finn's forehead before walking out of the kitchen.

Sean followed behind a few moments later and dimmed the light in their bedroom. "You know," he said softly, now sitting on the bed's edge with her, taking her hand in his. "We haven't had a date night in a while. We could use an evening out."

"Sounds nice," Tierney whispered.

Louie jumped up on the bed, head-butted away Sean's hand, and curled up under Tierney's palm.

"You really are Mom's cat." Sean stroked his purring body.

Tierney smiled but kept her eyes closed as she laid down on the pillow.

"I know you don't like discussing this, but I think you should consider meeting with that doc BB has mentioned. Someone to talk to? I know you've been trying to get more involved at school in order to occupy your thoughts, but struggling to get in with bitchy women doesn't seem like the best solution."

Tierney nodded slowly. "I'm planning to schedule an appointment. I just haven't been able to bring myself to make the call."

"Some of the women on my team openly talk about seeing a therapist like it's the thing to do, with a few even comparing their medication names casually in the break room. I know it sounds odd, but I'm telling you times have changed." Sean took her hand again. "And not to sound harsh, but your parents aren't around anymore to make you feel weird about it. I think your brothers would be accepting of it. I mean, if you ever chose to share with them. We already know they have such respect for what you've been through; no cop in your family has ever lost a partner."

"It's just this childhood stigma I can't get beyond." Tierney pulled the pillow over her head. "O'Shaughnessys are supposed to suck it up. I know it's not logical to anyone else. Heck, BB is my best friend and she's a therapist. Of course, I support what she does, but it's never felt like something for me—it's something others do."

"I want you to be happy and find something to fill your days while Finn is at school. You mentioned the baking again? Great idea. I sense your pull towards the investigation, and to somehow help the victim you met on the plane, but baking would be a healthier focus." Sean gave her hand a gentle squeeze.

She squeezed back.

"I know you thought the Squad's psychiatrist in Dublin was a waste of time, but BB's guy would be better." He playfully placed his ear against her back, listening to her heart. "At least that's what your heart is telling me. I actually think it's the strong people who ultimately ask for help."

"I promise to call," she said, pulling the pillow around her head more tightly.

"But bottom line—Finn and I love you too much to see you struggling like this. It's no way to live and you deserve better. What happened at the Embassy that night was not your fault."

Tierney remained motionless for a few moments as she processed his words. "Bottom line? You're such an accountant," she said in a muffled voice before pulling away the pillow to face him.

Sean perked up at the sight of her slight smile. "Well, think about it. I'll go check on Finn."

"Please make sure he knows it's nothing he did."

"Of course. I'll leave you to your purring security blanket." He kissed Tierney, gave Louie's cheek a rub, and closed the bedroom door behind him, keeping the room as dark as possible since migraines occasionally followed these episodes.

Tierney could hear him rotate the bulky leather "Do not disturb" sign on their doorknob, a souvenir from their wedding night. They really did need a date night soon. Their last one had been in Queen Anne.

Sean's comments were settling in—his push to call Dr. Mosely, and to find something enjoyable to fill her days. She knew he was right. The bustle of Finn's preschool years had just numbed her feelings of guilt, but now everything felt static. A change was needed, but it was hard to take the next step—especially when her first and last attempt at therapy had been so dreadful. She could still remember how ashamed she had felt in that Squad psychiatrist's waiting room.

~ ~ ~

Dr. Young's office was located at the far end of the station with a private entrance, so Tierney wouldn't have to see or be seen by any colleagues when going to her appointment. Her interim boss, the Chief Inspector, had arranged the session on the doctor's overbooked calendar—which his secretary confirmed the day prior.

"Two p.m. sharp. Don't be late." The woman's cold instruction and judgment shot through the receiver.

Tierney entered the small waiting room. The walls were painted a neutral grey and the air smelled like the attic of her childhood home. The only things in the space were a worn beige couch, a fake potted plant with a layer of dust smothering its leaves, a sign that read *The doctor will be with you shortly,* and the sound of a low, monotonous hum coming from a tiny noise-canceling device on the floor. She wished they made a device like that for thoughts.

Tierney considered turning around to wait for BB in the parking lot where she'd just dropped her off. But she knew that BB, the Chief Inspector, and his secretary would be furious if she didn't see this introductory appointment through. *A mental well-being screening; my family would be so disappointed.* She reluctantly took a seat and waited for Dr. Young to open his door.

—

"I realized within a year of graduating that the career path I'd chosen was more emotionally charged than anticipated, but I'd been able to handle things," Tierney said in response to Dr. Young's question while he continued to fumble through a large stack of folders on his grand mahogany desk, finally retrieving one near the bottom. "I mean—"

"I see here you were valedictorian at Trinity?" Dr. Young flipped through what looked to be her employee file.

"That's right."

"Miss O'Malley—"

"It's O'Shaughnessy, actually," Tierney politely corrected the doctor.

"Right. I see here that you had been a strong criminology student. And, ultimately, hand-chosen by Inspector Norah Boyce as her partner within the Squad?"

"Yes, I was quite capable when it came to studying the criminal mind, and while encountering it in my early Squad work and negotiation assignments. Even when things grew more violent in Dublin and involved colleagues getting hurt, it was very stressful but I still found the work energizing. I just didn't anticipate how Norah's death would affect me," Tierney said.

"I hear what you're saying." The doctor reached over for a clipboard and began checking boxes with a red pen.

"Perhaps this will better illustrate my situation. My eldest brother is a police officer in New York City. He encouraged me to get back on the horse last month with a part-time dispatch job. But after an hour on the calls, I had to step away. I mean," Tierney continued, "my brothers had always been the physically tough ones in the family, while I was the peacekeeper, with more nurturing skills—like emotional support, tolerance, and patience. Maybe it was silly for me to think that just because I had grown up in a law enforcement household that I'd be immune to violence occurring in my immediate—"

"You mention your brothers," the doctor interrupted. "Why don't we start with your parents. How was your relationship with them?"

"Oh, fine. Normal. But what does that have to do with why I'm here today?" An uncomfortable feeling shot through Tierney's body with the pointless questioning.

"Miss O'Mall, O'Shaughnessy, it's important that I ascertain a complete picture of my patients when offering diagnosis, and that must begin at the core family level."

"Sure. It's just that I was hoping to talk about what happened at the Embassy to help with the nightmares I've been having." Tierney wiped her palms against her jeans. "I find myself walking up to a glass room, and can see all the dressed-up women inside but no one can see me. And when I try to open the door to let them out, it's stuck, and the sound of their voices grows louder and louder until I can't breathe and—"

"I'm happy to prescribe a sleeping medication. And you'll need to be careful when operating a motor vehicle, of course, until you see how the dose affects you." The doctor scribbled on a small pad.

"Um, okay."

"Now, let's start with your mother."

The session moved slowly along. It was about as pleasant as Tierney's recent shoulder surgery, but at least that had offered a sense of purpose.

As she felt the appointment wrapping up, she picked up her purse in anticipation of leaving and Dr. Young flipped through his calendar.

"I'll be away on holiday for a bit, but my next available is in seven weeks. Same time of day work for you?"

"Um, sure. I'll be starting physical therapy for my shoulder soon but I imagine I'll be able to work around that."

"Excellent. I will see you on the third at two p.m. Should any problems arise in the meantime, please contact the hospital directly at this number." He tore off the top sheet from his pad and flipped it over to write down the number.

Tierney took the paper and began to leave through the same door through which she arrived.

"This way, please." Dr. Young aimed his pen towards a door located to the side of his desk.

She surprisingly hadn't noticed the secondary exit during the session but it made sense—an escape hatch. *For doctor or patient?* Regardless, she was happy to leave any way she could.

She walked outside into the overcast afternoon. No sign of BB yet. Tierney glanced at her watch and was surprised to register that the fifty-minute session had only lasted thirty-seven minutes. She felt the weight of the paper in her hand—a Valium prescription. She cringed at the thought of a family member finding that in her medicine cabinet on their next visit from the States.

She tore up the paper and tossed it into a nearby garbage can. She leaned back against the brick wall and closed her eyes, hoping BB would be her usual five-minutes-early self.

"Have you been waiting long?" BB watched her roommate slump into the passenger seat at 2:45 p.m.

"He thankfully booted me early."

"Aw, man. How'd it go?"

"Utter waste of time." Tierney kicked off her shoes. "As I knew it would be."

"So sorry." BB slowly made her way towards the parking lot's exit. "These things take more than one appointment, you know."

"I know. But he kept interrupting me, and spent the whole time asking about my relationship with Mom. Like what the hell?" Tierney continued, eyes still closed.

"Unfortunately, many government-supplied employees are either overworked or not yet experienced enough—like me," BB said with a cautious laugh. "I can ask my boss if she can recommend someone in private practice, a better fit?" She glanced encouragingly at Tierney for any sign of interest.

"That sounds expensive," said Tierney. "And I can't ask my brothers to help, especially after handling my parents' funeral arrangements last year. They'd say no anyway, like my parents would've."

"Right. 'Cockamamie quacks,' just like me," BB replied.

"Their words, not mine. You know I believe in what you do."

"I know. I've experienced my own share of misguided family beliefs. But perhaps if they knew how much you were struggling after what happened to Norah they'd think differently?"

"I don't want to talk about this anymore. I have another appointment with Dr. Young in seven weeks and—"

"Seven? Why so far out?"

"He's going on holiday." Tierney slumped lower into her seat. "I'm to call the hospital should any 'problems arise' while he's away."

"Lord. Sorry, Keats." BB picked up speed and gunned a yellow light.

~ ~ ~

Tierney woke from her rest feeling disappointed in herself, but determined to show Sean and Finn that her behavior had just been a blip—nothing to worry about.

She found Sean in the office, and Finn launching cars with his Hot Wheels ramp in his room, and gave each a reassuring hug before entering the kitchen to clean up the baking project. She warmed at the sight of a clean sink and the Porter Cake placed on her mom's marble pedestal. *My boys.*

With the extra time before bed, she hung up a few Thanksgiving decorations in the family and dining rooms. Better late than never. She loved setting out Finn's artwork from preschool, taping up assorted items on windows and walls and placing sturdier pieces on tabletops, like the elastic-trimmed fabric puff that took shape as a turkey when a roll of toilet paper was positioned inside.

The rooms were looking festive, so she closed up the Thanksgiving box and printed her shopping list for the emergency kit supplies. She made the decision to hit Target on Black Friday to help save the school some money after Lily and Hugh's departure. That way she could drop things off at Mara's well before the Sunday deadline.

It felt comforting to have a plan and finalize a project. Plus, she was giving more consideration to what Sean had said. Not only to finally call Dr. Mosely, but to think of another way she'd enjoy spending her time.

She knew deep down that Finn didn't need her on campus. He had settled in with friends nicely, so her one-sided mission to volunteer had grown pointless. But what else was of interest? She could stop by Bonnie's Bakery to inquire about project work. Or visit their competition? Or become the competition? Would the programming department at Park View Community Center next to Schick Pool be game for her to teach a baking class for moms? Or kids? She felt a flurry of excitement at the idea of teaching something useful. She simply wanted no more random projects with the school.

Tierney printed out her Target list and went to shut her laptop when a new email from Regina appeared. The subject line read, "Silent Auction Committee." *The time-suck role Laura mentioned?*

Hi Tierney!

We've had an opening on the Silent Auction Committee and thought you'd be a great fit. It's an exciting opportunity—securing donations from stores around town. Attached is the job description. Let me know if you have any questions, and welcome aboard!

Regina

You've got to be kidding. Payback for Sean's company being involved in Ian's investigation?

* * *

Sutton swiveled his monitor around to show Ayala a photo of a blonde Tatyana. "The Russian Math School sent over her employee photo."

"That's more like it. I mean, how she looked when we saw her body at Schick."

"And much different than her passport photo. This one was taken down from the company's 'Meet our Tutors' webpage the day she was fired." Sutton repositioned his screen.

"Their new HR manager is one tough cookie," said Ayala. "Much more thorough than our pal, Brad, and how he kept employment records at Schick. She's had experience with employees forging documentation, and Tatyana's apparently looked quite professional. Never would've been the wiser if it weren't for her standing policy to cross-reference non-US citizens' paperwork against the immigration database. Her predecessor hadn't bothered, so Tatyana had already been working for weeks before the catch."

"That is thorough."

"But nothing else of note during my conversation. Tatyana actually sounded like a solid employee, and great with the kids she tutored during the after-school program."

Sutton closed his screen and changed topics. "Any progress in reaching Josh Jeffries?"

"I've stopped by his apartment twice, in between his shifts at the school, but no luck. I know you asked me not to interrogate him at Apricot Grove because of the kids so I keep calling."

"Any known hangouts?"

"His landlord said he's always home, which tells me he's in avoidance mode. He doesn't have a car, just a bike. I'll try him again. Also, got a returned call from Treat salon and the number of Tatyana's stylist. I'll find out if anything of note was shared during their appointments."

"Sounds like a plan."

Ayala walked out of the room for his mid-morning soda from the vending machine and returned with a look of concern in his eyes. "Sutton?"

"Yeah?" Sutton looked up from his reading.

"Just passed the chief in the hallway. Said he wants to see you in his office."

"Ominous."

"Thought so, too." Ayala cracked open his soda. "Want me to join you?"

"I've got this, kid."

—

"You wanted to see me, sir?" Sutton stood in the chief's doorway. Aside from the vast display of Christmas ornaments set out months in advance at stores like Hallmark and Walmart, this office was the only place Sutton had ever known to completely skip over the Thanksgiving holiday.

"Help yourself to a candy cane and some fudge," Chief Marks replied while licking chocolate from his finger.

Sutton walked around the fresh, eight-foot Douglas Fir dripping in silver, gold, and blue globe ornaments, and reached for a candy from the Rudolph bowl before sitting.

"I'll get right to it. Why is no one behind bars for the Popov case? This Brad character looked promising from the get-go."

"I'm not entirely convinced Brad is our guy, sir. Ayala and I have been scouring the data and still have avenues to explore. We'll be speaking with a possible suspect shortly." Sutton hoped Ayala had heard back on Natalia's address.

"Really?" The chief leaned back in his chair, arms crossed behind his head, exposing the white undershirt in between the barely-held-together buttons of his dress shirt.

"Yes. I agree the CCTV footage shows Brad in the office at the time Popov was murdered, but we have no proof of him ever exiting the office in the direction of where the body was found. He could've been passed out on the futon, like in the story he's held to. Plus, we still don't have a murder weapon."

"I view the video differently. He was onsite, has the jealous ex-boyfriend motive, the strength to hit Popov on the head with whatever weapon you eventually find, and he's using the 'passed out drunk' story as an alibi. The cleaning crew probably arrived just after he murdered the girl and that's all he could come up with. Case looks pretty closed."

"But sir, the medical examiner did find traces of cocaine under Popov's nails—the exact same formulation as our bike messenger in a coma. Someone with a lifeguard's salary couldn't afford such high-end drugs. There must be a cocaine connection to Schick. The messenger was hit so close to the pool, right in front of the neighboring community center."

Sutton was growing agitated as he looked at the chief and how poorly he represented the uniform. To think this guy was chosen for the job over him was an embarrassment; the chief couldn't outrun an old lady with a cane.

"Humor me. We know the bike messenger had all that coke in his bag when he was hit by a vehicle, and had just come from swimming at Schick, but that's it. The DEA, and you for that matter, has had months to find a drug ring there and all we've come up with is a rinky-dink weed-selling outfit among the lifeguards. Cocaine on Popov proves nothing happening at Schick." The chief reached for a candy cane from the bowl.

"Maybe. But we're still in need of a murder weapon. We just need a bit more time. Plus," Sutton hesitated and cleared his throat, "things have taken longer with Ayala instead of, instead of Irene. No disrespect to the kid, but if I could just get your okay to reach out to her about the case—"

"That's enough. You're lucky you got assigned a new partner with the budget cuts. And no contact with anyone outside these station walls. Understand?"

Sutton nodded. He knew his request was inappropriate, but also wanted to just find out how she was doing.

"We're keeping a lid on this. We have enough going on with a stressed-out city and nothing yet solid. I do not want attention drawn to that." The chief looked at his desk calendar. "I'll give you and Ayala until I'm back from my cruise next week for an arrest—then I take matters into my own hands," he said, and crinkled the wrapper. "Understood? And I have the DA's support."

"Understood, sir." *You enjoy that cruise while a murderer remains at large.*

THANKSGIVING

Sutton finished his breakfast, a three-egg scramble with crumbled bacon, gruyere cheese, and green onions sliced on the bias, and switched off the Hallmark channel, which he'd begun watching after his last girlfriend accused him of being emotionally vacant. The latest movie wasn't keeping his interest anyway. Why was it always the farmer or firefighter who got the girl? Maybe the next storyline would feature a small-town cop, for Christ's sake.

He cleaned the egg pan, gave the stovetop a good scrub with a new scouring pad from the box under the sink, and bagged up his Thanksgiving lunch/dinner—leftover take-out from Chef Chin's. He topped off his beagle's water bowl and drove to the station.

Sutton got comfortable in his chair. Under the buzz of fluorescent lights, he clicked through Schick Pool's limited and grainy CCTV footage. Again. All camera wires on the property had intentionally been cut a few months ago, based on the spider webs and accumulated dried leaf debris, rendering them inoperable—with the exception of one inside the office. Whoever made that cut hadn't been thorough, which screamed of Brad's sloppy work. Regardless, he and Ayala at least had some visuals from the night of the murder.

Why the hell had Tatyana placed a manikin in the lobby chair after the check-in rush? Trying to block the camera's view of something?

He fast-forwarded the video to see Brad onsite around the time of Tatyana's death as estimated by the medical examiner, but only showing him stumble by the desk a few times with a vodka bottle. It never showed him exiting towards the pool, just passed out on the futon as he'd shared since the beginning.

Sutton opened the cartons of Mongolian beef and chow mein, savoring every last morsel. He didn't mind covering for Ayala on Thanksgiving and clocking overtime while the chief was away. They'd already been working nonstop, knowing each passing day meant one more reason for the chief to ridicule them, but everything was closed and it didn't make sense for Ayala to sit around with him.

Ayala was growing on him, but the change in process was frustrating. Irene might've had something by now. Sensed something he hadn't. Ayala was bright but inexperienced. Sutton felt despondent. The memory of Irene cleaning out her desk, now Ayala's, and moving on with life six months ago still stung.

It wasn't Irene but Sutton's sister who had encouraged him to take the Chief's Exam two years ago. He ultimately agreed the change would be good. Lord knows he had put in the time. But it was embarrassing to share with family that he'd been passed over for the a-hole from the Hillsborough station he now called chief. A friend of the mayor. He belched at the thought and picked up Tatyana's autopsy report.

Death due to blunt force trauma to the head . . . trace amounts of metal found in wound indicative of a metallic weapon . . . Toxicology—cocaine found on victim's hands but not in bloodstream.

The cocaine. The purest formulation the department had ever encountered at ninety-nine percent. *Where was Tatyana getting it?*

Ayala had tracked down Tatyana's stylist at Treat salon, but the only thing noteworthy was that she'd pay for hair appointments with cash, something unusual for their high-end shop. Most patrons would slap down a credit card. Less hassle. "And Tatyana had a reputation for being a big tipper, too, also with cash."

Surely the cocaine discovered on her body was related to her cash influx. He tossed the report on his desk and his dinner cartons into the trash. He rummaged through the top desk drawer, pushing aside an opened but full pack of Marlboro Reds (the only item Irene had left behind), and retrieved the pool patron interview transcripts Ayala had completed so far. He began flipping through the pages again.

Witness Interview
Name: Holly Oaks (Lap Swim Patron)
Page 1 of 1
HOLLY: I don't recall anything out of the ordinary at the pool on the day that poor girl was murdered, but I do remember an odd interaction with Tatyana back in September.

AYALA: And what was that?

HOLLY: I'd had a good lap swim and went in to shower but realized someone had put their lock on my things. Locker number eighty. Really inconsiderate.

AYALA: And Tatyana helped you?

HOLLY: Yes, well, at first. We walked out together to the pool deck and she blew her whistle. I just stood next to her, dripping wet without my towel and freezing.

AYALA: And what did she do?

HOLLY: She announced something like "Attention. Will the swimmer who put a lock on number eighty in the women's locker room please come open it?" Her heart was in the right place, but you know, her accent was a bit, shall we say, strong. You know how those people sound so it was hard to know if anyone even understood her. My Clemson girlfriends and I have been to Russia with a tour group, that was for my fifty-fifth birthday and—

AYALA: I'm sure the trip was lovely but could we please return to how Tatyana helped with the locker?

HOLLY: Yes, of course. Well, no one stopped what they were doing. How could anyone even hear her with all the splashing? Although a handful of swimmers turned towards us, primarily men, with eyes fixed on the attractive lifeguard. I mean, with that long blonde hair in a high ponytail and her suit hiked up just as high to show her nether region? Her goal was clearly attention seeking and—

AYALA: Please continue with the locker.

HOLLY: Well, no one exited the pool. So, after another minute of no response, we left the pool deck and she went to get bolt cutters from the mechanical room. I was absolutely shivering at this point, but she was trying to be helpful. It took her a few tries and the lock finally broke free.

AYALA: What was odd about that interaction?

HOLLY: She was just so rude after that. I mean, silly me, I did realize after she'd cut it open that I'd been mistaken about my locker number. I'd gotten it wrong and the items in eighty weren't my things after all. You see, I typically use eighty but someone had been in my way when I arrived so I went one row down that day and had forgotten. But I could tell right away with the large blue towel hanging inside that it wasn't mine. I prefer neutral-hued towels from Bloomingdale's and—

AYALA: Okay, so they weren't your things, and then what did Tatyana do?

HOLLY: She didn't do anything. She didn't acknowledge my apology, or ask if I was warming up or anything. She just kept staring at the open locker and was quite rude to not look at me, much less ask after me.

AYALA: What was she looking at?

HOLLY: That's not the point. Just a towel that I could see. But she kept staring into the locker and didn't say she was sorry for the ordeal I had just endured. I was so cold and she didn't care. So, I just opened the lock on my correct locker to get my shower caddy and hopped in a warm shower pronto. I was done with her.

AYALA: Okay, is there anything else to this story? Or was anyone else in the locker room with you that observed this interaction, too?

HOLLY: Not really, and no. It was just us. Even when I was done and leaving Schick, I passed her at the front desk and she was on her cell phone talking with someone in whispers and didn't even look up. She could've asked then if I was okay, but you know how people from that part of the world can be so rude and—

Interview end

Sutton leaned back in his seat. *What did she see in the locker? Cocaine?*

* * *

Tierney was focused on Thanksgiving and not going to let Regina's coercive email ruin her holiday vibe. Laura had broken free from that Apricot Grove "opportunity," and she wasn't about to be manipulated into it. Today would be the day she visited Bonnie's Bakery.

The *Daily Gazette* had written about a few downtown shops trying something new this year and holding morning hours on the holiday. The bakery was specifically of interest, although Tierney did find it odd how Thanksgiving was growing less meaningful to businesses with each passing year. She loved the holiday, and the Skype with her three older brothers she organized on their off years of celebrating together. But that just meant they'd all be together soon for Christmas.

She popped in the turkey, prepped the stuffing and sides, and went exploring downtown for an hour while Sean was home with Finn watching the Macy's Thanksgiving Day Parade. There was a spring to Tierney's gait as she approached Bonnie's Bakery and the idea of starting something new.

The mouthwatering scent of baked goods from the sidewalk dreamily pulled her past the outdoor patio, which Tierney had seen teeming with customers on warmer days, and inside. The bakery hummed with conversation as she entered the brightly decorated shop, its signature periwinkle and white-striped hues at every turn. The line of patrons at the cashier was almost out the door. There were a few round tables with chairs inside, all taken, and as Tierney stood in line, she found herself within earshot of an elderly group discussing how outraged they were about no one yet being apprehended for the lifeguard murder.

"I think we've all called the hotline by now, Gladys even a few times, but it hasn't done any good," a woman with a helmet of grey hair said in frustration.

"It's bullshit is what it is. Our tax dollars aren't doing a damn thing," a man replied, and took an aggressive bite of scone.

"We need to start policing the police is what we need to do," said another woman while bouncing a tea bag in and out of her mug as others nodded in sync.

"Agreed," the man added. "And if I hear dispatch say one more time that I should just follow the local news channel for details, the department is going to be the news!"

Oh my. Tierney neared the cashier. There was a posted flier advertising that the shop had recently begun offering baking classes during off hours. *So, there was demand for classes.*

After purchasing a few of Bonnie's "best sellers" and avoiding the group of thankless Park View senior citizens now readying their departure with coats and scarves, she headed outside with the small paper bakery bag. She still had time to explore Main Street before heading home for her O'Shaughnessy-clan Skype.

The treats she sampled while window shopping were flavorful, but the shortbread wouldn't pass the "Ryan test," what her family standard had been coined. Bonnie's used an English recipe, unlike her family's Irish version, which was heartier in texture—her preference. Tierney was feeling like she might be onto something as she continued her stroll downtown, now enjoying a gluten-free jam thumbprint cookie.

She passed a handful of restaurants, high-end jewelry stores, boutiques with upscale clothing on trim mannequins; hair salons, nail salons—too many hair and nail salons, she realized after losing count—but it was a gorgeous Thanksgiving display in the florist's window that caused her to linger. A magnificent mix of autumnal roses and mums was gathered inside an intricately braided cornucopia. Tierney had always loved the table accents that complemented her catering jobs, and the arrangement reminded her of Lily and Hugh's arrival in a few hours from Seattle. She finished the cookie, closed up the bag with the last one to enjoy later, and entered Deep Roots Floral to see what might make a nice addition to her dining room table.

The salesgirl looked up from the roses she was trimming and her eyes twinkled as they met Tierney's. "Welcome in. Let me know if I can help," she said, and returned to her project.

Tierney smiled and began her slow walk around the shoebox shop, to the sound of tranquil, atmospheric music. She was taken in by every item, especially the orange roses, lilies and alstroemeria, miniature maroon carnations, and yellow daisy spray chrysanthemums accented with white wax flower, red cottage yarrow, huckleberry, grevillea, brown copper beech, and preserved oak leaves.

The front door's wind chimes sounded as another patron entered, along with a gust.

"Morning, Detective Sutton."

Tierney glanced up at his reflection in the mirrored wall. It was the same man from the newspaper article.

"Hi Piper. I'm a bit behind this year."

"No prob. Are you thinking bouquet or arrangement?" she asked with an upturn to her cheery smile.

"Remind me what I sent for her birthday?"

"'Mums for your mom,' you had decided, in a glass vase."

"That's right. Let's go bigger. She's not pleased I'm missing Thanksgiving this year."

"Got it. Hopefully the case will wrap soon and you'll be flying to Denver before you know it. Mums again as the primary flower? Or roses or lilies?"

"I like your positive outlook," Sutton said, then looked perplexed. "Jeez, I'm not sure."

Tierney, holding a centerpiece she had chosen, walked over to get in line as Sutton faced her.

"How about orange roses, and those?" he said, pointing to Tierney's selection.

"Oh, sunflowers? My mom loved sunflowers," Tierney said. "They're so cheery, and my kindergartener thinks they're a cool shape."

"Great. Let's throw in a couple," Sutton said to Piper.

Piper winked at Tierney. "Excellent choice. Charge your account with the same note and address?"

"Same note, same address, but different room number. My sister said they've moved her to the memory care wing. One-thirty-seven."

Piper wiped both hands on her apron and began entering the order on the desktop computer with gentle keystrokes.

Sutton rubbed his hand through his thinning hair while awaiting confirmation.

"Thanks for your efforts on the case, detective," Tierney said, surprised by her desire to break the silence.

He nodded in appreciation. "Keeping us busy."

"I used to lap swim at Schick. Really miss the place. Think it will re-open soon?"

"Afraid that's up to the city. The drought has been rough on everyone."

Tierney enjoyed having an opportunity to speak with a detective. He might value hearing her thoughts firsthand, and perhaps learning her messages hadn't reached him. "I've actually called in some details to Joelle about the victim. I spent time with Tatyana on a flight from Seattle to San Jose, and thought someone from the department might've contacted me? I was also at Schick during the evening lap swim session on the night she was killed."

"Joelle?" His eyebrows raised. "I do recall seeing call-in notes regarding a flight. Joelle is thorough that way."

"Oh, I've no doubt. There was just something in the way Tatyana had spoken of there not being much for her back in Moscow. It was her tone. She was excited about starting a new job in America but, at the same time, like she might've been running from something? But her family would be able to shed light there."

Sutton stared at her.

"I mean, I assume you've spoken with her family."

"Of course," he said with a scoff. "We speak with family first."

Tierney was taken aback by his condescending attitude. *Had he contacted family?* She flashed to a Garda officer, early on in her career, making a derogatory comment to her face about having been a quota hire. She had grown used to being spoken to with disdain by male peers and, after a while, their insecurity amused her. Norah had taught her that. But it had been a long time since she'd encountered belittling and the feelings that ensued.

Tierney's thoughts turned to Finn's recent dependency on his cape and her body stiffened. She pressed the issue. "Tatyana mentioned having lots of cousins. Maybe they've shared some perspective to help solve the case?"

"We follow-up on every *relevant* lead, which includes contacting parties who had swum at the pool that evening."

Tierney felt a pilot light ignite inside of her. "Well, I haven't received a call."

"You've contacted us, no? So we have received your details?"

"For the most part yes, but—"

"Your order is all set," Piper said with a firm click of her keyboard. She glanced, without twinkle, from Sutton to Tierney and then back to Sutton. "It should arrive no later than two p.m. today."

Sutton gave her a thumbs-up and returned to Tierney. "Rest assured, miss, we have it covered. But if you think of anything *concrete* we should know, here's my card. Call anytime."

I've got something concrete for you. No call-in should be ignored. At minimum, to rule out the cranks. Tierney reluctantly placed the centerpiece on the counter and accepted his card, along with the florist's clear desire to maintain a peaceful space.

"Well, ladies, enjoy the holiday." He walked towards the door, nearly tripping over a bucket of pussywillow branches on the way out.

Tierney reached for her wallet to buy the centerpiece and noticed a tight, crumpled ball in her hand. She'd squeezed all life from the bakery bag she'd been holding, and the last cookie inside. She tossed it into the trash bin near the register, slid Sutton's card into her back pocket, and paid Piper.

That pilot light inside burned brighter.

—

"Auntie Lily and Uncle Hugh!" Finn flew to the front door in his cape. He'd been counting down days until their visit.

Tierney knew her son missed living by them; they'd been his favorite sitters in Seattle, especially when Ryan was around for cousin time. Staying at their home for a week in June while Tierney and Sean handled the Park View move had been especially memorable for him, since it was Ryan's last summer at home before college.

"How is my sweet cheeks?" Lily bent down to hug her nephew.

As they gathered in the family room, Tierney realized how much she'd missed living close to them, too. But the distance certainly didn't stop the relatives from spoiling Finn.

Hugh, an avid collector of Hot Wheels himself, presented his nephew with a small box topped with a red bow. "I've been thinking we need to ramp up your knowledge of older models."

"Cool, thanks! It's not even my birthday yet." Finn showed Sean after unwrapping the collector's edition Corvette Stingray.

"It's a beauty," said Sean.

"And I believe your grandpa had this one?" Hugh looked at Tierney.

"So thoughtful, guys," Tierney said. "Yes, it was my dad's car, until my middle brother totaled it." Tierney shook her head at the memory, and of said brother who'd just mentioned on Skype that he'd purchased one for his home's newly expanded six-car garage.

Sean helped Hugh bring in the suitcases while Tierney gave Lily a house tour, including their bedroom for the evening. They'd be staying for one night plus a day before continuing on to San Diego to visit Ryan for the remainder of the holiday weekend.

—

"Love the new hairstyle and clothes, by the way," said Lily as she rinsed silverware and dishes under the faucet from the stack brought in by the boys after dinner.

"Oh, well, when in Rome, as I keep saying."

"Oooh, remind me to talk with you about Rome. But you seem to be settling in well. Along with the rest of the family, I might add," Lily said and the two glanced over at Finn and Sean, happily talking with Hugh and watching the football game.

Tierney nodded as she opened the dishwasher.

"It's good you're staying home with Finn," Lily said.

"I'm lucky to be, in this pricey neighborhood."

"Do you ever miss the baking, though?"

"Funny you should mention that." Tierney shared her idea for the baking class/birthday party venue/whatever business as she loaded dishes.

"Dynamo idea. I'm wishing I had something like that with my empty nest—that I didn't give up my law career entirely with Ryan now off at college. Never thought my baby would be okay with spending Thanksgiving in San Diego to celebrate with his coach and other players instead of us. Bridget's busyness has been easier, now that she's married and settling down in Oregon, but I'm trying to be supportive of Ryan's new friendships."

"I'm sure he appreciates that. And how sweet of them both to call before dinner. Did you see Finn's face light up when Ryan asked to speak with him? We loved spending time with him earlier this month, and what a thrill for Finn when Ryan and some teammates were able to join us for dinner after their last game."

"He is a thoughtful son. It's been hard, though, as I explore Lily 3.0. I've been giving some thought to writing a legal thriller. Channel my inner John Grisham, and take some writing classes. Lord knows I have time now."

"I can certainly relate to having too much time to kill. And I think writing sounds like a great idea. You'd have lots of material to tap into from all those years as a legal secretary."

"Never too late to try something new, right? And you'll have the baking. I mean, definitely not the Squad work again. Do you ever miss it, though?" She reached for a sponge to wipe the counter.

"Sometimes I feel a pull. Like with the local murder investigation and victim I had met on the plane that we told you guys about. Not sure the detectives are doing a thorough job, and taking much longer than I'd expect. But I could never truly go back, not with a family."

"I do see these sticky notes by the phone, though. Doing a bit of moonlighting?"

"Funny. Just being a responsible community member." Tierney glanced up at the hotline number and was reminded of her conversation with Sutton at the florist, and how she'd be doing a better job to resolve the case.

"Well, I haven't seen a determined look like that cross your face since you negotiated that unplanned epidural with the on-call anesthesiologist during your labor with Finn," said Lily.

—

"What a nice evening," Tierney said as she squeezed out toothpaste, "but glad we're not turning in too late so we can get an early start for the Christmas tree."

Sean headed towards the bed for his pajamas. "I'm exhausted."

"You were a little distracted during dinner. Everything okay?" she asked through minty foam.

"Taking off today was hard enough," he said while yanking off his second shoe and throwing it aside. "I knew we shouldn't have closed the office tomorrow, too."

"Oh, really?"

"I told Ken it wasn't practical," he continued, now sitting motionless and staring into his lap. "He wanted to be Mr. Nice Guy and give everyone four days off for Thanksgiving, but I can't lose another day." His hands were now shaking.

Tierney had been so intent on making the holiday perfect that she hadn't even noticed he might be struggling. She dropped the toothbrush in the sink, wiping away remaining foam with a hand towel, and went to him.

"I'm sorry," he said as she sat by his side. "I know how important a holiday weekend is but I have too many appointments to prep for Monday. And now I'm recognizing names on the subpoena list." He let out a sigh. "One of them is a parent on Finn's soccer team."

She put her arm around his shoulders and thought of Ian. Sean leaned into her for support, which she knew was hard for him. She could feel a lump forming in her throat as he tightened his hold. "We'll get through this," she whispered, blinking back tears. "Together. We're a team, okay? And I can take the lead on entertaining Lily and Hugh tomorrow before their evening flight. They'll understand."

"I'll go with you guys to get the tree, but should break away after. I need to figure out who in the office I can offload my conflict of interest to. And I imagine this won't be the first."

"Of course, anything you need." *Do better, Tierney. What he needs is for me to be the rock for a change.* Tierney reached for his water glass. She sat with him, encouraging small sips as his muscles relaxed.

"Take as much time as you need tomorrow," Tierney said. "And you're right, by the way. What you said to me last night? I should be taking better care of myself. If not for me, for you and Finn."

"I know you're trying."

"I'll call BB's doctor friend tomorrow and see how soon he can meet."

Sean gave her hand a reassuring squeeze.

FRIDAY, NOVEMBER 23

"How do you guys like the neighborhood?" Hugh asked as the five embarked on their early morning drive south over Highway 17 toward the Santa Cruz Mountains in search of the perfect Christmas tree.

"It's been nice," Tierney said, handing Finn the rest of his breakfast burrito, now wrapped in foil, that he'd left on the table. "Thanks to Gem next door, I've been included in things like a book club, a yoga class, even a baby shower. She's such a kind person. I wish you could meet her, but their family is skiing through Saturday."

"Her husband Rob is great, too," Sean said.

"Hopefully we can meet them next time," Lily said. "You know, I can say this now that you're settled, but I was worried about you guys. We've encountered many self-proclaimed Silicon Valley 'refugees' in our area, happy to have escaped from the region and high cost of living."

"We've seen that trend, too, with families cashing out and choosing Washington or Oregon," Tierney said. "But we're still willing to give it a chance."

"Think you'll try to buy something in the cul-de-sac?" Hugh asked, having been in commercial real estate for years. "The land prices are outrageous in this mid-peninsula region. I can't even begin to quantify how much that new outdoor mall near the airport cost."

"We'll see." Tierney looked over at Sean, who was focused on the winding road ahead. "There's not really a rush. That's another reason we went the private school route—so it wouldn't make a difference where we bought."

"We've been happy with our little move, too, haven't we Hugh?" Lily asked. "The place at Lake Chelan as a second home has been dreamy. And there's lots of new vineyards popping up. We're becoming more knowledgeable about wine."

"We're happy with your move, too," said Sean as he moved into the slower lane. "Our visit last year was stellar, and the property will be a draw for Bridget and Ryan for years to come. Smart decision there."

Lily smiled at her brother's praise. "And speaking of your last visit," she clasped her hands together, "Hugh and I are thinking Italy this summer—an extended family thing, with you guys joining us?"

"Uh, yes, please," Tierney said. "I've never been."

"We're planning to rent a villa in Tuscany—one large enough to accommodate Hugh's side of the family as well as yours, brothers included. We can tour the sites, do a group cooking class, maybe even a baking one with decadent Italian desserts? And some of the properties have gorgeous pools on the grounds so you could swim whenever you'd like."

"We'd love to join you. Right, Sean?" Tierney said.

"A vacation sounds great," Sean replied. "I'll just need to see how my client schedule looks."

"And I can show Ryan how long I can hold my breath under water," said Finn. "I practiced all summer."

"Fab. Will keep you all posted on details." Lily turned her focus outside to the passing mountains.

—

When their crew returned home, Hugh and Finn got the tree off the car and into the house. Lily helped Tierney sort through the Christmas boxes and tested strands of blinking lights. And with Sean holed up again at his computer, she was reminded of her promise. She never truly gave therapy a chance in Dublin, with that one appointment. And if she was being honest with herself, that appointment had been over before it began. Alone in the garage now for a few minutes, it was as good a time as any to call Dr. Mosely, even if it was the day after Thanksgiving.

"You're for sure going to get his voicemail," BB had explained. "Mosely's outgoing message will say he's not accepting new patients, but leave a message anyway. Remind him you're an old friend of mine. He'll make room on his calendar, but you'll need to be flexible with dates."

Tierney scrolled through her contacts and found his name. She sat down on the cold step leading up to the laundry room and dialed.

—

The family's afternoon together passed in a blur. Before long, it was time to drive Lily and Hugh to the airport for their evening flight to San Diego.

"It's not goodbye," Lily said teasingly after their hugs by curbside check-in. "It's, 'I'll see you in Tuscany.'"

When Tierney arrived home, Sean surprised her with a date night on the calendar for Saturday evening.

"Tomorrow night? How sweet, but do you really think that's smart? Let's not add to your stress. Wait, did you say Chez Chloé? How in the world did you swing that?"

Sean smirked and shared that while following up on project updates with one of the grateful clients he represented, a Vibora board member, he'd learned that the man hadn't exactly enjoyed the recent holiday. "We were making small talk about our Thanksgivings and he mentioned it was the first time he'd been without family for the holiday."

"That's sad."

"The poor guy sounds exhausted. He has a standing reservation at Chez Chloé on the Saturday after Thanksgiving but said he can't bring himself to cancel."

"Their *Daily Gazette* review said it's booked at least six months in advance."

"Not much notice for us, I know, but he insisted. And I thought it could be that break for us? It's on the later side, though. Eight p.m. Think we can find a sitter?"

"I'm on it," Tierney said, and pulled him into her arms.

She spent the rest of the afternoon cleaning up Thanksgiving and preparing for Christmas, including the spreadsheet she'd promised to email her brothers' families so they could all get a jump on Christmas wish lists. After hitting send, she went outside to retrieve Saturday's mail along with the morning paper she had forgotten earlier.

She opened the *Daily Gazette* to a cover story about the bike safety protesters, and how they'd agreed to a temporary hiatus thanks to City Council's recent agreement to evaluate a bike-lane-widening proposal. At least something was progressing in Park View.

Tierney flipped the page and was met by the gaze of Tatyana Popov—a photo of her with blonde hair. No wonder Tierney hadn't recognized her at the pool. She skimmed the article for anything new, learning of Tatyana's odd jobs after losing the au pair gig, but still no arrest in the case or mention of significant progress. *Nice job, Sutton.* She sighed and her thoughts turned to another annoyance, Regina. Tierney was still in a state of disbelief over her email. She would rather do something outside of school than work on something of no interest.

There. It was decided. First, Tierney would wrap up her commitments with the emergency supply project. She'd head to Mara's after Target, not bothering to email or call ahead since Mara never returned messages anyway. If no one was home, she'd simply tuck the supplies somewhere neatly on the front porch. In and out.

Next, she would decline Regina's "opportunity" with the auction committee, and pass on Jennie's baby shower invite. While she liked Jennie, she couldn't bring herself to enter Regina's home—*the coven.*

Tierney sent Gem an email sharing her plans, and that she would drop off Jennie's gift this weekend—a family-favorite book of Irish folk and fairy stories she had seen in the downtown bookstore's window. Tierney knew Gem would empathize with her decision. And, if Tierney was being fully transparent with herself, she was relieved to not have to face a Norah doppelgänger again soon.

Before dinner, she headed to Target and braved the crowds.

* * *

Sutton was still bothered by that wannabe-detective mom at the florist who got up in his grill. What the hell did she know? Plus, he and Ayala had already called all patrons on the sign-in sheets. *The people in this town, I swear.* He was also agitated by the tongue-lashing he'd received from a mob of disgruntled senior citizens on the walk back to his car. It felt invigorating today, though, to be doing something more public with the investigation, letting onlookers see how hard their police department was working. He waited for walkers to pass and pulled into the driveway of what was the largest Park View home he'd ever called on.

He and Ayala stepped out of the car. Sutton couldn't help but notice the bins pulled out for collection the next day but not yet placed down at the curb. The recycling bin was close to his door and overflowed with empty alcohol bottles. He rolled it off to the side so he wouldn't bump it when they left.

Sutton showed his badge to the boy kicking a soccer ball on the front lawn. "Are your parents around?"

"They're at the country club. My au pair is watching me." He kneed the ball up into his hands.

"Impressive control," Ayala said, and the boy grinned.

"That's actually who we'd like to speak with." Sutton looked at the front windows of the house and noticed a young woman watching them from inside.

The boy headed the ball while walking up to the porch and entered the house. A moment later, the woman appeared in the open doorway.

"Did Max get that right? You are detectives?"

"Correct. Are you Natalia Blaski?"

The woman nodded and the partners showed their badges.

"What is this about?"

"We have a few questions about Tatyana Popov," Sutton said.

"How can I help?" Her eyes fixed over their shoulders at a group of female joggers slowly passing by. "Please come in," Natalia said, motioning them inside and quickly closing the door.

Sutton noted the vast number of framed family photos around the house, many including Natalia, as she led the way into the living room. He had never seen so many professionally-taken portraits in a family home. The one over the mantle, a family of three with wide smiles, set against a golden Northern California countryside, was larger than the big-screen TV in his townhouse.

"Max, why don't you go upstairs and play Nintendo?"

"Do I have to?"

"Yes. Or I'll take away your Minecraft time later."

Natalia and Max stared at each other for a moment before Natalia added, with a taut smile, "Now, please show these detectives what good manners you have."

"Fine," he said with a huff and left the room.

"Can I get you gentlemen something to drink?"

—

Natalia handed Sutton a coffee, Ayala a can of Coke, and placed two coasters on the sturdy oak coffee table. Sutton looked around the open space and noticed a bar in the dining room, before taking a seat. A bottle of vodka, the same high-end brand they had found in multiple locations around the Schick Pool property, sat unopened next to other spirits.

Natalia took a seat adjacent to the detectives, hands folded delicately over her lap, and crossed, uncrossed, then recrossed her ankles. Her eyes looked misty. "I still can't believe she's gone."

"You two were close?" Sutton asked.

"We weren't best friends, but we saw each other often, usually for weekend runs. I was assigned as her mentor when she first arrived and we kept in touch that way."

"We understand the situation behind her first host family divorcing, but things are a bit fuzzy surrounding her employment after."

"Well, I only know what Tatyana told me."

"Let's start there then." Sutton took out his notepad.

"She moved in with her boyfriend after the host family let her go. Au Pair Match tried to find her another placement but things didn't work out. They blamed the 'economic landscape,' whatever that means. Anyway, she lost it a little, like dyed her hair blonde and starting drinking more. But she found work at the Russian Math School, until they terminated her employment for having forged the expiration date on her work visa. She was lucky they didn't call the authorities." Natalia shook her head at the thought. "Anyway, her boyfriend gave her a lifeguarding job on an evening shift, which was sweet."

"We're talking about Brad Madrone?" Sutton noticed Natalia clasp her hands tightly.

"Yes. She didn't want to go back to Moscow and said her new goal was to make enough money to get by, although it was really to get engaged. One of the older au pairs in our circle recently got engaged so it gave her the idea." Natalia paused for a long minute; her knuckles were now pale as chalk.

"I see. Go on."

"Detectives, I want to be fully transparent. I may have known Tatyana, and that she was breaking the rules by working outside of her au pair visa, but I've nothing to hide. I realize now that I should've come forward with information I'm sharing today, but I've been fearful. I enjoy living and working in America and want no trouble."

"We understand, and appreciate your cooperation today with our investigation."

"How long have you been in the country?" Ayala asked. "Your English is quite good."

"Thank you. About four years."

"Four years? Don't au pairs typically stay for a year?" Sutton asked.

"That is true." Natalia's voice wavered. "My host family is well connected. They have a college friend in US Citizenship and Immigration Services who helped me bypass a little red tape to secure a green card. It's real, I assure you, and am happy to show you," she said, and began to stand.

"That won't be necessary, Miss," Sutton said, and gestured for her to remain seated. It was something he could easily check later. "Please, continue your story."

She nodded and smoothed her skirt. "Well, after a while, Tatyana told Brad that the lifeguarding hours weren't enough to cover her expenses and make her feel secure so she'd need to find something else if he wasn't going to ask for her hand. But Brad held his ground—told her he loved her but he'd never marry again. A bad divorce a few years ago, he'd said."

"So, they broke up?"

"Yes. She moved out and started dating other guys. Brad let her keep the lifeguard job, though, I think because he hoped to win her back? He just didn't want to get married, which I understand. My parents had a terrible marriage. Anyway, that's around the time I recommended her as an independent math tutor to my host family. But then things got odd."

"How so?"

"Her Russian accent grew more pronounced, as if she had tried to tame it before but was now just being her true self. And she started showing up for our runs with expensive Nikes, Lululemon outfits, Beats, Burberry sunglasses—things like that. Oh, and Prada running gloves that were way over-the-top. She'd also moved from hair bleach at home to a fancy salon downtown called Treat. A platinum shade like that is pricey to maintain with her brown hair. Like appointments every three weeks? It was all odd since I knew she wasn't making much money with the lifeguarding or tutoring."

"Where do you think the items or funds were coming from?"

"The boyfriends, I assumed. She joked one time saying the wealthy sure liked their cocaine. And asked me if I wanted in. Which, of course, I said no."

"She specifically said 'cocaine'?" Sutton asked and clicked open his pen. "When was this?" He pulled down his readers.

"About a month before she died." Tears began forming in her eyes and she reached over for a tissue box on an end table.

"The last time I saw her was over here for a tutoring session. I had talked Mara into letting Tatyana tutor Max once a week, to help with some income."

"Mara is Max's mom?" Sutton asked.

"Yes. Max struggles with numbers so Mara was fine with it. She didn't want him to repeat kindergarten again. Tatyana had worked with Max for about a month before I told her it needed to be her last session, since it felt wrong to have this new vibe of hers around him. He's like a little brother to me. But Tatyana couldn't stop crying and I felt so guilty that I told her she could have a bit more time to get away from the bad crowd." Natalia dabbed her eyes.

"When was the last time you were in contact with her?"

"She stopped replying to my texts two days before she died. I just assumed she was mad for what I'd said about her being a bad influence around Max."

Sutton nodded and wrote on his notepad. "Help me understand this. Why would she even bother with a tutoring gig, or lifeguarding for that matter, if she was making better money elsewhere?"

"I was hopeful she was trying to reset, and tutoring and lifeguarding were more wholesome than whatever that cocaine situation was."

"Okay, so cocaine and 'the wealthy' were mentioned regarding her mystery income. Any idea who these other guys were that she was dating?"

"She implied there were a couple. One occasionally swam at Schick Pool, a venture capitalist named DJ. He was actually her host dad. He sits on a few boards, too. I got the feeling Tatyana had something on him."

Sutton exchanged glances with Ayala and could feel his pulse elevate. Ayala had updated him on the host mom only. *Christ.* Irene wouldn't have let that slip; he should've been more thorough. "Last name?"

"Don't actually know. But Au Pair Match could tell you. Not sure what he looks like either. The only guy I ever saw was the one she moved in with after leaving Brad. Josh—he's the crossing guard at Apricot Grove. Not exactly one of the wealthy ones."

* * *

Tierney turned down the street lined with olive trees and instantly knew which house was Mara's. Not only had Gem mentioned it being the most impressive one in the neighborhood, but she had once shown her photos—on the pages of a *Sunset* magazine feature highlighting Silicon Valley properties.

Today, it was decorated with tasteful Thanksgiving ornamentation, and must've cost a fortune based on Tierney's knowledge of staging events from catering days. Underneath the decor stood a stately Craftsman with cedar siding and clay-colored trim. It was breathtaking.

Tierney indicated her turn signal. Backing out of the stone-paved driveway was a black Ford sedan. The driver looked like Sutton. *Interesting.* As he and his male passenger drove off in the opposite direction, she parked on the street in case anyone else would be leaving.

With receipts in hand, she walked up the path that bordered a well-maintained lawn towards the porch. An elegant display of fairytale pumpkins and gourds sat at the top. She rang the doorbell. No answer. Tierney reached out to ring again when the massive front door opened abruptly.

"Oh, hi Natalia, I'm Finn's mom from soccer." She hoped for some sense of recognition—unsuccessfully. "Is Mara home?" She could see Max sitting on the couch inside playing with a Nintendo DS.

"She and Craig are at a party," Natalia offered coolly.

"Oh, okay. Can I leave these receipts with you then?"

"Sure." Natalia took the papers from Tierney and started to close the door.

"Oh, before you go, I also have a bunch of supplies in my car. Want to just open the garage door and I'll stack them inside?"

Just then, Regina's au pair passed behind Natalia and into the kitchen.

"No, the garage isn't good," Natalia replied. "Take them around to the laundry room." She pointed her finger in the direction of the side yard. "The door should be unlocked."

"Okay," Tierney said, and the front door shut.

Friendly bunch.

Tierney began unloading supplies and headed to the laundry room. On approach, she could see an enormous wooden play structure in the backyard. Go big or go home, Tierney's contractor brother would say to that. The property oozed wealth and she wasn't even inside yet.

Tierney opened the laundry room door. The space was triple the size of the one in their ranch-style rental, and featured a commercial washer and dryer and two department store-sized clothing racks.

She made two trips, being mindful of her shoulder, and placed the items as neatly as possible next to large boxes labeled "rolling backpacks." She closed the door, remembering not to lock it, and made her way back to Betty. As she passed by the front kitchen window again, she could see what looked to be Natalia in tears being consoled by her friend. Not wanting to get caught staring, Tierney kept moving, but couldn't help but wonder just how close the two had been to Tatyana.

SATURDAY, NOVEMBER 24

The Gillespies had lucked out. Laura's favorite sitter was available to watch Finn, and the holiday weekend was proving quite festive.

After selecting an outfit from the clothes she'd purchased with Gem, and laying the dress and accessories out on the bed, Tierney found herself face-to-face with the bucket list on her cork board. She wrote, "Baking Class/Birthday Party Business" on a sticky note and smacked it directly over item number one.

She slid off her jeans and out fell Sutton's business card from the back pocket. Not wanting to lose it, she tacked it up on the cork board, too.

Tierney dressed for dinner and stood in front of the mirror. Feeling indulgent, she spritzed on her signature Bulgari scent, the first gift Sean had ever given her. She pulled out the new mascara from the drawer for a light application and grabbed Chapstick for a hydrating touch.

"So glamorous," Sean said upon seeing his wife in the hallway.

"Just a step up from my jeans, silly," she said, poking him in the chest with her finger, and continued into the kitchen to prepare Finn's dinner.

The sitter Laura had recommended was from Italy, and the young woman's boyfriend had kindly dropped her off en route to his night-shift job. Finn had already mapped out their evening together, announcing it would be spent "all in" at the Grand Prix he'd tracked across and around the dining room table.

"I hope there's a Lamborghini Countach in there somewhere," she said to Finn at the sight of the room.

His eyes doubled in size at his sitter's knowledge of fancy Italian cars. It was trending to be a good evening for all.

—

"Heavenly," said Tierney with closed eyes after the first course of their six-course tasting menu—pommes soufflé with golden Osetra caviar.

Not knowing much about wine himself, Sean took the sommelier's recommendation—a bottle of pinot noir from the Russian River Valley—to complement their dining experience. Tierney could never have imagined spending so much money on wine, but Sean's position now made their life comfortable in a way she'd never known.

Sean was looking more relaxed, and opened up about his projects during dinner. "Vibora's executive team is being escalated on the depositions list. There's been more evidence than anticipated of illegal backdating by their VP of HR, CFO, and CEO."

The irony of the situation wasn't lost on Tierney; Sean, too, could potentially have issues with a Regina cohort—her husband, Ian. But she pushed recent Regina events from her mind, choosing to keep the conversation upbeat instead of rehashing the upsetting incidents again with Sean.

"Will be interesting to see how it all goes down." Tierney took another sip of wine. She was feeling more at ease herself and shared the latest with her baking class idea. "And the kid-friendly recipes I've been working on after school with Finn's input have been awesome, in case I end up going the children's-class-party route."

"Sounds like a great use of your expertise. And I'm thrilled you've given serious thought to finding an outlet that excites you." He reached for Tierney's hand.

"Oh, and I forgot to tell you earlier. While I was buying that Thanksgiving centerpiece downtown, I met a detective working on the lifeguard case."

"Really? What are the odds?" Sean's tone had a note of trepidation.

"Didn't learn anything new, and he was kind of an ass, but he gave me his card in case I remembered other details. You know, about the victim from the plane, happenings at the pool. I got a weird feeling he hadn't pursued any details I called in already, like following up with Tatyana's family. But I didn't push it."

Sean squeezed Tierney's hand. "I know law enforcement is part of who you are, but it would be healthier to focus your energy on this new baking business. It's a great idea. Plus, a happier topic than a murder investigation that dredges up things, you know?"

She smiled at the love in his eyes. "I see why you'd say that. It's just, I feel a connection with this girl—we were both new to the area and starting fresh. If there's some way I can help with the case, I want to at least try. I'm just not sure how."

"That's fair. But enough of the investigation. Back to our dinner."

"Yes. And cheers to your client's kind gesture."

"Indeed. Cheers to Dean Javits. He's a big golfer, but likes to lap swim like you."

Tierney hesitated, mid-drink, at the name Dean. Tierney knew a Dean from the pool. Well, knew of. But Dean was a fairly common name.

"What's that look?"

"Oh nothing, sweetheart," she said in a light voice. "Just trying to identify those notes of raspberry on my tongue like the sommelier mentioned. I clearly need more practice in my savoring technique." She wasn't about to bring up the pool again.

—

Tierney didn't mind driving the sitter home—or to her boyfriend's apartment, as she learned would be the case. It had been a while since they'd hired a sitter and Tierney missed hearing how an evening with Finn had gone.

The boyfriend lived across town in Park View's new development. Tierney had only been to the area once before, during summer while dropping off a boy from Finn's soccer camp, but she knew of it. It was the lower-income location that Gem and other wealthy private school parents were up-in-arms about over the number of families it housed, and what that was going to do to the neighborhood and property values.

It was a three-story community with over a hundred new units, with some, allegedly, housing extended families living in spaces designed for a single. That trend was soon expected to cause enrollment issues in local schools, larger class sizes being just one of the problems an increased population presented.

Having seen all walks from growing up in New York City and working for the Squad, she could imagine and empathize with the plight of residents. She considered herself lucky to be on the private school side of things now, but was torn on where her opinions stood since the community had garnered a reputation for being a drug-dealing spot.

After watching the sitter walk inside the complex, Tierney drove away but absent-mindedly turned right instead of left through the neighborhood. While making a U-turn, she was surprised to pass by Bell's weathered white VW Scirocco parked on the street near the complex's south entrance.

She knew from BB as well as her work in Dublin that hoarders were frequently functioning people in society. But then again, Bell did seem to have other issues. She pondered the idea of Bell potentially having a home nearby. *Or maybe this was Bell's new parking spot since the pool closure?* Regardless, Tierney circled back.

With the pencil and sticky notepad she kept in the cup holder, she jotted down Bell's license plate number as Sean's dredging comment floated back. He, and BB for that matter, were probably right to assume the investigation was making her PTSD worse. She decided to not dial Sutton's number and, instead, just hang onto the license plate in case it was needed. Before she put down her pencil, though, she scribbled one more thing: "Dean Javits." At the sight of the name, she paused. *Initials DJ.* Hadn't the au pairs mentioned a DJ?

Tierney learned years ago to trust her intuition. The Dean she had interacted with at the pool didn't strike her as a killer, although he had made that throttling comment about the Stingrays.

SUNDAY, NOVEMBER 25

Tierney was busy chucking ornaments and other Christmas items that had broken during their move. It was her latest attempt at distraction since her late-night Google search while Sean was getting ready for bed—confirming that his client, Dean Javits, former board member of Vibora, was indeed the same man she had shared a lane with a few times at Schick Pool. She was still contemplating its significance when she heard Gem's family rolling out their trash and recycle bins.

Tierney headed outside with a plate of cookies and saw it was Gem. "I missed your arrival home this afternoon. Made you guys a Happy Thanksgiving welcome back. They're chocolate ginger."

"They look delish."

The two friends hugged and shared holiday highlights.

"By the way," Gem continued, "I've been dying to tell you my Mara scoop from Jennie's shower this afternoon."

"Oh, do I want to hear this?" Tierney made a cringe face.

"You do. Granted, she was quite tipsy, but said mid-bite of Regina's sub-par dessert that 'Finn's mom should handle Mrs. Ferber's holiday party before winter break.'"

"Really?"

"Honest to goodness. In front of everyone, she said your cookies are amazing. Anyway, I know you're currently working on that new business idea, but if you've any interest in still doing something in Finn's classroom, you are in!"

"I thought this day would never come." Tierney pretended to pinch herself.

Gem continued sharing the latest, including their unexpected traffic, snowstorm and five-hour road closure on Highway 80, all en route to Tahoe, and how they had met an adorable Irish couple in the lodge during a lunch break. "Much younger than us, but the guy went to Trinity."

"How fun. I really did enjoy my time there." The heaviness around Tierney's heart had softened a bit this weekend. Finding a haven with family, being there for Sean, following through on her promise to call Dr. Mosely, and knowing she had a genuine new friend in Gem had all made an impact. Tierney hesitated, but then felt oddly okay with continuing. "One of the most meaningful things was during my second year. BB and I had the same graduation requirement—to fulfill twenty-five volunteer hours with a community outreach program. She had already begun volunteering on campus with the Crisis Hotline Call Center and roped me in since they were understaffed."

"I could see why that would be meaningful, but also stressful?"

"It was, but wasn't at the same time? It was as if I had uncovered a calling of my own. This innate ability to read others based on voice intonations. And after three years with them—"

"Three years? What happened to twenty-five hours?"

The comment made Tierney smile. "I know. But I loved helping fellow students, even the staff and faculty members who'd sometimes call in. My confidence grew. I even took over the manager spot from BB once her labs became too time consuming."

"Impressive."

"The experience developed this crisis management skill set in me, and honed an ability to persuade people. Which is so funny now since I couldn't negotiate my way into Finn's classroom."

Gem giggled. "What happened to change all that for you? I mean, because you switched to baking."

Tierney took in a breath. "As graduation approached, I pretty much bypassed having to be a police officer and landed a highly-coveted position with the Crisis Intervention Squad, thanks to graduating at the top of my class. Plus, the Head of the Criminology Department was a former classmate of the Squad's Chief Inspector."

"Nice connection. They always say it's not who you know, but who knows you. That's how Rob got this new job of his, from a former colleague."

"Exactly. I mean, I still had to pass a few phases of the Garda's training program to secure the opp, but that was a piece of cake. I was super fit back then, and had a solid knowledge of the work already from watching my dad and older brother while growing up. The job I ultimately found myself in with the Squad, though? Not so much cake."

"How so?"

"I had this amazing mentor named Norah," Tierney said and hesitated. *It's okay, it's Gem.* Tierney breathed in courage. "She identified something special in me after seeing how well we'd worked together in a highly charged incident. She pulled me up through the ranks of the Squad to serve directly with her. She had already been with the organization for a few years and held the lead hostage negotiator position."

"Wow. A hostage negotiator?"

Tierney nodded. "She was my strength. She helped me build on the confidence I'd developed while working those Trinity phones—to take risks and lead with my intuition in the moment while on duty. It was amazing. She made me realize I was genuinely good at the work, and didn't just have the role because I'd fast-tracked in." Tierney could feel her eyes tearing up.

"I bet you could handle any situation, no matter how wild."

Tierney slid her hands into her pockets. "I could, but then one day I couldn't. That was the night Norah died—"

"Oh no!" Gem's hand flew up to her mouth.

Just then, a loud bang shot from across the cul-de-sac and the friends flinched. Their eyes flew around to see Mildred on the street side of her recently slammed gate, trash bin rumbling behind. Their catch-up time was over.

Gem returned her attention to Tierney and whispered, "I'm so sorry to hear about Norah. That must've been unbearable. I can understand the appeal of baking after that."

Tierney held back tears. She could hear in Gem's voice that what she'd shared had been intense, so decided to change topics and force a smile. "Yes, overcooking something or catching an oven mitt on fire was about as horrible as things would get from that point on."

Gem giggled.

Success.

Mildred yelled hello, waving to the two friends who did so in return.

"Thanks for listening. We'll talk more later," Tierney said.

MONDAY, NOVEMBER 26

"If I don't get a call back this morning, I am sending officers over for an arrest on the grounds of interfering with a murder investigation," Sutton said into the receiver and slammed down his desk phone.

Ayala pulled up a chair next to Sutton's desk. "Still trying to get the host dad's last name and number from the agency? Sorry again about my oversight. Guess I had taken the reason for Tatyana's exit at face value—just another divorce."

"Not entirely your fault; I should've asked about him."

"Well, bummer regardless. And that he and his wife have different last names, so my notes don't help. That does seem to be a trend nowadays."

Sutton swiveled around to face him. "It's absurd. The agency piece, that is, not the last name thing. Am I the only one who checks messages over a holiday weekend?"

"I know. Same thing with the host mom."

"And what's that in your hand? More bad news?"

"Thought I was done following up with the list of lap swimmers from Schick Pool's sign-in sheet on the night of the murder, but this last page just arrived from Facilities."

"Seriously? Just now?"

"It fell behind the check-in desk and wasn't discovered until recently, when the cleaning crew moved furniture. City's apparently taking full advantage of the closure to spruce up things."

"A lot of names left? Any DJ?"

"Not too many. And nothing DJ-related. That was the first thing I checked. But, uh, would it be okay if I disappeared for about an hour? Take care of an errand?"

"Personal business should be handled outside of work. Station policy." Sutton couldn't help but notice how awkward Ayala looked at the request—and his damn full head of hair.

"I know, it's just that, my mom doesn't really like taking taxis alone and I don't want her to miss—"

"Your mom?"

"She's in town for Thanksgiving and I'd like to run her back to the airport so she doesn't miss her flight."

"Why the hell didn't you say you needed to help your mom? Hand me that list."

"Great."

"And when you're back, I want an update on Josh Jeffries while I stay on top of this DJ character. And finish typing up the interview transcripts, would ya? You don't want to get so far behind and forget something."

"You got it."

Once Ayala left, Sutton was reminded of the call with his own mom on Thanksgiving. Maybe he should consider a move back to Denver after this Popov case wraps. That's where his family was—his sister's brood plus his mom, who was growing less like the mom he knew with each passing day under dementia's grip.

His mom was the best. A stay-at-home mom in the truest sense. Always there for him after school, making his favorite snacks, driving him on rainy days for his paper route, teaching him practical things like how to cook and balance a checkbook. She said she never missed having a job out in the world while his dad supported them financially with the law practice. Trusts and estates, wills and probate were what kept them comfortable.

Sutton's thoughts returned to work, and he pulled down his readers. He reviewed the lap swimmer names and paused at the sight of one, written in neat, tidy script. *Tierney Gillespie.* Sounding familiar, he wiggled his mouse and typed the name into the station's database. Up popped a few entries of past calls Joelle had fielded. Ah yes, the woman known around the station for leaving her name, spelling it out, and providing a phone number, despite the line being anonymous. He snickered but could appreciate the professionalism.

Her call-in list included a drug-related sighting during a youth soccer game, a call to say she had been at Schick Pool the evening of the murder and was available for any questions, a hit-and-run incident with a crossing guard at Apricot Grove, *Josh again,* and an encounter with Tatyana on a flight to San Jose. *Wait. That wannabe-detective mom from the florist? Christ. She had signed in that evening.*

* * *

Across town, Tierney sat in standstill traffic just four houses beyond their cul-de-sac, thankful to have grabbed her travel coffee mug on the way to Apricot Grove. One of the neighbors had commenced with renovation work and the crews were jostling for parking space. *Stay clear of Mildred's.*

Tierney wished she could discuss her DJ concerns with someone, but it still didn't feel right to worry Sean unnecessarily, or BB. Should she check in with Sutton, or wait for something to hit the news? Or could Mosely be of assistance? Maybe yoga would help her process a decision. Tierney had agreed to meet Gem at the studio again, and it felt good to have somewhere to go after drop off—even if it was yoga.

Finn was still wearing his cape as they approached Mrs. Ferber's classroom. Transitions after a break had always been hard for him.

Tierney dabbed his eyes as they reached the door, and asked him to tap into his super powers. "Imagine yourself walking out of the classroom in a few hours and seeing me right here waiting for you."

He sniffled and nodded. "Are you and Dad going to be okay while I'm at school?"

"Of course. Why wouldn't we be?"

"I don't want the pool murderer to get you." His damp eyes narrowed with worry.

"Oh, bud. That's not going to happen." Tierney gave Finn a bear hug until she squeezed out a smile, which was good because she'd need to remove his cape. Class rules—no costumes. But Mrs. Ferber was already on it, inviting Finn to put it in his cubby where he could see it. Tierney untied the fabric and he reluctantly entered the classroom. *Gretchen was clueless. Mrs. Ferber is fabulous.* Finn turned back to face Tierney and waved.

Now it was her turn to be strong, and speak with Mara about the opportunity Gem mentioned. It certainly couldn't hurt to get more visibility for her baking skills if she wanted a successful business launch. Heck, maybe Mara would even be looking for her this time for a one-on-one chat. She stood up taller at the thought and walked around the kindergarten wing until she spotted a girl gaggle. Mara was, of course, in the center.

"You can do this, for God's sake. You're a grown-ass woman." Tierney envisioned BB yelling at her.

She saw Laura on the perimeter so began there, sharing the fun her entire family had enjoyed that evening thanks to her sitter recommendation. When the final bell rang, and with all kids now inside, parents began to disperse. While looking towards what remained of the circle, Tierney's eyes met Mara's.

"Hey Tierney."

Tierney was surprised Mara remembered her name, but she could hear in her eager tone that some critical news was about to unfold as Mara approached. The French roast percolated in her gut.

"Oh hi, Mara. How was your holiday?"

"I so enjoy this time of year." Mara started in: "You know, I wanted to tell you that every December I host this fabulous holiday party for my mom friends and I'd love it if you could join us. It's a cookie exchange as well. Are you free on Saturday?"

"Oh, I think so." Tierney was dumbstruck by what she'd just been asked.

"Nice. I'll send you an invitation with the details. Just no chocolate chip, and only homemade recipes. Not that I really need to tell you that," she said, her wide smile a perfect white. "I hear you're a professional baker, is that right? That must explain the quality of your cookies at the class party."

"Yes, I was. I mean, I am." The invite was sinking in.

"Great, talk soon."

Mara walked off to join another group before the volunteering question could form on Tierney's lips, but did she hear Mara correctly? Had she just been invited to Apricot Grove's party of the year? She turned around, as if in need of someone else to verify the invitation. But as she took in the space, a feeling of happiness spilled in.

On her walk back to Betty, questions followed. Was she willing to be uncomfortable and attend an event inside Mara's house? Knowing Regina would be there, too? She would have Gem at the party for moral support. And she'd be able to showcase her cookies—another great advertising opportunity for the new business. *Tons of potential customers.* Her stomach twisted at the mixed emotions, right alongside the ones still churning over Dean Javits.

While driving downtown, her cell phone rang from where it rested on the passenger seat. *Dr. Mosely calling back.* She reached over for it without taking her eyes off the road and accepted the call on speaker.

"Hi, this is Detective Sergeant Howard Sutton with the Park View Police Department. Do you have a few minutes?"

Tierney cleared her throat. "Yes, of course." She felt a twinge of excitement.

"I believe we met at the florist the other day."

"I remember. What can I do for you?"

"I'm making calls about the investigation. And this call is being recorded. Okay for us to proceed?"

"Certainly."

"And my apologies. Looks as if you haven't been contacted yet about your swim at the pool on the evening of the murder. Bit of a paperwork glitch."

Tierney smiled but wasn't going to waste time gloating. "I didn't actually swim that evening. I was onsite to retrieve fins I'd left behind but still signed in. Following protocol and all."

"Yes, of course. Did you notice anything out of the ordinary that evening?"

"I've actually been going over it in my mind since our conversation. Now, I did show up on the later side, after the check-in rush. I found it odd that Dummy, oh sorry, that's what they call him—the life-size water rescue manikin the staff uses for training? It had been propped up at the check-in desk instead of there being a real person who usually punches lap cards." Tierney could hear the detective typing.

"Go on."

"I had assumed the lifeguard staff was being silly, or maybe busy and didn't want to get in trouble if a coworker saw no one manning the front?"

"Please continue."

"I just proceeded through the lobby to search the lost and found bin."

"Do you recall seeing Brad Madrone, the manager, on site?"

Tierney thought for a moment, as she turned into the yoga studio's parking lot. She motioned to Gem, waiting outside, that she would need a few more minutes to wrap up a call. Gem nodded and went inside.

"You know, I did." Tierney proceeded to relay the interaction she observed with Josh, Brad, and a girl she now believed to be Tatyana. "I later realized it was her, based on her height and the way she carried herself. I mentioned to you at the florist that I'd encountered her on a flight from Seattle earlier this year?"

"Yes. And I see you've called in miscellaneous details around town to the station."

"Correct. So, she wasn't a blonde when I met her on the flight, but, like I said, the way she carried herself—with a slouch that made me correct my own posture—was the tell-tale sign for me."

Sutton gave a loud exhale.

"Anyway, it was a peculiar exchange among the three near the lobby doors at the beginning of the evening shift—as if they all knew each other but not in a good way. Total speculation on my part, though, for the record."

"For the record, yes. Did you see Brad on the property once inside?

"I didn't."

"Anything else noteworthy about the victim, Tatyana Popov?"

Should she mention a possible DJ-Dean pool connection? No, she'd already shared enough speculation. "Nothing I haven't already mentioned. And I assume you've already questioned the crossing guard?" *Ugh. But it would be horrible for Sean to potentially be representing a murderer.*

Sutton cleared his throat. "Yes, well, thank you for your time. If there's anything else you think of, please—"

"Actually, there is a swimmer named Dean Javits I should mention. Although, he may go by DJ."

"Oh?"

Tierney heard an upturn in Sutton's voice as his typing started again, which made her stomach twitch. She clearly not only owed further exploration to her husband, but to Tatyana as well. And Sutton needed to be the one to sniff it out.

"It's just a hunch, but I think he may have known Tatyana, from what I've heard around school. I'm not sure if he was at the pool for an evening swim that same night, but I did see him during the morning session."

"Good to know. All leads appreciated."

"I don't think it's anything, by the way, but wanted to cover all bases. He never gave me a violent vibe. Tired, maybe agitated, but I'll leave that for you to investigate." Tierney felt her shoulders relax upon sharing the details, and Sutton seemed more open to her feedback this time.

"You've been most helpful and—"

"Oh sorry, there is one more thing. Someone must've mentioned this already but there's always been this old white VW Scirocco parked onsite. The woman who drives it may have seen something. I don't know her name, though. But I'm sure if you asked the beat cops, they'd know of her. Maybe track her down for questioning?"

"Thanks for the insight," Sutton said.

"Although, she might startle if you approach her too quickly," Tierney continued. "And, actually, her car might have even been involved in an almost-hit-and-run a few weeks back near Apricot Grove with Josh, that crossing guard I mentioned earlier who walked the victim to work? You might have a record of that, too, with a license number?"

Sutton sighed. "I will look into it."

"Oh wait. I got her license plate number the other day but it's at home on my cork board. Happy to call it in later today before I pick up my son at school? In the meantime, be careful approaching her if it was her car from that school incident. She's a bit unstable."

"Yes, ma'am. Will do."

Tierney registered Sutton's sarcasm but was too busy jotting down a reminder to call back with the plate number to dwell on it. Sean's "dredging" comment from their date night is what came to mind, but he would understand. She was just doing her civic duty; he'd do the same.

Sutton ended the call, and Tierney waited patiently for a woman from the prior class to re-roll her mat that had taken a waterfall dive from her hatchback. Talking with someone in law enforcement made her feel at ease despite now running late.

Tierney entered the lobby with two minutes to spare. While tossing her things in a cubby, she saw Regina but didn't flinch. The woman was busy telling the small group still gathered outside the classroom door something about the victim.

"My friend's husband oversees Parks and Rec and heard that she died from a blow to the head—with some kind of spear. One of his guys was there onsite the night her body was found," said Regina.

A spear? Tierney froze, sneaker in hand. She hadn't heard or read that in any news report. And she had never reported their harpoon missing. Should she now?

"It's all just unbelievable, in our town," said Gretchen.

"And so tragic for a young person wanting to find a new life for herself in the US. Tatyana had subbed for our sitter a few times and my kids really liked her," said another woman whose puffed lips and expression didn't move when she spoke.

Tierney reminded herself that hearsay wasn't helpful, but didn't know what was true anymore. She tabled the spear comment in her mind and grabbed a lavender-infused meditation eye mask (she was going to need it), followed the women inside to the sound of a centering gong, and found her place near Gem.

The classroom was quiet but still abuzz with the latest *Daily Gazette* article about the investigation.

"Aren't there any suspects?" Gretchen whispered to Regina as the women took their mats.

Marc sounded the gong again.

Tierney was thankful for a structuring sound. She wondered how the Stingrays would react to an underwater gong as she refocused on Marc, who audibly filled his lungs with classroom air, and began to lead the morning mantra.

Om…

She was still finding the spear comment unsettling when her body jumped at the blaring sound of a cell phone's ringtone—the song "Celebration" by Kool & The Gang. She opened her eyes to see Jennie lunging from her mat to silence her phone.

"Oh my gosh," Jennie gasp-whispered.

"Class, just a reminder to leave your phones outside in the cubbies or silence them. Now let's recenter," Marc said, calmly irritated.

Jennie's cheeks turned rosy as she sat back down. "So sorry, guys," she whispered, and shut her eyes tight, joining in the class's deep inhale and, more likely, to hide from glares.

—

"Hope that wasn't bad news on the phone earlier?" Gem asked Tierney after class.

"Sorry again to be late." Tierney spoke softly and shared basic details of her detective call.

"To think you were at the pool that same evening the murder happened," Gem whispered, a bit too loud, and Regina's head swiveled in their direction.

Tierney knew then that she'd need to take a yoga hiatus, at least until the investigation was over. The vibe had never been the relaxing experience she had hoped for—for herself or her shoulder—and it certainly wasn't now. She longed for the pool. *Damn drought.*

Gem and Tierney encountered Jennie in the lobby distributing thank-you cards. Tierney apologized to her personally this time for being unable to make it to the shower.

"It's okay. Things come up," she said in a kind tone. "By the way, I loved your gift—such a unique book for our shelf. I've already ordered copies for my nieces and nephews for Christmas."

"So nice to hear. The collection is a family favorite," Tierney said while registering Regina's glare.

"Speaking of parties," Gretchen said, as Jennie walked over to another group with her cards, "I need to decide between two recipes for Mara's cookie exchange."

"I've already chosen mine," Regina said. "And Mara will be making Kolaczki. It's a Polish recipe Natalia has loved since childhood. Isn't that sweet?"

"Adorbs," said Gretchen. "This is her biggest party of the year," she said to Tierney, as if she'd know nothing about it.

"Oh, Mara mentioned it and I think I can make it," Tierney said.

"Awesome to have you there!" Gem said.

It was clear Gretchen was processing what she'd just heard. "Yes, I suppose the more regular moms the better. Mara's Junior League friends are plenty enough in the fancy baker department."

Gem and Tierney exchanged glances.

"She's actually worse—a professional baker," Regina said.

"Seriously?" Gretchen said.

"This isn't the World Pastry Cup, ladies. And it's the holidays, for goodness' sake," Gem said.

Tierney couldn't believe how quickly the topic had centered on her, and as if she wasn't standing right there. *Regina must have a real problem with Sean working on the Vibora investigation.*

Gretchen dismissed Gem's remark with a shrug. "Anyway, will the poker party for the dads be at your home again, Regina?"

"Definitely. And I told Ian he should make it a small pay-to-play fundraiser for the school this year."

"Excellent idea," Gretchen said.

"And Mara told me she's thrilled Justine can make it to the exchange this year."

"She's usually out of town or busy with work," Gretchen said. "But oh, my God. Did you see her Christmas letter? I think they must plan their vacations based on the pretentious factor so they can brag about it come December."

"And she always has to be the first one to get her cards in the mail like the day before Thanksgiving so it's first to arrive in people's mailboxes," Regina continued.

Tierney and Gem walked outside to distance themselves from the negative energy and stopped on the sidewalk for Gem to re-tie her shoe. Laura exited the studio with them but passed by and over to her car without saying a word before Tierney realized it was her. *Odd.*

Gretchen and Regina exited the studio moments later, but continued their gossip run on the short walk down to Starbucks. "And every time I drive by Bob's Bar, I see Craig's Porsche in the parking lot. Maybe this 'in-between jobs' time is getting to him," Regina said, and their conversation trailed off.

Aren't all these women friends?

Gem rolled her eyes at the remark. "It's been great having you, a normal person, in class. And why does Gretchen need to make the cookie exchange so competitive? I'm already feeling stressed enough about the holidays and my parents arriving this week."

"Sorry to hear you've been stressed. Maybe we should read Laura's holiday book."

Gem giggled. "I do need to keep things in perspective. I mean, someone last year did bring soccer team cookies to the party. From a cookie dough fundraiser that year in March."

"That doesn't scream freezer burn. Would you like help with deciding what cookie to make?"

"I was planning to do the one I did last year—molasses cookies, which people enjoyed. But I'm guessing I should mix things up?"

"How did you like the ones I gave you yesterday?"

"We all fought over them."

Tierney beamed.

"Think I could handle a chocolate ginger recipe?"

"Absolutely. It's simple. I'll get you a copy and you'll be dazzling the ladies yet again."

"Thanks for having my back."

"Ditto. Just pop over when you get home."

—

Tierney checked messages in the car and saw that Dr. Mosely had returned her call. As she listened to his appointment options, she noted how calming his voice was. *This is really happening. I'll be trying therapy again.* Tierney shifted uncomfortably under the seat belt. *My parents would die. My brothers would die.* Times were changing, though, just as Sean had said. There was no shame in asking for help with one's mental health. *There was no shame in asking for help with one's mental health.*

Once home, Tierney passed through the kitchen to pull down the cookbook for Gem and was reminded of Lily's moonlighting comment about the sticky notes. Not wanting Gem to ask specifics about what she'd called in, she moved them to the cork board by her bed. *Don't forget to call Sutton with the plate number. And mention the harpoon? No, the license plate was the concrete piece.*

She made a copy of the recipe for Gem on their home copier and placed it with the cookbook on the dining room table.

—

"Things are looking tidy, miss," Gem remarked while walking through Tierney's front entry.

"I certainly have more free time with the pool closure."

Gem followed her into the dining room. "I'm sure my chocolate ginger won't be as delicious as yours, but at least I'll have a tried and trusted recipe. Is that the cookbook—all Christmas cookies?" Gem flipped through the dog-eared pages. "Looks well loved."

"I've had it since high school. So many creative recipes. More ideas for us next year," Tierney said as a Polaroid fell out and fluttered to the ground.

Gem retrieved it and noticed the same thing Tierney had on their first day of yoga together. "Holy cow, that lady is Jennie's twin." Gem pointed to a woman's face.

Tierney's heart sank. She hesitantly peeked over Gem's shoulder to see a photo she hadn't laid eyes on in years, of three friends: Norah, BB, and herself, at Toby's Tavern. Toby's had been the pub closest to the station where they'd meet for drinks after work. Gem turned it over to the July 22, 1999 date written on the back. Tierney's birthday—the last one Norah had been alive to celebrate.

"I thought the same thing when I first saw Jennie. That's Norah," Tierney's voice cracked. "My mentor I told you about? And this is BB."

Gem looked up at Tierney. "I'm sorry. Seeing photos of old friends can be hard. Is BB visiting anytime soon? I'd love to meet her."

"Nothing planned yet, unfortunately. Holidays are a therapist's busiest time of year." She tried to sound casual while taking the photo and sliding it back into the cookbook. Tierney wasn't in the mood to discuss more, already feeling drained. Their discussion would need to be just about recipes.

"It's an effort to keep in touch with old friends now that we all have families and live in different places," Gem said.

"So true."

"I'd better head back," Gem continued, seeming to sense the change in Tierney's mood. "And get to a grocery store to make sure I have all ingredients for my new baking project before my parents arrive. I should get as much prep done as possible. Thanks again for this." Gem waved the recipe in the air as she headed out.

"Of course, anytime." Tierney closed the door and stood for a moment before pulling out the Polaroid again.

She sat on the arm of the leather chair and looked at her younger self. She glowed back in 1999, in a way Tierney couldn't recall having seen in years. This present moment, though, she felt oddly okay in looking at the three young faces. Maybe Jennie's presence at yoga was helping her subconscious process? But how she missed Norah. She could almost feel her blue eyes smiling from their favorite table near the stage. It reminded her of when she'd gone out to dinner with Norah at a nice restaurant downtown after her last review, and credited her mentor with the independent, more confident person she'd become.

"That's kind, Tierney, but no one can give you confidence," Norah said. "That comes from within. And be proud of yourself? I might've shown you the ropes, but I don't walk in your shoes. Only you can walk your path. And may I remind—"

Norah paused to glare away a group of gathered businessmen who'd loosened their mouths along with their ties, dropping one too many *fucks* within earshot of children dining with parents at a nearby table, and returned to Tierney (the sound of multiple 'sorry, lasses' in the men's wake).

"—a path that includes taking over the Inspector role when I retire at fifty. Philip's already purchased tools and begun work on the beach house his grandfather left him in Malahide, looking rather devilish in a toolbelt without his trousers, I might add."

Tierney snorted and a mouthful of lager shot across the table.

Norah smiled in an alluring way and tossed Tierney a napkin from an extra place setting. "In all seriousness, with that intuition of yours, it's the only way I could ever imagine stepping down from the Squad."

Tierney returned the cookbook to the shelf and thought about how she'd describe Norah to Gem next time.

TUESDAY, NOVEMBER 27

Sutton was feeling energized about the case. With the Thanksgiving weekend in his taillights and a number for Dean Javits, progress would be forthcoming.

While awaiting a callback from Dean, who apparently traveled a lot, he replayed Tierney's voice message about the mystery VW's license plate number. Still agitated by her air, he added the details to Tierney's witness file anyway, and did the same for a few other call-ins. He was reminded of his attorney father's words when he was alive, on how best to keep clients happy. "Mind the billable hours."

Sutton thought of Tierney's remark at the florist about Tatyana seeming to be running from something in Moscow. *Yeah, that loveless mother who was of no help.* And lots of cousins? That would take forever to investigate, so he focused instead on the birds in hand. He looked across to Ayala at his desk. "Any luck with Josh Jeffries?"

"Hasn't returned my calls. Time to interrogate him during his school shift?"

"Leave him another message with a choice—to be interviewed this afternoon at the station or patrol will pick him up at the school."

"Will do."

"And any update on a murder weapon?"

"Nothing yet. I thought for sure it would've been found at the bottom of the pool or in that dense jasmine. But I have a second call into Facilities to see what was affixed to that 3D mural in the pool's office. And when was the last time someone saw it there."

"Good, but review the medical examiner's report again. Take in the crime scene and autopsy photos, and the shape of the wound? Put on your weapons wonk cap. Maybe it will spark something new.

"What else could've been used on the property that's metal, like the medical examiner said in his report? Forensics swept the place for possibilities."

Hearing Ayala's question jarred Sutton's memory. "Wait, the Holly Oaks interview. Tatyana had used bolt cutters to open the mistaken locker that day, right? Let's check the pool's inventory list. See if bolt cutters are accounted for." Sutton held out his empty mug to Ayala. "And get me a fill up while you're at it. Black, no funny business."

—

Sutton looked outside through the station's row of awning windows and spotted a guy in his early thirties, wearing old jeans that hung three inches below the waistline. *Must be Josh*. While reaching over to lock his bike to a pole in front of the station, Josh revealed a large bruise on his upper arm before his T-shirt sleeve fell back into place. He checked in with reception and was led to Interview Room A.

"Mr. Jeffries. You're a tough man to track down." Sutton put his notepad on the table and introduced himself.

"Always in demand." Josh sniffed, wiped his hand across his nose, and crossed his arms over his chest.

Sutton lowered his readers and flipped through a folder. "Does the room look the same?"

Josh's expression grew less cocky. "The walls are painted darker, I guess. But that was back in high school. My juvie days are over."

"Junior high, too. Anyway, as mentioned on the phone, I'd like to talk with you about Tatyana Popov, and this session is being recorded." Sutton pointed to the video camera, which Josh indicated he'd already noticed. "What exactly was your relationship?"

"Met her a few months back while guarding at Apricot Grove, bro. She was picking up someone's kid for a playdate and we got to talking." He adjusted the rim of his Oakland Raiders cap and Sutton noticed another bruise near his temple.

"I'm not your bro. Was she your girlfriend?"

"I guess. We were together." Josh couldn't sit still.

"When was the last time you saw her?"

"That would've been a Thursday morning. I left early to guard and she was still asleep."

"So, the morning of the date her body was found?"

"Yeah, I guess."

"Take me through that day."

"My morning shift is about an hour. My boss likes me to stay past the bell for stragglers."

"Do you know where Tatyana went that morning?"

"Naw. I assume the pool? She was working odd shifts there. Taking what she could get for money. She lost her au pair gig so was crashing with me. You should ask her manager, Brad."

"I see. Do you know what other jobs she might've had to 'take what she could get for money'?"

Josh scowled. "Why don't you ask those rich families at Apricot Grove who hired her to do stuff, instead of riding my ass?"

"And which rich families might those be?"

"I'd start with the one that has their name on the parking spot out front."

Sutton scribbled some notes. "Alright. Now, where did you go afterwards? I mean, if you didn't see her again that day."

"Here and there."

"I'll need you to be more specific."

"Um, I went back to the school around two-forty-five to do my afternoon shift for another hour. Tons of parents would've seen me there."

"Let me clarify. Where were you that evening, around five p.m. onward?"

"Didn't see her."

"We have a witness that saw you walking her to Schick Pool for her evening shift."

"Then maybe I did." Josh's tone turned defensive. "I can't remember everything."

"Right. So, you didn't see her after her shift? Later that night? Or even speak with her on the phone or text at any point?"

"I'm not a phone guy."

"Never leave a trail, eh?"

"Naw. We just had a routine. We'd meet up at my place at night after her shift but she never made it home."

"Yes, sorry for your loss." *This guy couldn't give two shits about her.*

"Um, yeah."

"Then talk to me about specifics. Where were you that evening between five p.m. and nine-thirty?"

"I might've been at the gas station, the one over by Peet's downtown. I sometimes help out the manager with projects, I can't really remember."

"Gas station projects, huh? Okay, let's focus on how you got those nasty bruises near your temple and on your arm. Crossing guard life rough these days?"

"Slipped in the shower."

"Based on the location of the bruising, and the fact you obviously haven't showered lately, I'm thinking the cause might've been something else. Hanging with a rough crowd near Schick Pool?"

"Hell no. I've never stepped foot in that place. Brad would kill me."

"Brad again?"

"Yeah, in fact, why don't you ask him where he was that night? He was pissed that me and Tatyana had been dating."

"I do see here that you two went to the same schools. A few years apart?"

"He was my older brother's age. They were friends. We weren't."

"I can follow up with Brad on all that. But right now, as Ms. Popov's self-proclaimed boyfriend, you're our prime suspect. So, unless you can provide an alibi on the night of the murder, you're going to be here a while."

Josh began tapping his fingers on his hat. "Okay, bro. I mean, detective," Josh said, and leaned forward. "I was dealing with a guy who broke into my apartment. He wore a ski mask and was looking for something when I walked in on him."

"A ski mask?" Sutton said, his tone clipped. "Let me guess. Didn't get a look at him?"

"Naw."

"Any idea who he was?"

"Naw."

"How about his size?"

"Taller than me. And fit. He roughed me up pretty good. I was out flat for a couple hours. My neighbor can attest to it. He heard the commotion and ran over. The guy left out back when he saw Nick. You can ask him. Nick in apartment 125."

Detective Sutton wrote on his notepad. "Did you file a police report?"

"Why would I do that? Cops don't do shit. Sorry, at least from my experience."

Sutton sighed. Getting him to elaborate was growing tiresome. "Did Tatyana keep personal effects at your place?"

"Naw. She traveled light and always kept things with her—even her toothbrush—in a duffle stashed at Schick. Mechanical Room, I think she once said. Kept saying she'd move her stuff in once we got engaged, but that wasn't my plan. I mean, I'm in my prime."

"Clearly. So, what do you think this guy was looking for?"

"He yelled about something Tatyana had of his. Came back a few nights ago too so I've been crashing with friends."

"Interesting. Any idea what this 'something' was that Tatyana had?"

"You'd have to ask her." Josh leaned back and sneered.

Emotionally vacant much? This guy's a sociopath. And involved in her death somehow. But how?

———

Josh left the station and Ayala met Sutton in the hallway.

"Nothing to hold him?" Ayala said.

"Not yet. Do me a favor. Call Apricot Grove. Find out whose name is on the parking spot out front. We need that info today. Drive by if you have to."

"You got it."

"I'm going to check out Josh's apartment complex and his alibi with a neighbor."

"And what about the white VW that lady called in about? Need me to follow up?"

"Already on it. The car's last known location was near Josh's apartment complex."

* * *

After school, Tierney settled Finn with Hot Wheels playtime so she could return Dr. Mosely's call. His first available wasn't until January, but he offered to fit her in next week due to her relationship with BB. Surely there would be insight about Dean Javits in the news by then if anything was pertinent, but she'd at least have Mosely to talk with if not.

After the call, Tierney heard a commotion in front of the house but remained focused on selecting her cookie recipe for Mara's party. She retrieved the cookbook she had been looking at with Gem and flipped right to it: Finnish Ribbon Cookies. She rubbed her finger along the indentation the old tavern photo had made on the page from bookmarking the recipe. The cookies were Norah's favorite, which Tierney had made a few times for her mentor's birthday. It was the perfect choice for Mara's party.

Tierney now felt a rumbling outside and approached the front windows. It was quite the scene—a full-sized truck from the construction crew down the street had stalled in the middle of her cul-de-sac. Its hood was up, a steamy kettle trailer attached to its hitch, and another truck was parking in front of it to help get it started. She smiled at the sight of Mildred, wearing an orange Clemson vest, barreling out her front door with a determined look to supervise anything and everything to ensure a quick departure of the men untangling jumper cables.

Tierney's windows were shut but a hot-asphalt smell from the kettle's steaming slurry began seeping into the house through the cracks. It struck Tierney like a fist to the diaphragm, knocking the breath from her, and the cookbook from her grip. Her memory from that night at the Embassy flooded in.

* * *

Sutton hung up the phone with Ayala. *Wright.* The name sounded familiar. He reached for a folder and his readers on his desk, and flipped through the lifeguard interview transcripts Ayala had finally finished.

Witness Interview
Name of witness: Riley Winkler (Lifeguard)
Page 2 of 2
AYALA: What do you think the two were fighting about from inside the mechanical room?
RILEY: I didn't give it much thought. We all knew they broke up a while ago and they were always kind of snippy with each other. Not sure why Tatyana still hung around. It's not like lifeguard pay is that great.
AYALA: Where did the two go after their argument?
RILEY: Hmmm. Tatyana started to organize the bins outside the mechanical room, separating the pull buoys that always get tossed in with the kickboards—an annoying task, really. And Brad stayed inside the room, probably to take a shot. I'd seen him do those multiple times during shifts. He kept vodka bottles in random places around the facility.
AYALA: Did you see him take a swig during your shift that evening?
RILEY: No, so I guess I shouldn't speculate.
AYALA: Did you ever see him use drugs?
RILEY: Brad? No way. Drugs weren't his thing. Just alcohol. And I know that because some of the guards are potheads, even dealers. This guy Brent, who only works in the summer when

he's home from Dartmouth? He's a business major and always trying to sell us weed. Sometimes patrons, too, when they catch wind of his connections. There are other dealers too among the staff, but Brent is the most consistent. Brad didn't care, though. Rumor was that he just wanted no trouble with cops.

AYALA: Anything else you'd categorize as out of the ordinary that evening?

RILEY: Hmmm. I do remember seeing Mr. Wright hop out of the pool to check his phone. Which was odd since he had arrived late and then up and left the facility after seeing a message. It was an uncharacteristically short swim for him. And he bumped into Tatyana, like literally, while she was looking at something on her phone, and he looked upset.

AYALA: Did the two know each other?

RILEY: Well, everyone knows Mr. Wright. He was like the captain of the Masters, I mean, if they had one.

AYALA: Did the two have a conversation?

RILEY: Something short. I was on duty, Detective, so had to keep my eyes on the pool. Safety first, you know.

AYALA: Yes, of course.

Interview end

Paydirt. Sutton typed the name "Wright" into his search screen but up populated an entry for Natalia Blaski. *Tatyana's au pair friend?* He scrolled down to the notes section. "Host family residence of Mara and Craig Wright." *Christ.* He and Ayala had been in his home.

Sutton pulled his notepad from his pocket to jot down their phone number but two cell phones were listed. Craig's was the 415 number. He reached across for Tatyana's phone records and compared it to the only 415 number on that list—a text she had sent the evening of her death. It matched.

Sutton picked up the phone and dialed Craig's number.

* * *

Tierney broke from her Embassy memory when the double-wide truck backfired in the cul-de-sac. Still braced against the window casing, she wiped tears from her eyes as the sound of radio interference reverberated in her head.

She registered Finn still playing in his room, so she maneuvered into the family room and sunk into the couch next to Louie. His paws stretched out to her and she rested her hands on his warm fur. Her gaze fell to their framed family photo on the mantle—Sean, Finn, and her, all smiles on vacation last summer at Lily and Hugh's lake house. Tierney as wife and mom. Her new phase of life, one Norah would never get to see. *Because I'm here and you're not.*

Tierney forced herself up to a standing position and walked into the garage. She flipped on the light and could see the Squad box clearly—right where she had last shoved it, having nowhere left to go. She peeled back the tape and sifted through the old clothes and knickknacks.

It must be there. BB had told her it was. She dug down further, all the way to the bottom, until Tierney could finally feel it. She removed the navy blue leather album and sat with it on the hard steps leading inside.

~ ~ ~

"Happy work anniversary!" Norah exclaimed as Tierney opened the gift box to reveal a gorgeous album with the Squad shield embossed on its cover.

Norah had wanted to commemorate the milestone of Tierney's latest work anniversary with a house party. Her husband, Philip, made the home-cooked meal, Irish stew being the main dish because it was a Tierney favorite. The party was small, with BB and a handful of colleagues, but a celebratory evening nonetheless. The two women had been through so much together.

"Now you have a designated place to put your newspaper clippings and memorabilia, my little scrapbooker."

"It's beautiful."

"Like you. Sláinte!" Norah embraced her partner and then all clinked together their overflowing glasses of cider.

Tierney had earned a reputation for being the Squad's historian, but it was her way of processing what had gone well during a negotiation and what could be improved upon. She had learned the technique from her dad. Frequently found at the staffroom table after hours, she'd be cutting out and taping in clippings that invariably made their way to her desk, along with the tactical notes from her debriefs with Norah and the team, as well as pieces of congratulatory memorabilia from jobs well done.

~ ~ ~

Tierney ran her palm across the textured cover and remained seated on the garage's concrete step. The album's leather still retained the historic scent of the station.

She opened the soft wrap closure and the pages cracked apart. The earliest photos were of her parents and brothers in attendance at her graduation from training, her posing with her gun in full Garda attire at the egging on of her eldest brother, and one with the entire Squad soon after she had been recruited. Then there was the first newspaper clipping, of the gun-toting wife at Trinity College.

She flipped to the next article, which she reset on the page after it shifted off center. It recounted the tourist who had begun an argument with a local DART bus driver that resulted in standstill traffic for two hours during the evening commute, and thirteen passengers held hostage at gunpoint with an assault weapon the tourist had purchased on the black market.

Then there was the disgruntled postal worker who, for some reason, thought he could hold twenty patrons hostage to get his job back. That assignment had been the first time their Squad appeared on the front page of *The Irish Independent*. After a few more successful negotiations, the paper had discovered Norah and Tierney's identities and begun calling them "The City's Dream Team." The women would occasionally be recognized out on the town, much to Tierney's dismay. Attention wasn't something she ever enjoyed or got used to.

With care, Tierney continued to turn the pages dried by time, filled with articles documenting successful negotiations. No lives lost, she and Norah would proudly say to each other—until that was no longer the case. Their calls eventually took a more dangerous turn, with the IRA's activity in the city on the rise. That group had begun using more violent tactics, including grenades and tear gas, to leverage demands from the Garda—and in many cases, before she and Norah arrived on site with the team. Civilian lives had become increasingly expendable.

The Garda had begun to work more closely with their Squad out of sheer necessity. "We need you two over at the Irish Army Ranger Wing next week for advanced firearms, and explosives training and certification," the Director of Diplomatic Security Service had informed them after their most dangerous job to date had gone south. Three civilians dead. Wearing bulletproof vests as part of their daily attire had become standard protocol.

Tierney had previous exposure to dangerous experiences during her high school years, when her dad and eldest brother were called in to help with riots around New York City. But that violence had never proven as deadly as what she was witnessing around Dublin.

A few months later, though, there was the breakthrough case, putting their Dream Team back on the upswing. There had been an attempted heist at Dublin's International Financial Services Centre that she and Norah had successfully shut down before two gunmen, code-named Mam and Gram, could harm any of the twenty-three onsite for a conference, including two high-profile hostages, American billionaires. One of the gunmen had lost his life that day, which would later prove problematic. But the United States government had been grateful for the turn of events, giving high praise to Dublin's Lord Mayor on the Dream Team's behalf.

Tierney and Norah had been called into the Embassy for a few debrief sessions with the Ambassador and American dignitaries, and learned of a gala being organized in their honor, to be held in the Embassy's stately Grand Briefing Room. It was slated to be a special night for Dublin women in law enforcement.

Tierney reached the final item in the album, a sole party invitation stuck in the seam. A gala where she and Norah were to be presented with a key to the city. An event Tierney had never made because she had been late. So stressed over not wanting to botch her co-speech with Norah, she'd changed her outfit at least ten times and absent-mindedly forgotten her mobile phone on the way out. BB had been away at a conference or would've most likely noticed the phone before Tierney drove off, but that wasn't her roommate's responsibility. It was all Tierney's doing, unable to warn Norah from—

She clapped the album shut and hugged it tightly against her chest. But Tierney knew it was pointless to try and keep it all together; everything inside was already coming apart. Too much time had passed for it to not be.

She began to rock back and forth on the step, fighting back tears and ruminations until they all flowed out. The partner she'd failed, the mentor she missed, the person she no longer was, the person she didn't know who to be now, the family she was never fully present for, the—

Finn! Tierney bolted up and quickly tried to dry her eyes on a shirt sleeve. She returned inside and saw him off in the living room, playing and content with his tractor set. She exhaled. He needed her less and less these days. She slipped the album in between two books on a shelf, Finn's *My Book About Me*, and Park View's *Chamber of Commerce Guide*. She'd figure out what to do with it soon.

—

Tierney wasn't up for cooking dinner so texted Sean and accepted his standing offer to grab take-out on the way home. She thought about mentioning the Squad box but didn't. She needed to process her heavy feelings with someone who had been there, by her side, living through that darkest time in her life.

She and BB were overdue for a proper chat anyway instead of miscellaneous texts, so she set the table for dinner and checked in with Finn again.

"How about a DVD until Dad gets home?"

"Best day ever!" He hugged her and ran to the media cabinet to retrieve his new favorite, *Ratatouille*.

More like "worst parent ever."

She microwaved a bag of popcorn and started the movie. She headed into her bedroom, sank into the cushion on her mom's antique rocking chair, and texted BB.

I've opened the Squad box. Can you chat?

Tierney's laptop buzzed within a minute and the two connected via Skype.

"I'm proud of you," BB said with her own tear-brimmed eyes after hearing Tierney's account of the album experience. "That was a huge milestone."

Tierney blew her nose. "Thanks for always being there. For hanging in with me until I could see for myself that I can't do this guilt thing anymore. Guilt changes nothing, I now get, and want to stop feeling this way. To get better. To get back to that earlier time in my life when I felt I was, like I was—"

"You."

"Exactly. The person I saw in those early album photos? I miss myself. Does that make sense?"

"Of course it does. I miss that Tierney, too. Sometimes you get to the point where the guilt of surviving feels like it's all you have left of a person, and it's hard to let that go. But something tells me you're ready."

Tierney rubbed her eyes. "I'm actually looking forward to my appointment with Mosely next week."

"Ditto. And don't be surprised if your memories about that Embassy night filter back more vividly now that you've opened the box. It's all part of healing, and Mosely can help you process it."

"I'm afraid I've already started experiencing that."

BB sighed. "I imagine you have. Well, then, let's talk about something more light-hearted. We have so much to catch up on."

Tierney wondered how the next few weeks would unfold. She knew she was on the right path, but still felt uneasy. "How was your Thanksgiving?"

"Amazing. Sue's brother is a hoot, and we all got along well. Steered clear of politics, which can always be dicey."

"I've had my own share of politics, but have tried not to burden you with the latest school mom BS."

"Oh, do tell. Just a taste."

"Mara's sidekick, Regina? She's proven to be the bigger problem."

"Interesting. Like that old adage, 'Talk to the organ grinder, not the monkey.' The second in command can typically be more menacing than the leader."

"How it's been feeling for sure. Oh, and I don't think I've shared yet, that your 'assert yourself' plan to bring cookies to the class party worked. Mara was impressed, and she's personally invited me to her holiday cookie exchange."

"Congratulations?" BB's tone was hesitant.

"I was leery at first, too, and a total last-minute add, but think it will be a great opportunity—for my business, at least."

Tierney went on to share the latest happenings, and having opened up to Gem about the Squad. BB listened to it all, with the same sensitive ear as always. "Gem has been a godsend, especially without you nearby."

"That's wonderful. And remember, let's both try not to wish away our struggles in life. Just that we'll be strong enough to handle whatever comes at us. Like all those past relationships and rough conversations with my parents you've always been by my side to help unpack." BB shivered out her own memories.

"I think you've just given me a new morning mantra: 'to handle whatever comes at me.'" Tierney's mood brightened. "How are things with Sue? And the pups? Actually, did you bring them to work? I hear dogs in the background."

"Don't get me started. Would you believe a pet psychiatrist moved into the office space next door? It's been a circus around here. I'm in the process of strategizing a master plan."

"If anyone can handle a difficult situation, it's you."

The two friends continued their catch-up and it was lovely to hear how well BB was doing—her meaningful work, and especially her relationship with Sue. It warmed Tierney's heart to reinforce acceptance with BB.

"And if there's space in the villa that Lily will be renting this summer," Tierney continued, "we'd love for you ladies to join us. I miss our trips together."

"Yes, me joining you guys in Nantucket seems eons ago."

"I'll keep you posted on details."

"And speaking of Sue, she just texted and is on her way. It's my night for dinner so you know how that goes."

"Gotcha. Take-out." Tierney laughed, recalling BB's distaste for cooking.

"Thinking about trying a new Chinese place in Ballard."

"Funny, Sean texted on his drive home and we're having Chinese, too."

"Then it's a sign."

—

The Chinese restaurant Sean chose in San Jose was delicious, and known for its custom fortune cookies that use vanilla extract instead of almond.

"My client's receptionist said they're a hot ticket. I bought the variety pack since I couldn't decide on one flavor."

Tierney admired the detail work. The cookies were toasted a golden blond, perfectly crimped, had meticulously curled edges, and dipped in either milk chocolate, dark chocolate, or white chocolate with a variety of embellishments like gold shavings and colorful sprinkles.

"These are beautiful." She tasted a dark chocolate one first. "And delicious." She read the fortune which featured a tiny lady-bug logo. "You will find success in your next venture." Wouldn't that be nice? The message was a reminder to download and get started on a class proposal for the Park View Community Center.

Sutton could hear Craig Wright checking in and looked on as an officer escorted him to Interview Room B. Through the open doorway, he could see Craig remove his blazer, fold it neatly, take a seat, and drape it across his knees. He then stood up, hung it on the back of his chair, and smoothed out the sleeves.

"Greetings," said Sutton as he entered and shut the door. "Appreciate you coming in today." He was genuinely thankful that he and Ayala hadn't needed to track Craig down, being acutely aware of time dwindling under the chief's directive.

"No problem." Craig took a seat. "How can I help?"

"I have a few questions. About your relationship with Tatyana Popov." Sutton pointed up to a camera and mentioned their meeting was being recorded.

"Sure, but I don't know how much help I'll be."

Sutton noted Wright's knee bouncing up against the underside of the table, causing a wave in his coffee mug. "Could you please share your activity on the evening of November 15th when you arrived at the pool and until nine-thirty p.m. that evening?"

Wright leaned forward. "I, uh, went to Schick for some laps and hoped to catch a guy who's looking for funding on his project. A programming prodigy fresh out of Cal. He usually swims early with the Masters or on Thursday evenings, but has been a no-show lately. I'd been juggling a few work opportunities. But I think all that is irrelevant here?"

"Let us determine what's relevant, thank you." Sutton reached into his shirt pocket for readers and opened his notepad. "So, we have a staff member onsite who witnessed you talking with Ms. Popov after you abruptly hopped out of the pool, and then departed the facility—'an uncharacteristically short swim'—and that you appeared upset by your interaction with the victim. What exactly did you two discuss?"

"We didn't discuss anything. And I wasn't upset. Who told you that?"

"I'm not at liberty to say. Please continue."

"Look, I heard my ringtone so hopped out to check messages. I'd been hoping to confirm another business meeting for that evening. And okay, so I might have been a bit distracted after that call and accidentally bumped into her on my way out. I didn't even know she was my son's math tutor, by the way. That was something my wife had organized. As far as I knew, the girl was just one of the newer guards at Schick." Craig took a long exhale.

"I'll ask you again. What did you and Ms. Popov discuss?"

"She said something like if I ever needed her help with anything to let her know."

"And what did she mean by 'her help' and 'anything'?"

"To be honest, I was in a rush to get to my appointment, so didn't give it much thought. I just said I was all good, or something like that."

"And how did she reply?"

"Just to enjoy the evening. That was it. I guess I thought she was propositioning me or something, but I ignored it. I'm used to women hitting on me. You know?"

"Yes, I know." Sutton resisted rolling his eyes. "So, she's been to your home a few times?"

"That's right, from what my wife tells me. For the tutoring. But I've only seen her at the pool. She was friendly. That's it."

"You two have never texted or talked on the phone?"

"Never."

"Well, she must've known you. Otherwise, how else would she have gotten your number?"

"I never gave her my number. Why?"

"Her cell records say otherwise. Ms. Popov texted your number shortly after your pool departure with, 'I meant what I said.'"

"Oh, that," Craig replied. "I do recall seeing something come through. But I didn't recognize the number so dismissed it."

"How did she get your number, if you didn't give it to her?"

"No idea." Craig's knee bounce grew more rapid and Sutton picked up his mug from the table. "Maybe from my wife or our au pair for emergency purposes? My son has a severe allergy so we always make sure one of us is available."

"Regardless, you left the pool around the same time you received her text. Also, Ms. Popov departed the property shortly after your departure. You see how this looks. Did you two meet somewhere offsite?"

"Absolutely not. I told you I didn't know her. She might have known who I was. Lots of people do."

Sutton scoffed at yet another arrogant remark but then recalled the absurd quantity of family photos around the Wright home. It was possible Tatyana recognized him from those alone, so Sutton changed gears. "Then where did you go?"

"I'd rather not say, but it has nothing to do with that girl."

"I'll need more information than that."

"Ugh, fine. But my wife doesn't know about my appointment."

"And maybe she doesn't have to. Where were you and can anyone vouch for you?"

"Yes. I went to talk with the owner of Bob's Bar."

"You were at a bar? How much did you have to drink?"

"No. I mean, I was there for a meeting with the owner."

"You were at the bar all evening having drinks with the owner?"

"No, I was at the bar for a meeting with Bob. And I may have had a few beers, three tops, while I was there."

"Okay, so what was this meeting about?"

"I'm interested in buying a vacant piece of property downtown that he owns. Turn it into a brewery. Something family-friendly, with homemade root beer, too? You know, a local gathering place for kids after team events, and somewhere in town families can walk to. It would really revitalize the area. And offer the best burgers, BBQ, fish and chips, and pizza in town. And only serve local beers. Would you come to a place like that?"

"Sure, whatever. If I contact Bob, he will confirm there was an actual business meeting that evening and you were not there to just drink or to meet someone else?"

"That's correct."

"And you never saw Ms. Popov again after leaving the pool that evening?"

"That's correct."

"Where were you the rest of the night through nine-thirty p.m.?"

"I went home. My family can vouch for that. But please don't mention the brewery part to my wife? I haven't told her my business idea yet. I want her to be a partner with me. She's amazing with interior design and would make the place shine. But she's been, well, on edge."

"Because of her math tutor's death?"

"No, not that. I mean, sure, she's been upset by that. We've all been. But, it's a difficult time of year." Craig got quiet and looked down at his hands resting on the table. His leg had stopped bouncing. "Our OB calls it an 'Anniversary of the Heart.' I wouldn't wish it on my worst enemy."

Sutton felt an itchy sensation in the back of his throat and sat back in his chair. "We have no need to be involved in your personal life, but I'm afraid that depends on the investigation," he said, followed by a dry cough. "I'll be in touch again if your story with Bob and the timing of events don't line up."

Craig looked up at Sutton. "They will. I'm sure of it." He then gestured to his blazer on the back of the chair.

"Yes, you can go." Sutton followed him back to the lobby.

Once inside the break room, Sutton dumped his half-full coffee into the sink and refilled his mug with water from the Alhambra cooler. He hated when interviews got personal. He drank the entire mug of water and cleared his throat. *Stay focused.* He looked up at the clock. It was time to try Dean Javits's number again.

* * *

Tierney downed the leftover Kung Pao shrimp for lunch and printed her draft business proposal. When she returned to the kitchen with the document, she found Louie in the sink, face down in her bowl. She shooed him away but not before he ran off with a shrimp tail. *When will I learn with the damn shrimp?*

She followed him around the chair, unsuccessfully grabbed for him, continued down the hallway where he ran, and finally cornered him under Finn's bed. As she slid him out by the scruff of his neck, Sean's missing harpoon appeared between his tightly clutched paws.

"What the—"

Tierney sat on the floor with a retrieved shrimp tail in one hand and their harpoon from the garage in another. She stared at the latter in disbelief. The thought of Finn feeling as if he or their family needed protection from the lifeguard murderer made her heart hurt. Some badass mother she was for her son to not feel safe in his own home; she was failing him, and with this stay-at-home mom thing. If she hadn't already scheduled her appointment with Mosely, today would've been the day.

Tierney thought about calling Sean to discuss how best to speak with Finn about the harpoon and his worries, but no. This was her conversation to handle. She should've thought to ask him directly about it earlier and not assume it had been one of the neighbor boys. He could've easily used all the stacked boxes as a step ladder in the garage.

She'd talk with Finn solo after school and reassure him. And thank goodness she never ended up reporting the missing harpoon to the station.

*　*　*

"It's DJ to family and friends, but I go by Dean otherwise," Dean said on the phone to Sutton, who was back at his desk. "And yes, I knew Tatyana. She was my family's au pair earlier this year before my wife left me. My wife has been upset about some litigation I'm involved in. Business dealings, to clarify, nothing violent. She took the kids with her to Chicago, which is where I'm calling from now."

"I see. So, I have a witness account that says you and Tatyana were involved. Is that correct?"

"Involved? I guess, but not in a creepy way."

"Care to explain?"

Dean lowered his voice. "Hold on a moment."

Sutton could hear a door open then close, and background noise that sounded like wind.

"Look. Once my wife and the kids left, and the agency couldn't find a new placement for Tatyana, I felt badly for her. Genuinely. She didn't want to return to Moscow defeated, so I said she could stay in the house a bit longer to find her footing. I've admittedly made some dumb decisions lately, but getting into a relationship with her was not one of them. And Jesus, I'm old enough to be her father."

"And Tatyana was fine with this platonic relationship?"

"At first. But then she started saying things like she could be my new wife, my new world. But that's not what I wanted. I've missed my family desperately, and we're trying to work things out now. My life has been pure nothing without my wife and kids, so I finally told Tatyana she had to move out."

"And that was the end of it?"

"Well, she got a little crazy."

"Was cocaine involved?"

"Cocaine? No, never. That's not my style. But I did give her some cash, to help secure an apartment. You know, just a few months' rent and to help with the security deposit."

"Alright, please continue." Sutton jotted down a note in his pad about Dean not being a cocaine link for Tatyana.

"She knew about the trouble I was in. She'd overheard details about business dealings during arguments with my wife, come across legal papers in the house, things like that. She ultimately tried to blackmail me into a deeper relationship. By then, though, the Feds had everything on me, so any leverage she did have had fizzled. It was pretty laughable on all fronts."

"Well, I hear that you swim at Schick Pool, where she was lifeguarding? I imagine you'd seen her there?"

"On a few occasions, yes. But I kept my distance. My office is in downtown Park View, and their pool is the most convenient outlet I've had to help with stress. Swimming became more desirable than rounds on the golf course where colleagues were learning of my legal troubles."

"The thing I'm struggling with is that you swam at the pool on the day of Tatyana's death. How do I know you didn't hide away on the property somewhere and then confront her later that evening? Maybe she had something else on you that you're not sharing with me."

"I did swim at the pool that morning. But I couldn't have been further away in the evening."

"Is that so? And where was this further away?"

He let out a long sigh. "Look, I was a mess that day. Hadn't slept for days. I typically swim in the evenings but thought a morning swim would help jump-start my day. It proved otherwise. I began experiencing chest pains and drove straight from the pool to Stanford Hospital to check myself in for observation. I was there for at least twenty-four hours. Thankfully, just a panic attack. You can call and verify."

Sutton gave a frustrated shake of his head. "I'll do that. Anything else I should know?"

"Look, what happened to Tatyana was terrible, but I'd never kill anyone. And I was certainly in no position to do so that day."

———

An hour later, Sutton walked into the staffroom and saw Ayala banging on the side of the vending machine. "If you drank coffee like the rest of us, you wouldn't have that problem."

"Right." Ayala hit it again and his soda released. "Finally got in touch with the retired facilities manager. Employees there now are too new to know what had originally hung on the mural, but HR tracked down the guy's number."

"Anything helpful?"

"He told me the antique harpoon was removed years ago when a swim team parent complained of its 'dangerous nature.' It was moved to the Park View History House and is currently on display in a case onsite. I've personally checked it and the dimensions are a match."

"Nice work, but all these dead ends. Wright's alibi pans out, so does Josh's, and same with Dean Javits."

"You reached him?"

"Yeah. Stanford Hospital confirmed his whereabouts on the night Tatyana was killed."

"Damn. Any news on the VW?"

"Not yet. We just need a murder weapon so we can bring in Brad again and nail him. It's gotta be him."

* * *

Tierney was able to refocus after finding the harpoon and still make the day productive before returning to Apricot Grove. She picked up ingredients for the Finnish Ribbon Cookies and continued on to Park View Community Center to speak with their Activities Program Manager. She had a few questions before submitting her baking class application for the spring session.

It was a cold but beautiful fall day—the sun up high and not a cloud in view. Tierney was beginning to understand the appeal of California living. Parking in the area was a challenge, though, with young playgroups out enjoying the weather, too. She parked in front of the apartment complex, walked by Schick Pool and around to the nearby Community Center's administrative offices.

After the meeting with a helpful associate, Tierney was feeling optimistic about her class idea when she spotted Joan, the water fitness instructor, decked out in '80s stone-washed denim and hot pink leg warmers. Their eyes met and Tierney introduced herself as a lap swimmer.

"Sad state of affairs, eh?" She shook Tierney's extended hand.

The two continued outside along the path and Joan shared that she'd been looking for another exercise gig with the city to no avail. "I've been with them for years. The water class wasn't much but it was something, you know?"

Tierney certainly did. "I imagine many have been affected by the closure. I mean, I get it—the city waiting to fill the pool. But it's hard."

"Sure is. I've run into many former students. The one with the waterproof cane? She's back to using her walker. Without water fitness, her PT efforts stalled. And remember the pregnant ladies?"

"Did they all have their babies yet?"

"Two I know of. I saw the group meeting over at the park last week. They've been dying to get back in the water. Baby weight and all."

"Oh, I recall that desire. And the grandmas with the daisy caps? I think they live over in that apartment complex, so no doubt the closure has been a disappointment there, too."

"Haven't seen them. They never listened to me anyway. Did their own thing during class, which I found frustrating."

Tierney recalled the behavior. The lifeguards seemed to adore the two, though, always exchanging smiles and waves, and wouldn't think of blowing the whistle on grandmothers for hanging onto lane lines while they chatted. "Maybe they didn't understand the instructions—I think there was a language issue. Must be tons of pros and cons that come with being a teacher, though. I'm proposing a baking class at the Center. How do you like working with management?" The two stopped walking near the stroller parking to continue their conversation. Tierney, one hand shielding her eyes against the bright sun, enjoyed hearing how supportive the city was.

While sharing her business idea, a bouncing ball from the playground passed by their feet and into the thick jasmine. Joan retrieved it, tossed it back to the toddler, but reached back down at something both women could now see glistening through the leaves.

Joan went to pick it up when Tierney yelled, "Wait!"

Joan yanked her hand back. "What is it?"

Tierney bent down and carefully separated some leaves. She could see a blade covered in dried blood. *Bolt cutters?*

Joan gasped.

Tierney reached for her phone, which she'd left in Betty a few blocks away. *You've got to be kidding.* "Joan, you need to call Detective Sutton. I know his number."

* * *

"Civilians." Sutton snickered, hung up his phone, and relayed the bolt cutter find to Ayala at his desk.

"And Tierney Gillespie was with her? Who is this woman?"

"Just another busybody Park View mom. More observant than most, though. I'll give her that."

"But wait, didn't Forensics search that area first? And with metal detectors?"

"I believe so."

"What, did the murderer return it to the scene of the crime after the fact?"

"The world works in mysterious ways, kid. Regardless, Gillespie and the water fitness instructor are giving statements to patrol now, and the bolt cutters are headed to the lab." Sutton clicked away at his pen. "Hopefully we'll get a match soon with the murder weapon from the medical examiner along with Brad's prints from Forensics."

THURSDAY, NOVEMBER 29

"What is taking the lab so long? It's not like they have anything more critical around town." The large vein over Sutton's right temple pulsed as he slammed the sedan door.

"Sure you don't want me to drive this time?" Ayala asked.

"I'm not a good passenger."

Ayala opened the take-out bag with sandwiches they'd just picked up from Poor House Bistro, one of Sutton's treasured eateries, and unwrapped a fried oyster po-boy sandwich. It was Ayala's first time being invited to join him on a lunch run. "Oh my God, this is delicious."

"Told you."

"So we haven't ruled out the mystery VW yet," Ayala said with a full mouth. "Want me to follow up with patrol again? Maybe the local mom got the license plate wrong."

Sutton turned on the ignition and a maintenance alert illuminated on the dash. "Christ. Put in a service request when we get back to the station, would ya? And that license number isn't wrong. It was just last registered to a red Miata.

"So stolen plates?"

"It appears that—wait, hold on. It's Forensics calling."

Ayala lowered the radio's volume.

"Sutton here . . . Really? . . . And the medical examiner? . . . Excellent, thanks for letting me know." Sutton ended the call and put the car into drive.

"Positive news?"

"The bolt cutters are a match. And Brad's prints are all over them."

—

Sutton found Ayala enjoying an afternoon snack at his desk. "Patrol finally found Brad. Picked him up at a blackjack table— Cache Creek Casino up in Northern California—after checking his credit card usage. Appears he started living up there a week after the murder. Should be arriving in a few. Want to join me for the interrogation?"

"Definitely. Unless it happens at the same time that guy picked up for DUI last night frees up. DEA got first dibs on him at the Elmwood Correctional Facility in Milpitas, but brought him back here for further questioning after his bail hearing," Ayala said, followed by a loud crunch.

"What the hell are you eating?"

"Chocolate-covered coffee beans. Want one?"

"No. But at least you're trying. Who's the guy?"

"Some rich a-hole picked up driving high on coke, and he's agreed to cooperate—share his dealer's name and such—in exchange for lighter sentencing."

"And let's hope a connection with Schick."

"Exactly. The DEA should be done soon, and I need to finish reviewing my list of questions before his wife posts bail."

"Refer to that cheatsheet I gave you?"

Ayala nodded. "I'll have time. The wife doesn't seem to be in a hurry. Hasn't arrived yet."

"Nice. I'd let him stew, too."

—

"Look, I don't touch the stuff," Brad said. "I let the lifeguards go about their business as long as it doesn't bring the cops. I'm not their dad, for God's sake. And besides, there's some guy named Yuri who runs the coke scene."

"Yuri?"

"I've heard his name a couple times around deck. But I mind my own business. He should be sitting here instead of me."

Sutton shook his head in disbelief. "Let's discuss Josh. We have a witness who saw you acknowledge Ms. Popov's arrival for her shift with a Josh Jeffries, her boyfriend, on the night she was murdered. You told me previously that you 'weren't quite sure' who she was with after you two broke up. Why did you lie?"

"I was pissed. I mean, to let that asshole walk her to work and rub their relationship in my face?"

"Fine, but that doesn't explain why you'd lie. Why would you cover for him?"

"We have a past. The less I'm connected to him, the better. He's no doubt involved in her death."

"Well, he has an alibi. You don't. Now, moving to later that evening, another witness saw you and Tatyana arguing by the mechanical room during the evening lap swim session. What about?"

"I told her I thought it was bullshit how she flaunted Josh in my face. The pool was our place."

"I see. She left the pool grounds a short time after this argument. Do you know where she went?"

"I never saw her leave. Assumed she was in the office manning the front desk and then left after her shift."

"You never saw or spoke with her again after your argument?"

"No. I shut the place down once everyone left, and then played video games. And had some vodka."

"Yes, the vodka. You drink an expensive brand, and a large volume, based on the bottles we collected around the property. How can you afford it? Drug sales treating you well?"

"I already told you. Drugs aren't my scene. Find Yuri!"

Sutton scoffed again. "Enough of this Yuri game. How can you afford the vodka?"

"The bottles were gifts. They'd appear in the bottom drawer of my filing cabinet."

"You mean, to buy your silence at what was taking place at the pool?"

"Maybe. I didn't really think about it. Was just glad they were there. Kinda hoped, though, they were gifts from Tatyana."

"And why would she leave you bottles of vodka?"

"She and I used to do vodka shots together. It was our thing. We'd pop in a Netflix movie and get drunk and then—"

"Romantic. Let's move on. Explain how you could be in the office and not hear someone being murdered by the pool."

"I already told you. I passed out. I've been having a rough go of things. With my ex. Bills. The workload. Schick is always lightly staffed this time of year. Things were all crashing down on me. So, I drink a little to cope. That's no crime."

"But murder is."

Brad's head fell forward into his palm. "I loved Tatyana. I'd never hurt her."

"Yes, you loved her so much you didn't even know her last name."

Brad looked up at Sutton and pointed his finger at him. "I'd had a lot to drink that first night you asked me, and was overwhelmed by her death. But I remember it. Petrov."

"Close, but no. Popov."

Brad's face went blank.

"Regardless, the murder weapon confirms your hand in her death."

"What murder weapon?"

"Nice try. We also have record of your violent tendencies." Sutton opened a file on the table and lowered his readers. "You and your car were involved in a reckless event at Apricot Grove on November twentieth. With witnesses. The license plate on your white VW Golf matches the caller's info as having almost killed Josh Jeffries. A coincidence that he was the guy your now deceased girlfriend left you for? Sounds like motive to me."

"I only wanted to scare Josh. We've known each other since junior high and he pissed me off by doing God knows what to get her killed. But I never meant to hurt the guy. Just shake him up."

"You weren't pissed enough to seek revenge?"

"I would never kill someone. She started dating that loser to get back at me, when I told her I'd never marry again. My ex took the shirt off my back so another wedding is out of the question, even though Tatyana proposed it as a green card marriage. Said we could divorce after she had her papers, but I have trust issues. I told Tatyana I'd get her a ring and everything, that we could be engaged forever. But she became obsessed with getting hitched and dumped me."

"Then she targeted Josh for a proposal?"

"Yeah, like, so gross, right?"

"Questionable taste in men, for certain."

Brad nodded before registering the insult. "Hey."

"Look, I'm afraid this discussion is going nowhere. So, unless you can deliver this mystery man Yuri to me, you're our guy."

Brad opened and shut his mouth a few times in reply. "I want a lawyer."

—

"What do you make of this Yuri thing?" Ayala asked after hearing Sutton's interrogation recap on the other side of the station, still awaiting his DUI guy to free up.

"Brad is getting desperate, making up things to distract us."

"Okay, but do we really think Brad could be a ringleader? He doesn't strike me as all that together, nor the murdering type. An alcoholic, for sure. But a murderer?"

"His prints and Tatyana's are the only ones on the bolt cutters. That was the final piece we needed."

"I still find that odd. Wouldn't other lifeguards have touched them at some point, or maintenance workers while cleaning? Or our murderer wiped the weapon clean and then pressed Brad's hand against it while he was passed out?" Ayala said.

"Possibly, but murderers typically want to flee quickly. Maybe lock cutting just wasn't needed often."

"I guess. But there's something unexplored with Josh. My gut tells me he's involved. Should we tail him?"

"I feel something is off there, too, but—"

Sutton's desk phone rang. He sighed at the caller ID. "The chief. Must be back from vacation."

—

"Remember, follow my lead," Sutton said quietly to Ayala before knocking.

"Enter," said Police Chief Marks.

The partners made their way towards the chief's desk. Ayala tripped over the snowy tree skirt and fell into the seat next to Sutton.

The chief waited, expressionless, as Ayala adjusted himself before starting in. "Gentlemen, are we finally convinced Brad is our guy? Because I am."

"We think it's a definite possibility, sir."

"A definite possibility isn't definite."

"He's still a person of interest, but we received a new bit of information during his interrogation," Sutton continued.

"A potential suspect named Yuri," Ayala blurted out.

Sutton shot him a what-the-hell-happened-to-following-my-lead look.

"Yuri?" the chief asked. "Like this is now a Russian situation? Please."

"What Ayala means is that we still have more to explore before your deadline, so a few days—"

"Look, gentlemen, we're staying the course with Brad. The scumbag probably gave himself a cute nickname. Yuri." The chief's belly bounced as he laughed. "We have the murder weapon and Brad's prints. Waiting longer will uncover nothing. So, unless you have hard evidence about a shady Russian drug lord being involved in the case," he said and wiggled his fingers in the air, "I consider the bike messenger in a coma to simply be a guy who liked to swim—from another town with the designer drug problem—and Popov to be a dealer who got herself mixed up in a deadly love triangle. Case closed."

"But sir, one more day would even—"

"I said case closed, Sutton. I want him charged. Residents need to understand that a murderer is not running loose in their community. Plus, tomorrow is a Friday. Perfect day for a press release to start the weekend off right—show our townspeople how professional their police department is with a murderer behind bars."

Ayala was speechless.

Sutton nodded.

"And this professionalism of yours won't go unnoticed, gentlemen." The chief twirled a Christmas tree pen around his sausage fingers. "I know you two have been working long hours, and Sutton, you're overdue for a promotion. Maybe there's something I can do about all that."

Sutton processed the remark, while Ayala's expression turned to one of disbelief.

The chief glared at Ayala. "Do we understand each other?"

"Yes, sir. We understand," Sutton said on their behalf and signaled to his partner it was time to leave.

Sutton was agitated but Ayala looked enraged as they headed to the station's back courtyard.

Sutton pulled out Irene's pack of Marlboro Reds from his coat pocket.

"Since when do you smoke?"

"I don't." He placed one in between his lips, unlit. "Look, I've been at this longer than you. Park View hasn't had a murder in years and," Sutton lowered his voice as two officers passed the door, "the chief and DA both want this case wrapped ASAP. Having the case still open over Thanksgiving was difficult enough—the largest number of angry calls from community members Joelle has ever fielded."

Ayala's eyes opened wide. "Listen to yourself. Wanting a pleasant holiday should not be the reason to accelerate a murder investigation."

"Keep it down. It's not just the holiday. With the chief's retirement coming up next spring and the DA entering an election year, you know, a drug ring running wild doesn't look good on anyone's record."

"Like that detail makes this situation better?"

"There's enough on Brad to nail him and be done with it. This is what we've been working towards."

"I know but there are still questions. Not just this Yuri, but Josh's vibe. He'd be getting away free and clear—of something."

"It's off our plate now," Sutton said, and rubbed his head. He could feel his years of being a rule follower wavering. Plus, did he really want a promotion this way? His gut told him Ayala's outrage was justified. He was pissed at the chief, too. Hell, maybe he should support the kid's perspective. *Crap.* Sutton cleared his throat and, to his surprise, added, "Technically."

"Technically?"

Sutton stood taller. "With an arrest under way and the chief approving a press release as we speak, we'll be assigned other cases. Most likely a flurry of drunk drivers this time of year with all the bougie parties. But those cases are easy as far as paperwork, so we'd still have bandwidth to keep our feelers out on the pool investigation."

"I like where this is going."

"Ayala?" An officer appeared in the courtyard doorway. "All clear to talk with our DUI."

"Great," Ayala said and started to follow the officer before turning back to Sutton. "Wanna join me?"

"You've got this, kid. I have a call to make and then I'll find you."

—

Brad was transported and booked into the Santa Clara County Main Jail. Sutton walked through the lobby looking for Ayala and passed a woman signing release papers. Her intense smile, aimed at no one, caught his eye—a look he had seen numerous times throughout his career and romantic life. An enraged, unstable smile of a woman barely holding it together. He was happy to not be on the receiving end of it this time.

A man with an officer escort sheepishly walked in from the corridor. "Thanks for coming," he said to the woman.

"You prick," she hissed in a quiet voice. "I've got enough going on without having to deal with your stupidity."

"I'm sorry." The man didn't appear to know where to land his eyes.

"Do you think I had time to pick up your fucking car from impound? And if I hear anyone say they saw you getting pulled over last night," she continued, "it's humiliating."

The people in this town, I swear.

The man walked behind his wife out the front door. Sutton followed a short distance after them to continue listening for any details that might help the case, as he drank his coffee and awaited Ayala.

"I'm sorry. It won't happen again," the man said.

"Damn straight it won't. You'd better keep your shit together. And be on your best behavior at poker. Not a drink, not a snort, nothing. Do you hear me?"

"I hear you."

"The lawyer said if you're caught using again before your court appearance, your record will be unsalvageable." The wife unlocked the doors of a gleaming silver Tesla Roadster prototype.

"I'm so sorry, Regina. We'll get through this." The man slipped into the passenger seat.

"I'll get through this for sure. Don't know if that will be with you." She took her place in the driver's seat and slammed the door.

As they pulled out, Sutton noticed the CHP 11-99 Foundation license plate frame. So stupid for people to think that meant a get-out-of-jail-free card.

"Wouldn't want to be him on the drive home." Ayala appeared by Sutton's side and cracked open a soda.

"Seriously. How was your talk with him?" Sutton sipped from his mug.

"Cooperating fully. Just had to mention the word 'obstruction.'"

"Works every time."

"He babbled on about how he started using a few months into his role as VP of Sales at Vibora. Knew he was in over his head when board expectations were more fast-paced than he was used to from the big corporation he worked at the prior twenty years. Apparently had to work longer hours, and discovered coke would keep him more alert and productive."

Sutton grunted at the thought of how many late nights he'd worked over the years just fine. "Hard to feel sorry for these types."

"Totally. But great news. He gave us a positive ID on Tatyana as one of his dealers."

"One of them?"

"She apparently sold to him on the evening of her murder. Around six-thirty p.m. in the Vibora parking lot, which would've been around the time she was seen leaving the pool."

"Nice. Maybe that's why she propped up the manikin, to buy time should Brad or fellow lifeguards glance through the window before she returned from her field trip."

"A reasonable possibility. But get this: this Ian guy also ID'd one of the men in the DEA file you left on my desk—an Enrique Salazar. Said he was his original dealer, until the location was changed by Tatyana a few weeks later."

"Interesting. But I didn't leave a DEA file on your desk."

Tierney pulled out the last baking tray of Finnish Ribbon Cookies from the oven and heard the breaking news-themed music on the family room TV. She left the tray to cool on the stovetop before glazing, noting she had gone a bit overboard with quantity, and took a seat on the couch. The lead story was Schick Pool. She hoped fingerprints were found on the bolt cutters, or something to help the case and Finn's peace of mind. Her little Superman, who'd apparently considered taking her chef's knife for protection but opted instead for Sean's harpoon since it's never used.

"The Park View Police Department announced moments ago that they have formally arrested Brad Madrone, pool manager and head lifeguard, for the murder of Tatyana Popov," the news anchor began.

Brad? Tierney stared in disbelief. *Thank God not a Dean or DJ, though.* She needed to trust Sutton's follow-up here. *Right? But what about Josh?*

"The investigation uncovered that Madrone had been involved in a love triangle with the victim and his former school friend—a Josh Jeffries."

Ok, there's Josh.

Brad's mugshot appeared on the screen and he looked a mess. But a murderer?

"His Volkswagen had recently been reported by parents at Apricot Grove School for an attempted hit-and-run of Jeffries where he works as a crossing guard."

Not Bell's car? Tierney's thoughts ticked back to summer. She had seen Brad open his trunk in the parking lot one day to retrieve a new set of kickboards. It was a white Golf, not a Scirocco. But still a VW, and a small white one. Finn had been right about the white car piece, although Tierney had assumed it was Bell's VW Scirocco. Pool employees did typically park on side streets to make room for swimmers, which could explain why she hadn't seen Brad's car more frequently to recall it earlier.

Regardless, the news didn't sit well. Not because her family had potentially interacted with a murderer, but whether the police had the right guy. She never sensed Brad capable of violence, much less murder, as she had intuited with perps numerous times in Dublin.

Her attention returned to the broadcast, which had switched to a live scene in front of Schick Pool's shuttered lobby.

"The County Medical Examiner has confirmed," the reporter said, "that Tatyana Popov died from blunt force trauma—a single blow to the head. She died instantly, most likely taken by surprise, as no defense wounds were found. The weapon was discovered in the dense jasmine surrounding Schick Pool and the nearby Community Center by the city's water fitness instructor, Joan Pratt. Lucky for us to have Ms. Pratt with us here now to share her account of the find with viewers. Joan, thanks for joining us."

Tierney smiled at the sight of Joan on TV. Joan had told officers she'd be happy to come back anytime and speak with reporters. Tierney was pleased to have assisted with the discovery, and that Sean hadn't freaked out when she'd shared her involvement in finding the murder weapon, but she wanted to stay out of the news. She and Norah had been burned in the past by inaccurate reporting.

"Yes, hi, Joan Pratt here." She took the microphone from the reporter. "Water fitness instructor with the city and I also teach jazzercise for any organization who may be in need of a seasoned instructor."

"Yes, thank you for that." The reporter reclaimed the mic from Joan's grip. "Please share your find with our viewers."

As Joan recounted the story about the boy and rolling ball, Tierney was distracted by the activity taking place on screen behind her. A group of women with candles and a sign, "Justice for Tatyana!" was gathering. She recognized Natalia, Regina's au pair, Laura's sitter who had watched Finn, and a few others from soccer games. It was an impressive turnout, and Tierney was touched by the scene.

As Joan's interview wrapped, the cameraman focused his lens on the gathering.

"Now, as you'll see behind me," the reporter said, "representatives from Au Pair Match, where the deceased originally worked upon arrival in America, along with fellow au pairs, have organized a candlelight vigil in light of an arrest being made. A group to pay homage to a woman who tragically lost her life too soon."

A life lost too soon. The words struck Tierney and the TV screen in front of her grew hazy.

~ ~ ~

Tierney could barely think straight, much less get out of bed. Thank God for BB.

"Keep telling yourself, 'I'm doing this for Norah,'" BB instructed as they slowly made their way to the bathroom.

Tierney somehow showered, being mindful of her recently dislocated shoulder and torn rotator cuff, and dressed. But she needed assistance in selecting something to wear. Of the options

BB had pulled from her closet, Tierney chose the black dress with the lace-edged sleeves and deep pockets, which she'd stuff with tissues.

She couldn't believe her partner and mentor was gone. Tierney's insides felt hollow. She wanted to go back in time to change the outcome. A do-over. But the world stopped for no one. It. just. kept. spinning.

They'd need to depart soon to make it through the city on time to Glasnevin Cemetery. As Tierney readied herself, she picked up her mobile phone but crumpled back onto the bed. "I should have been with her, or could have at least warned her with this damn phone."

BB sat next to her and rubbed her back. "It doesn't feel like it now, but it will be okay," she said softly. "Breathe in through your nose, and out through your mouth."

Twenty minutes later, the roommates headed out in their Ford Cortina. But on the drive, Tierney panicked.

"I'm not sure I'll be able to get out once we park," she said, taking in deep breaths that fell short.

"You'll make it. You'll see." BB shifted gears and reached for Tierney's hand.

Tierney's words continued in between shallow breaths. "I don't think I can speak. Form a sentence."

"I'll be with you the whole time. We'll get through this together, okay?" BB kept her eyes on the road.

"Promise you'll help me interact with as few people as necessary—and skip the reception? I want to get back home, before I lose it again."

BB nodded.

As they parked, Tierney saw off in the distance what looked to be the whole Squad onsite, and then some. No surprise it was standing room only around the clover green lawn by the time she and BB reached the edge.

The ceremony was heartfelt but Tierney's stomach remained clenched. Beautiful words were woven by Norah's parents and the family's priest, as well as the Chief Inspector, who spoke of Norah's life being lost too soon.

The bagpipes played regally as Norah's casket was lowered into the ground. Tierney's tears continued to flow. "Once in the earth, they are at peace," she whispered to herself, remembering Grandma Molly's words years ago after scolding her and her brothers for playing tag around the O'Shaughnessy plot in Ireland while she re-planted flowers for long-passed relatives. *Norah at least would be at peace.*

On the walk back to the car, Tierney and BB saw familiar faces; Tierney simply nodded in acknowledgement. She had never met Norah's extended family so offering a similar response as she passed them was fairly easy, until it was not.

Philip met her bereft gaze with his own. BB slowed her gait, giving Tierney no choice but to engage.

"Thank you for coming." His voice broke.

"I'm sorry for your loss." Tierney replied mechanically, not knowing what else to say.

He reached out for her hand, being mindful of the other in a sling. "I know how hard this day is for us all."

"I wish I had been at the gala on time to help her. To somehow protect her." Tierney's tears now streamed down her flushed cheeks.

BB put her arm around her.

"Believe me, I understand," he said. "But you could've been killed, too."

"Maybe. But it's shitty on this side as well."

"Time heals all wounds, as my mother keeps telling me," he said with an awkward laugh.

"Things will get easier, with the passage of time," BB added in a textbook way, glancing between the two.

"Maybe. But if I had just gotten there on time, or been able to call and warn her so she could've gotten out." Tierney retrieved the last tissue from her pocket.

"You shouldn't feel guilty for Norah's death. It's important you understand that," he replied through damp eyes. "Norah knew the risks with this job. And that man was on a mission—revenge for the great work the Squad had been doing in Dublin. You never could've known that."

"Exactly," BB added.

Tierney cried into the tissue, surprised she had any tears left.

"I'm sorry, Tierney. I just wanted to thank you for being such a special friend to Norah. She adored you, and always said you were destined for great things," he continued.

Tierney looked up and was tongue-tied.

"Thank you for that," BB replied on her behalf. "We're all going to miss her."

Philip glanced at remaining guests. "I'd better get back to Norah's parents."

"Yes, of course. Please give them our best," BB replied.

The roommates crunched along the gravel path back towards the car park. Philip's words echoed in Tierney's ears—*destined for great things*. She could feel her heart pounding all the way down to her toenails. She reached the passenger side door and steadied herself. "I'm not going back."

"You don't need to. The reception isn't as important as the service."

"I mean I'm not going back to the Squad."

BB and Tierney locked eyes across the top of the sedan. "Don't decide that now. You're not in the right frame of mind," BB said.

"She thought I was destined for great things," Tierney swallowed, "and I failed her. I'll never find that strength again. She was my strength. I can't do this without her."

SATURDAY, DECEMBER 1

Norah's favorite. Tierney squatted eye level with the cookies and evaluated each treat with decorating tweezers. She had baked her most beautiful batch of Finnish Ribbon Cookies yet, ones that would impress party guests with her skill while showing Mara she'd be the ideal candidate to lead a memorable holiday class party for the kids. But she was growing uneasy about the cookie exchange only a few hours away.

There would be a lot of women at the party, more guests than at book club, although Gem would be with her again. Instead of watching the clock, she opted for a change of scenery. *Get gas, and swing by the police station with the extra batch.*

"Going to fill up the tank," she yelled to Sean and Finn. "Back soon!"

Tierney pulled up to the pump and saw Laura one bay over. She was certain Laura had noticed her arrival but for some reason chose to keep her eyes down on the nozzle filling her tank.

Tierney was a bundle of nervous energy but felt like now was as good a time as any to warm up on small talk. Plus, interactions with Laura were typically friendly. "How's your weekend?"

"Hi there." Laura's voice sounded defeated. "Didn't see you much around campus this week."

"I've been in and out pretty quick. A new business idea has been taking up my time." Tierney opened her gas tank, happy to have somewhere for her own eyes to be.

"Sounds exciting. What business?"

"I've been toying with the idea of teaching a baking class at the community center. Maybe even as a venue for kid's birthday parties? I recently submitted my Prospective Contractor Packet."

"How nice to have a plan for reentering the workforce. That makes one of us. And such a creative idea. My kids would love a baking birthday party. It's always a challenge to conjure up themes each year."

"Same for Finn. You can tell me what you think of my baking skills tonight at Mara's."

Laura reached for her keys. "Yes, that. I've been bumped from the group. I must've done something to offend her."

Tierney panicked for a second but refocused. "No, I'm certain I saw your name on the list. Come to think of it, your name was the only one who hadn't yet replied when I double-checked the start time."

"What list?"

"On the evite. I was a late addition myself."

"Mara always mails her invitations." Laura looked confused. "And on the prettiest Crane stationary."

"Guess she decided to go digital this year. Probably better for the environment."

Laura's face brightened. "My God, Tierney. I'm so glad I ran into you. The evite must've gone to my spam folder. I never even thought to look. I'll head home now and RSVP. But, wait, what will I bring?" She looked at her watch. "There's no time to bake anything this late."

"You could swing by Bonnie's. They might still be open if they haven't sold out."

"Would they have anything good left?"

"Might just be their gluten-free options, but if that's the case, their jam thumbprints are tasty. Oh, and if you need a sitter, Regina has options. You'll see those details on the evite, too."

"Never would've thought to try a gluten free cookie, so thanks, and for the sitter scoop." Laura hugged Tierney and got in her car. She peeled out of the gas station in the direction of Main Street.

I swear, this town.

A few minutes later, Tierney walked into the police station lobby with a large plate of Finnish Ribbon Cookies, covered in cellophane and a sticky note affixed to the top that read, "Thanks for All You Do for Park View! Warmly, The Gillespie Family." The department had juggled a lot over the past two weeks, and she'd always loved when civilians brought in treats to the station.

She approached the tall desk where a uniformed officer working reception was speaking quietly into a cell phone, his free hand against his forehead, before looking up at her.

"Hold a sec," he said into the phone, sat up straight, and placed the phone face down. "Can I help you?" he said in a curt tone before registering what Tierney was holding.

"Oh, nothing important. Just wanted to drop these off." She handed him the plate and explained what they were and for.

The officer's face softened as he accepted the gift. "Thank you for thinking of us. It's much appreciated." He read the note to himself, skimming his finger across the words as he did, but hovered over Gillespie for a second longer than the others as if it was familiar. He smiled.

"You're very welcome. It must be a relief to have the lifeguard case all wrapped up," she said graciously, as another officer entered the lobby with a grave-looking expression. The space grew cold.

The two men exchanged glances and then forced smiles Tierney's way, without further comment.

Time to leave. "Yes, well then, enjoy the evening, officers."

"You too," they said in unison.

Tierney turned on her heels and headed outside. Something was amiss.

* * *

The Starbucks barista placed a long, green straw next to the beverage on the counter. "Venti White Chocolate Mocha Frappuccino for Antonio?"

Sutton shook his head from the corner table at the sight of the milkshake-like beverage Ayala returned with.

"What? It's technically coffee. Progress is progress," Ayala said.

"I suppose." Sutton drank from his steaming cup of dark brown.

"Not bad." Ayala licked his lips, put the cup on the table, and pulled the DEA folder from his backpack.

"What the hell are you thinking, bringing that from the office?" Sutton's eyes darted around the coffeeshop while covering the folder with napkins. "It's classified."

"I wasn't going to show it to anyone else." Ayala returned the folder to his backpack. "Pretty sure it was the cute new records specialist who pulled it for me. She's always chatting me up by the fridge, although she's an orange soda gal."

"You have a lot to learn about station dynamics."

Ayala looked at Sutton curiously, not knowing what to make of the comment, but moved on. "I ran names of the potential suspects in the folder and the only one with possible ties to Schick is Enrique Salazar."

"The guy who worked on the evening maintenance crew for about a year."

Ayala nodded. "Although, don't you think a co-worker would've noticed him doing shady things? Like stuffing the lockers or toilet tanks with drugs?"

"Hard to know how their crews divvied up work."

"True. Or maybe others are in on it, too, and the DEA doesn't yet have eyes on them?"

"Maybe. But I did speak with the Facilities Director who oversees Schick's janitorial services. He said Salazar hasn't shown up for his past few shifts."

"Think he's already fled? I can check his last known address. Any landlord—"

"Hold on, I'm getting a call. It's Maureen," Sutton said with concern in his voice.

"The chief's admin?"

"Sutton here . . . What? . . . When? . . . Oh my God. Is he alive? . . . Of course . . . Who? . . . Seriously? . . . I, uh, yes. Ayala and I can leave now." Sutton hung up and stared at his phone.

"Everything okay?"

"The chief collapsed in the staffroom." Sutton stood and put on his jacket. "They thought he was choking on a piece of fruitcake but it's looking more like a heart attack."

"Where is he now?"

"They've rushed him to Good Samaritan Hospital."

"Is he going to be okay?"

"They don't know yet."

"Alright, let's go."

"I'll meet you there when I can. I'm supposed to report to the City Manager's office first. Actually, can you drop me on your way?"

"Sure, but why not the hospital?"

"I need to be sworn in as Interim Police Chief."

* * *

"Coooookies. My superfoooood. Bring me back coooookies." Finn flew by his parents through the kitchen.

"I second that," Sean replied.

"You know I will. We each bring five dozen, plate one of those for the tasting table, and depart with four dozen of everyone else's—so there will be plenty," Tierney said. "You can bring some to the office with you on Monday."

"Excellent," Sean said, reaching for a sample.

She playfully pushed his hand away and finished adding the last of the cookies into reusable, holiday-accented containers. "Sorry you don't get an evening out, too."

Ian had included all soccer team dads in his poker night invite, but Sean declined due to a handful of Silicon Valley heavy-hitters being in attendance. He didn't want to risk potential questions about projects or clients.

"It's fine. Never a shortage of work to catch up on. But," Sean said and looked up at the kitchen clock with a wide smile, "Finn and I have our own guy's night with pizza, popcorn, and a movie, commencing in thirty-three minutes."

"Way better than poker. Plus, that party is at Ian's home. You certainly don't want any association there due to his involvement in Vibora's backdating scandal."

Sean hesitated at Tierney's comment. "Ian isn't the parent on Finn's soccer team being investigated, hon. It's Justine."

"What?" Tierney froze.

"She's not with UnityHealing anymore, but she's been indicated. All of their board members have been questioned."

"Oh, God. I had no idea. I assumed it was Ian."

"I can understand why, from my comment last week. He is a mess. Maybe even an addict, for having shown up high to his son's event. But his deposition was clean, and he joined Vibora too recently to be in any legal trouble. Their CEO, CFO, and a few board members, however, not so lucky."

"Well, it's all still terrible." And to think how envious she had been of Justine's career. *Where nothing bad happened.*

"Agreed. But lucky for me, our new VP has taken over the biotech clients so I can remain focused on high tech. The devil I know, but individuals I don't."

"So, you wouldn't be personally on Justine's case?"

"Exactly. I hope investigators find that Justine had no involvement, but it's surely a stressful time for her and Coach, and unfortunate PR."

"Seriously."

"Papers are expected to run the UnityHealing story any day upon verification of a few more facts. But regardless of Coach potentially being at poker tonight, I have no time for games."

Tierney took Sean's chin in her hand and planted a kiss on his lips. "How did I get so lucky to have such a good-looking and above-board husband?"

—

Tierney pulled down the outfit she'd bought with Gem, the one set aside for a special holiday occasion. Mara's party was it. She felt stylish in the slim black slacks with crisp pleats, and emerald green blouse, but didn't feel complete. She spritzed herself with Bulgari, which elevated her mood, but something was still missing. *Lipstick tonight?*

She reached into her vanity drawer and retrieved the sample. It had been a long time. She thought of Norah and smiled. She slid the color across her lips and paused at her reflection. Her partner would've approved. While closing the tube, the white label on the bottom with the lipstick name drew her attention. She pulled it closer—"No Guilt." *No way.*

"Double wowza," Sean said at the sight of Tierney walking down the hall.

"Sweater or no sweater?" she asked, modeling both versions.

"Either looks great. Just bring it. At least you'll have it if it gets cold."

Tierney decided to wear it. "I'm going outside to pack up containers in the trunk and wait for Gem. My cell is on," she said, tapping her back pocket to verify its location, "so call if you boys need anything."

"We'll be fine. Go dazzle the ladies with your talent."

Finn flew up to his parents at the door. "I think I should be able to stay up until ten."

"Funny, my little negotiator," Tierney said and ruffled his hair. "It's nine o'clock tonight. Don't give Dad any trouble."

Although it was a crisp evening, Tierney's nerves were in full force and she was overheating. Her palms were already damp at the thought of entering Mara's home. She removed the sweater but her sleeve caught on her watch. She carefully released the snag, tossed her sweater into the back seat, and made room for Gem's cookies.

She had offered to drive so Betty would be at the ready in case she decided to call it an early night. But as Tierney looked at her watch for the third time, she saw they were running behind.

"Tonight has been an utter mess," Gem said breathlessly on approach, passing by Tierney with containers in hand towards the trunk.

Tierney followed behind and saw her neighbor's handiwork as she loaded the treats. "Your cookies turned out beautifully."

"Thanks so much, but I'll need you to bring them."

"What?" Tierney's heartbeat quickened.

"My parents arrived last night and my mom slipped on the bathroom floor while getting ready for bed. She hurt her ankle and it's black and blue."

"Oh no, I'm so sorry."

"We thought it was a sprain but the swelling won't stop. I need to get her checked out at the ER and probably an X-ray. I'm so sorry to miss. Hope you understand?"

"Of course. Go. And call me if I can help with anything."

"Will do. Now show off those gorgeous cookies of yours." Gem placed her hands on Tierney's shoulders and faced her. "And I want a full report, everything that goes down tonight, including which prizes you win."

"I didn't realize there would be prizes." Winning something couldn't be further from her mind.

Gem returned to her house and Tierney stood in disbelief. How could she attend this party alone? Gem wouldn't be there to walk in and talk with, and Laura might be a no-show if the bakery was sold out. Her stomach turned over. No, she couldn't do this alone.

She removed her containers from the back of the car and stacked them on the driveway. But at the sight of Gem's cookies, her arms fell to her sides. *Dammit.* She had to at least deliver Gem's cookies. How could she not? And hers, too, if she wanted customers for a new business.

Tierney sighed at her voice of reason. She repacked her cookies in Betty and slammed the door. *Leave them inside the foyer and return home.* It would be quick.

—

Tierney was now a late arrival and forced to park ten houses down—disappointing, due to the load she had to carry. She pulled two grocery bags from Betty's trunk organizer, a gift from Lily last Christmas, and gently placed Gem's five dozen inside of one bag and hers in the other. She balanced both and shepherded them to Mara's.

She could hear the party from the street as she followed the path to the front door. It was ajar and displayed a handwritten sign in calligraphy:

Come on in!

No nuts invited

Tierney remained standing on the porch, but was running the risk of her sweaty palms disintegrating the paper bags' handles if she waited any longer. A faint buzz in her ear was growing louder but her thoughts returned to Gem. She forced one step inside and placed the bags down by the door. Someone would see them and add them to the mix.

She turned to exit when her voice of reason struck again. She looked back at Gem's cookies. Knowing how hard her friend had worked, she couldn't leave them sitting in a grocery bag. If Tierney was the last arrival, they would remain there all night. No, she'd have to go inside and display them. At least do that. *Like any other catering event.* She took a deep breath and pushed through.

The front door swung open and Tierney was mesmerized, the fruity fragrance of Tahitian vanilla enticing a step inside. The spacious foyer was a mini version of a five-star hotel lobby. She had only caught a glimpse of it when she came by earlier with Mara's supplies, but she could see clearly now that the Wrights spared no expense on home decor.

A chandelier hung above a polished, round mahogany table, which shimmered in reflected crystals, and showcased a glorious floral arrangement in a large nickel vase. It overflowed with red roses, a medley of white flowers and dark green accent stems.

Tierney refocused on her mission to find the cookie display table. She entered the large room off to the right and registered the sound of Pearl Bailey's "Five Pound Box of Money" playing through the home stereo system. She was in awe again, but this time by the dining room table—on it the most stunning cookie display she had seen in all her years of catering.

She spotted thirty-some women in the house already, but thankfully only one guest in the room with her.

"Mara has outdone herself this year," the woman said upon noting Tierney's arrival.

Tierney gave a knowing smile and followed her lead, filling out a placard to identify Gem's cookies and arranging them on a platter in an open spot. The woman checked her appearance in a side wall mirror and joined the others. Tierney glanced over to the large group where she'd need to enter next and her throat began to tighten. She folded Gem's bag, tucked it into hers, and bumped into another guest as she turned to leave.

"Tierney! Happy holidays. So lovely to see you."

"Oh, hi, Franny. You, too. Quite a party."

"I know, right?"

"Which ones did you bring?"

"Oh, I haven't set them out yet," Tierney said with an exhale.

Franny looked down at Tierney's bag. "Those are gorgeous. What kind?"

"Finnish Ribbon Cookies. An old family favorite."

"Here, let me help you find a spot near my graham cracker sprinkles and get you a name tag."

Dammit. Tierney mentally revised her plan—make an appearance and pull an Irish goodbye.

Franny helped Tierney with her cookie display and accompanied her into the next room, passing a small table with three meticulously gift-wrapped voting boxes, labeled "Prettiest Cookie," "Most Unique Cookie," and "Best Tasting Cookie." Small slips of paper with pre-printed guest names, and a hammered pewter tin with candy cane-shaped pens, were set nearby.

When Tierney turned the corner, she saw Mara—looking every bit of perfection in her short red holiday dress with a cluster of decorative buttons in the shape of a flower on one sleeve. Mara appeared to teeter a bit as she spoke, though, with an empty champagne glass in hand, to the women gathered around her, including Laura. The topic was something about oven frustrations.

Tierney and Franny approached Laura and exchanged friendly embraces.

"Thanks again," Laura whispered to Tierney. "I ran into Mara at the bakery. Her oven's temperature gauge died and kept burning batches so she was there buying something last-minute, too."

"No way," said Tierney.

"I got the gluten-free ones you recommended, and Mara chose the only thing left: chocolate chip. Totally against the rules!"

"I'm glad things worked out," Tierney said, and they returned their attention to Mara, who was relaying the same Bonnie's Bakery adventure, which gave the group a big laugh. Mara's eyes then fell on Tierney and she stopped cold—breaking a smile.

"So glad you could join us tonight, Tierney."

"Oh," Tierney was taken aback by the kind comment and attention. "Glad I could make it."

"I bet I'll immediately know which cookies are yours when I pass the dining room table," she added sincerely yet with a slur. "Now if you'll all excuse me, I need to check on Nat in the kitchen."

Laura turned to Tierney after Mara's departure. "Looks as if your baking has already made quite an impression."

"Let's hope she likes them," Tierney replied and simultaneously cringed at her insecure response. "I mean, yes, thanks."

A few women registering Mara's praise walked off in the direction of the display table.

"I'll have to claim one myself," Laura said.

"They are lovely," Franny added, and the three of them moved to the nearby conversation, including word that Justine wasn't able to attend tonight's exchange after all—apparently not feeling well. Tierney had an idea how Justine might be feeling.

Tierney was trying her best to enjoy the party and meet new moms. She felt proud for staying as long as she had and realized she was no longer feeling desperate to escape. Was she actually having a nice evening?

Mara's baking compliment had helped her feel at ease. And with Tierney's stylish outfit and makeup à la Gem, she was feeling confident, maybe enough to mention her baking business to guests and to bring up the holiday class party with Mara. Tierney looked around to see if Mara had returned, but no sign of her yet. The house was expansive, though, so she'd keep a lookout.

As a few more guests headed over to cast votes, the conversation turned to the Popov murder and Brad's arrest.

"I can't believe it was Brad. I mean, my family has been around him for years," Lisa said.

"I'm just glad they caught the guy. Having a murderer on the loose is too much, especially around the holidays," another woman added. "I was calling the hotline daily to demand justice."

"Me, too," said another.

"Well, I'm glad the case is resolved for another reason," said an outdoorsy-looking woman with a cat-eye tan from sunglasses. "Now authorities can go back to finding the culprit who hit that bike messenger who's still in a coma. Just deplorable, really."

The other women nodded as she continued her story.

"City Council threw our organization a bone with a bogus bike lane-widening proposal so we'd ease up on protests, but until Park View is more supportive of biking around town, like they are in Amsterdam, we won't be silenced."

"I've never been to Amsterdam," said Lisa.

"The respect among cyclists, cars, and pedestrians is seamless. I've been on a few bike tours there, so know a safer solution can be found in Park View," the woman continued.

The road safety discussion continued and Mara returned with a full champagne glass, along with Natalia and Regina's au pair at her heels carrying the three voting boxes and unclaimed paper slips. The young women placed the materials on a small table. It was the first time Tierney had seen the au pairs at the party.

The room had grown stuffy so Mara opened the sliding door before ringing a ceremonial bell. "Okay, ladies, I'd like to keep the votes moving," she said, fumbling over her words. "If you haven't already, please swing by the cookie display to peruse and taste, and drop your ballots here. So excited to see our winners this year."

A few returned to the display, including Tierney, who hadn't yet voted. Some of the bakers stood by their treats, including a few whose platters matched their cookies, and two women who color-coordinated their outfits to complement their sweet creations. Who knew cookie exchanges were such serious business?

As Tierney circled the table, she noted some tough competition, including Italian fig cookies and a few Chanukah-inspired designs like a cookie menorah with frosted candles and flames. There were also sugar cookies cut into mitten shapes, tied together in pairs with real ribbon. Then there were minty cream wafers, little cookie sandwiches held together with buttery red or green filling, shortbread mice with thin red licorice for tails, mascarpone clusters, and gingerbread snowflakes trimmed with white-lined icing.

After one full sweep around, the cookie Tierney deemed most unique was, surprisingly, Regina's—homemade chocolate-dipped fortune cookies with red, white, and green sprinkles, not only impressive, but tedious to make. But could she bring herself to cast a vote for that woman? *Hold on.* Tierney examined them more closely. *The unique curled edges, and the sight of a ladybug logo peeking out on one of the fortune papers.*

Tierney looked around for Regina, who was busy exchanging whispers in the corner with another guest. *What a piece of work.*

Tierney surveyed the offerings one final time and, after sampling a few, she returned to the table by the slider to cast her votes—all three for Gem's chocolate ginger. Her neighbor had outdone herself, and friendship should always be rewarded.

As voting came to a close, Tierney caught a chill from the backyard breeze. She put down the wine Laura had handed her earlier and went to find her sweater. It wasn't by her purse, but then she remembered it was still in Betty. Tierney whispered to Laura that she'd be right back and scooted out the front door.

She continued down the sidewalk and retrieved her sweater from the back seat where she'd left it. She realized while putting it on that her original plan to get out as fast as possible was now outweighed by the fact she was enjoying herself. Such an emotional roller coaster today had been, but how nice to feel a part of something for a change.

* * *

Sutton shook hands with the City Manager and Mayor, and stepped into the lobby to take Ayala's call. "How's the chief?"

"Stabilized. But that's not why I'm calling."

"What's up?"

"I'm leaving the hospital now. You weren't answering your cell so Joelle contacted me. The uniforms you had watching Josh's apartment?"

"Yeah?"

"Josh had an altercation with someone. Perhaps our ski-mask guy returned? Anyway, we've got a tail on the suspect going westbound on Highway 85. They'll send his location soon."

"Swing by and pick me up."

* * *

Tierney walked back to Mara's and recognized Bell's VW amidst the many parked cars along the street. *Weird.* Tierney had assumed she lived near the new apartment community. Bell was full of surprises.

Tierney stepped up to the front door, now wide open. She had left it ajar; maybe the wind or a late arrival moved it. She saw Natalia through the kitchen window talking to a man, and Tierney glanced down at the time. *The guys should all be at Ian's by now.*

Tierney neared. There was a look of fear set across Natalia's face. She tiptoed into the house and looked for Mara but halted at the sound of threatening conversation.

"We've seen you with her, and that stupid boyfriend of hers said our coke is in this house. Where is it?" the male voice said in an aggressive whisper.

Tierney neared the kitchen door to listen while scanning for Mara in the room off to the right, which had grown crowded as women flowed around the cookie display. She pulled her phone from her back pocket and could now hear Natalia crying.

Tierney backed away from the kitchen door. As she turned to exit the house and call Sutton, she saw an officer wearing a DEA jacket entering the foyer. Tierney stopped short as her mind processed the scene. The officer brought her finger up to her lips on approach, holding her sidearm at the ready with at least four other unit members closely behind.

Tierney looked into the officer's eyes—a piercing amber. She'd know them anywhere. *Bell.* She returned the phone to her pocket.

In a low voice, Bell instructed Tierney to stay calm, and asked if she could help identify the homeowner.

Tierney nodded.

"We need to get your friends out the back door and around to the street. You up for that?"

Tierney nodded again.

Hair pulled back tautly in a ponytail and wearing a bullet-proof vest, Bell directed Tierney to enter the living room solo—to calmly help begin the evacuation and find Mara. Bell hung back, out of sight momentarily, as not to cause alarm among guests seeing an armed officer. Tierney noticed Bell continue to monitor activity in the kitchen, the angry conversation still discernible despite the Christmas music, as other officers kept surveillance.

Guests were initially confused with Tierney's instruction, but she calmly kept noise to an unalarming level amidst some tipsy partygoers. She finally eyed Mara. "I need your help getting guests out quietly. There are burglars in the kitchen but officers are onsite."

Mara blinked a few times, but nodded instead of becoming incensed. Tierney had been lucky. Her training had taught her to keep details to a minimum, and she didn't want to incite concern over Natalia and a blotto Mara to go rogue.

Once guests had been informed of the situation, Bell joined Tierney and Mara with the evacuation. Despite her intoxication, Mara's instruction to guests she clearly knew better than Tierney was working well.

"There's a side door through the laundry room off the kitchen which is sometimes unlocked," Tierney whispered to Bell, and felt a surge of adrenaline.

Bell acknowledged the intel as Laura passed by the pack, wearing a frantic "What the heck is going on?" expression. Tierney motioned that she continue outside, and was almost out herself when Mara shot back from the group, passing her and heading towards the kitchen.

"I didn't see Nat. I need to find her," said Mara.

Tierney grabbed for her arm but missed. She followed behind to try again, with Bell now on their heels, and both attempted to stop Mara before entering the kitchen. As Tierney grabbed for Mara's arm again, she made contact, but her watch snagged a large button on Mara's sleeve at the same time a muscular woman from inside the kitchen pulled Mara—and subsequently Tierney—inside before the button tore off.

Bell swore and retreated to the entryway. All other guests had mercifully exited, but now watched in horror from across the street, through the front window, as Tierney and Mara appeared in the kitchen.

Tierney had only seen a man earlier.

"Good, Ruby. More hostages to leverage." He laughed and waved the gun, directing his two new arrivals to join Natalia across from him.

Mara hugged her au pair and Tierney took a spot beside them. Tierney couldn't believe what was happening. Her ribcage tightened around her lungs, making it harder to breathe. She thought of Sean and Finn and couldn't catch her breath. The scene felt all too familiar, but worse. She had a family this time. And the top rule of hostage negotiation began flickering like a strobe light in her head—*don't be in the same room as the hostage taker*.

Her hands felt like drenched gloves and her vision began to blur. She felt unsteady and registered the blood draining from her face, down her neck and arms, and weaving through her core towards her feet. She was either going to pass out or vomit, uncertain which, or maybe both, when Jennie opened the bathroom door off the laundry room and walked straight into the commotion.

Tierney locked eyes with Jennie but didn't register it was her. Tierney's eyes glazed over for a moment. It wasn't Jennie she now saw—it was Norah. Tierney had the urge to reach out and hug her partner but felt suspended in time. Then, her muscle memory engaged.

A combination of adrenaline and an outpouring of inner strength rushed back through Tierney's limbs. She inhaled calmly amidst the situation that now registered in Mara's kitchen, and exhaled deeply. BB once shared that anxious people do better in highly charged situations since it's closer to their baseline. Tierney hoped that theory was correct. Her eyes fastened on Jennie, a wide-eyed vision in shock who instinctively wrapped her arms across her stomach and began to cry.

The woman named Ruby grabbed Jennie and pulled her over to the hostage lineup. They all now faced the barrel of the man's gun as Ruby became aware of the large crowd gathering out front, and the blue and red blinking lights from SWAT cars. She moved stealthily and lowered the blinds. The show was over.

Tierney still felt off-kilter, like her former self but removed. Déjà vu. She knew what to do. What had to be done. But could she do it? It had been so long. And Norah had always been by her side. But, maybe, she still was? She owed this to her—a second chance to get things right.

"Now where was I? Yes, where are my drugs, bitch?" the man yelled an inch from Natalia's face.

Survey the scene. Bell would be standing down near the front entry with gun drawn. Just start talking. Get the conversation going and keep it going. There are four of us and one gun, one weapon visible. The crack between the two window coverings in front. I can still see Bell's team. Some now inching their way up to the side door, including SWAT. The laundry room info being utilized.

"Tell us exactly what you're looking for," Tierney asked. "We're all innocent women here." *Listen to the voice. Get them talking.*

"Shut up. We do the talking," the man snapped nervously.

So talk, asshole.

"This one has been hiding drugs for Tatyana," he said, pointing his gun at Natalia.

He sounds afraid. He's not strong and in control here. An extra hostage has overwhelmed him. His hands are shaking. He's starting to sweat, profusely. He's not holding the gun confidently. Yes, the safety is still engaged!

"I told you. I don't know what you're talking about. I hardly know Tatyana, I, I mean, knew Tatyana," Natalia began crying louder.

"I don't believe you. Her loser boyfriend gave up this address when I beat the shit out of him. You're next," he directed at Natalia. "Tatyana had been hiding her stash here—our stashes she's been stealing—and we're going to find it all. Tonight. Actually, you're going to find it or I'm going to start killing off your friends here. Now show us," the man continued, waving his gun around the kitchen.

"I don't . . . even know . . . where . . . to look," Natalia spluttered.

Mara stood close to Natalia's side, squinting at what was happening.

"Natalia, stay calm and think." Tierney lowered her chin to generate downward inflection. "Where has Tatyana been in your home? Was she ever upstairs? Did she use the bathroom? Did she go in the garage?" Tierney pointed around as she spoke to distract the two perps away from the window as Bell's team made its way further up the side yard. *Not too close, guys.*

"We ask the questions," the man said, leveling his gun at Tierney's chest.

Tierney nodded and turned to Natalia for a response. *Keep the man and Ruby's backs to the side window so they can't see what I can.*

Tierney looked at the man while awaiting Natalia's reply. Something about him was familiar.

Natalia's sobs grew louder. Mara held her more tightly, motherly, in an effort to comfort her.

"She doesn't know this Tatyana," Mara said, her words slurring, clearly feeling emboldened. "You heard her say they were hardly friends. And I would've noticed if anyone had brought drugs into my home."

"So, this is your home?" the man said, now directing his gun at Mara. "You're probably in on this, too. Supplying your neighbors instead of us."

"What are you talking about? I'm no drug dealer." Mara latched hands to hips and stood in defiance. "And I certainly don't associate with druggies. I'm calling 911 right now." She reached for her phone.

Oh my God, Mara. The police are onsite!

"Give me that," Ruby yelled, swiping the phone from Mara's hand. "And the rest of you, give me your phones."

"That's mine," Mara shouted at Ruby and lunged towards her. Ruby shoved her back against the counter and Mara recoiled. *God, Park View women are entitled.*

"Shut up. I don't believe you don't know where it's stashed," the man yelled at both Natalia and Mara now, moving his gun between the two, behaving more nervous and now sweating profusely. Jennie and Natalia handed Ruby their phones, and she pulled Tierney's out from her back pocket. She tossed them all out of reach into the kitchen sink.

The man wiped his brow on his sleeve and yelled at Natalia again. "Where is it?"

That sweaty smell—Drakkar Noir. Oh my God, cologne man from the pool! His face. The Stingray looking up at me in the water. Tierney glanced over at the woman. *His kettlebell pal. Snake tattoo for sure under that turtleneck.*

"I don't know. This house is so big. How do I know where to start?" Natalia continued, tears now rolling down.

Keep. Talking. "It's okay. Try to stay calm. Did she ever bring anyone else to your home?" Tierney asked.

Mara put her arm more tightly around Natalia.

"Step away from her," the man yelled at Mara, now aiming his gun at her.

"How dare you wave that in front of me. Nat didn't have anything to do with your drugs," Mara yelled as Natalia leaned into her, and Jennie sobbed louder.

Dammit. The unpredictability of civilians. Mara has no clue of the danger we're in. "I know this is a tense situation, Mara, but please keep it together," Tierney said. "Natalia, anything can help."

"She was always with me, and brought nobody else over," Natalia said through sniffs. "Here in the kitchen. I think she helped me put away groceries once. And maybe she did use the bathroom there." She pointed to where Jennie had vacated. "And I showed her my room upstairs one time."

"That's it. A more private space. Let's go," he said to Natalia.

"You're not taking her anywhere," Mara said and stepped towards the gun, liquid courage enabling her boldness. *Recklessness.*

"Get in the bathroom, Mouthy," he snarled at Mara, shoving her towards the door. And your friends, too," he instructed.

"You don't need to do this," Tierney offered calmly, knowing once their group was separated from Natalia it would be harder for Bell's team to act.

"Ruby, take the gun and aim it at the bathroom door. If they try to escape, shoot them. I can handle this one upstairs," the man said, grabbing a now ashen-faced Natalia by the arm. "I'll be back." He watched Mara and Jennie enter the bathroom first.

Tierney caught a glimpse of officers holding their position inside the laundry room behind the pyramid of rolling backpack boxes, as Ruby gave her a final shove inside. *Thank God for those boxes.*

"Please let us go," Jennie sobbed, her chest beginning to rise and fall rapidly. "I have a family who needs me."

The door slammed in their faces. From within the quiet space, Tierney could hear the hum of "Run Rudolph Run."

* * *

"I'll drive," Sutton said.

Ayala put the car in park and moved to the passenger seat.

"We've been to this address before," Ayala said while scrolling through notes on his cell phone. "It's the Wright residence."

"Where we interviewed Natalia?"

"Yeah. Funny, I never sensed she or the host family had any involvement."

"It's hard to be certain what's going on with people."

"Guess we'll find out soon enough. And brace yourself. There's a holiday cookie exchange in progress onsite."

"What?"

"About thirty-five moms have been evacuated, but a few remain hostage inside."

"Jesus Christ. That's all we need—some idiot killing the wives of people wealthy enough to buy this town." And that was not how he wanted his biggest murder case to go down.

"Idiots plural. Apparently two perps inside and four female hostages. Tierney Gillespie is one of them."

"Seriously? And who from the department is in charge onsite?"

"Not sure. They were ro-sham-bo-ing last time I heard."

Sutton turned on lights and sirens and floored it.

* * *

"You, move it." Tierney overheard the man instructing Natalia from behind the door, and the muffled sound of shoes climbing the stairs. *One creaky floorboard on the third step, another at the top of the landing.*

Tierney flipped down the toilet seat and asked Jennie to sit before she hyperventilated. Jennie slumped onto the porcelain and reached for toilet paper from the roll. Her tears streamed as she blew her nose.

"How can this be happening?" Mara asked, still staring at the closed door.

"I don't know, but it is," Tierney said quietly, not knowing how closely Ruby was listening. "We're getting ourselves out of this, though. We just need to keep level heads."

Mara didn't move or respond.

"Mara, did you hear me?"

"I heard you." Mara turned around with puddled eyes. "Thank God Max is safe tonight at a sleepover. But if anything happens to Nat, I don't know what I'll do."

"It'll be okay," Tierney said loudly. She then motioned the women closer to her and whispered, "The SWAT team has already made its way into the laundry room. They're close and keeping an eye on us. Understand?"

"I guess you're more observant than I am," Mara replied and sniffled. "But I should've gone upstairs with her."

"You didn't have a choice. She'll be okay. They won't find anything, right? So, they'll be back down in no time. I'll need you two to remain calm and follow my lead."

"I want to go home," Jennie cried. "I shouldn't even have come tonight. Aaron has a lot going on at church this weekend and he was so sweet to give me a break."

"It's okay. Tierney's right. We're going to get through this. I won't let anything happen to you, or the baby," Mara replied, regaining a bit of composure at the sight of Jennie's stomach.

"That's the attitude," Tierney said while intently listening for outside noises.

They heard footsteps from above, along with yelling.

"That's Nat's room above us. He'd better not lay a hand on her or I will kill him," Mara replied with more anger in her voice.

"The guy just wants his drugs. He's not looking to hurt anyone. I imagine he wants out of here as much as we do. And besides, the head lifeguard from the pool is the one who killed Tatyana, not this guy—I mean, that's what the news report said," Tierney said without believing her words, especially after her police station visit.

A loud thud sounded above and Jennie began to ugly cry. Mara bent down to comfort her. As the two women embraced, Mara, too, became a bubbling mess.

"I'm trying to be calm, but the reality of what's happening, and us all at risk, is overwhelming," Mara said. "Nat is like a daughter to me. If anything bad hap—" Her voice grew softer and she drew in a big breath. "If anything happens to her, I don't think I could survive. I've already lost one daughter. Melody," she said, her voice breaking as she spoke the name.

Jennie and Tierney exchanged a confused look, but Tierney could hear the ache in Mara's voice. The kind that never goes away, but sits in wait until some trigger brings it right back up again. Tierney put her hand on Mara's shoulder.

Jennie reached up for Mara's hands. "I'm so sorry. How did I not know this? What happened?" she asks, almost breathless.

"No one knew except family. I wasn't far enough along to share my pregnancy news with friends before we left for France. Remember that summer we rented an estate in Provence?"

Jennie nodded.

"The stillbirth happened at twenty-two weeks while we were abroad. I haven't been myself since, especially this past year. We've never been able to get pregnant again, and all the changing plans last-minute this year when the doctor's office would reschedule, racing home to take a shot on time, missing Max's soccer games." She shook her head. "And the hormones made everything worse. I finally had to stop those. The mood swings, the bloating and bruising—the body issues that followed became unbearable."

"Oh, Mara." Tierney gave her shoulder a gentle squeeze. "It is so hard to lose someone you love." In a heartbeat, the past few months pulled into focus. *Mara had been distracted by life. Her own complicated, messy life. Like everyone else. My stupid volunteering requests couldn't have been further from her mind.*

Jennie and Tierney remained quiet as Mara continued.

"The nurse practitioner back then told me the best way to move on is to just get pregnant again. Wonder what the witch would say to me four years later, huh?" She laughed through tears. "Craig and I have tried every fertility treatment."

"You two have been seeing a specialist?" Jennie asked.

"Up at UCSF. Four rounds of IUI, then a few IVF. But the doctor called after my last cycle saying we should consider adoption or surrogate," Mara said through sniffles as she repositioned the center stone of her wedding set. "I know adoption is a noble thing, but my aunt was adopted and her life has been so complicated—such abandonment issues. I just don't think it's an option for me. And certainly not a surrogate. The thought of another woman carrying Craig's baby instead of me is—" Mara's body shuddered.

"I wish I could've been a support to you," Jennie said.

"It can be hard to ask for help," Mara said. "Today's date, December first, was Melody's due date. I actually started this party four years ago to distract myself through the holiday season. But having the date fall exactly on the first this year has been hell."

Tierney swallowed deeply. Tragic anniversaries were brutal.

"And I'm sorry I didn't follow through on your shower." Mara looked directly at Jennie. "I know I had offered a while back, especially because you had thrown one for Max. I've just been so depressed lately. I couldn't bear to host something that I wish I was celebrating myself."

"Don't feel guilty. I hosted your shower because I wanted to, not because I expected anything in return." Jennie adjusted her body to the side and winced.

Tierney winced, too, at Jennie's discomfort sitting on the lid's hard surface.

"Holy cow, the baby is doing a gymnastics routine," Jennie said.

Great. Her going into labor is not what we need. Tierney heard footsteps above move towards the back of the house and—*Wait. Or is it?*

"I'm sorry you've felt this way," Jennie continued.

Mara sniffled. "After all this tonight, I realize it's time for me to—"

"Sorry to interrupt ladies, but we need to take advantage of Ruby being downstairs alone. We're going to pretend Jennie's water broke." Tierney helped Jennie up from the toilet seat to a standing position. Not wanting to risk the sound of sink water turning on, she lifted the toilet lid and quietly splashed water onto the floor below Jennie and along her legs as the two looked on in horror.

"Will this work?" Mara whispered.

The gun's safety had better still be on. "The longer we stay in here, the harder things become for us. We need to at least get Jennie out and then," Tierney stood to face Jennie, "you can give the officers an account of what you've seen here, understand? Two criminals who were swimmers at Schick, one named Ruby and—"

"They swam at Schick?" Mara asked.

"Yes. And they're looking for their cocaine. Three of us hostages left inside. We're waiting for Natalia to rejoin us downstairs with the man."

"What if Ruby doesn't believe me?" Jennie sniffled. "I'm a terrible actress. My ward always cast me as an extra in their annual summer play."

"Well, you're going to prove them wrong tonight. Like your baby's life depends on it. Understand?"

Jennie nodded, a look of fear in her eyes.

"Start crying harder, like you've gone into labor. You have experience there, right? Channel it."

She blew her nose, took a deep breath, and started to cry out and bend over in pretend pain.

Tierney banged on the door. "Open up! She's gone into labor. Let us out!" They'd need to be quick before the man returned with Natalia.

No response.

"Open the door! A woman in labor is not a hostage you want. It's her third baby. It'll be here any minute."

Jennie cried louder, adding to the frenzy.

"None of us can help find your drugs if we're delivering a baby," Tierney yelled.

The doorknob slowly turned and Ruby opened the door to peek inside, gun barrel aimed. Her eyes moved between Jennie's doubled-over stature and the wet floor.

Gotcha. "Just let me help her to the front door before her next contraction." Tierney watched as Ruby processed the offer. "Your partner isn't going to want to deal with a baby, right?"

Ruby sighed and opened the door wider, eyes nervously darting around us. "Fuck. But only she walks out. By herself. You two stay put."

"Fine. Let her go now."

"You, out," Ruby motioned to Jennie with the gun and re-aimed at Mara and Tierney as the two stepped back.

Tierney couldn't make the safety's position as Ruby looked back over her shoulder into the kitchen.

"Straight out the front, holding your stomach, and don't look back," Tierney motioned to Jennie before Ruby turned around.

Jennie slowly exited, playing the role perfectly—hunched over and moaning as she made her way towards the front door before Ruby shut the bathroom door. *Dammit.*

Tierney listened for sounds from the floorboards above. Nothing yet. She then placed her ear up against the door as she held her breath, her heart thumping and stomach flipping inside out as she prayed that Plan A worked. *It had to.*

The front door slammed, followed by footfalls down the stairs as the man and Natalia returned.

"Why did the door slam?" Tierney heard the man's muffled question, followed by Ruby's recap. Jennie had made it out safely. *Thank God.*

"You idiot. They've played you," his voice continued. "Now you, hurry up and get looking. In the cabinets. In the pantry. We're running out of time before I start shooting."

Natalia's cries grew louder. Tierney leaned back against the door to think while Mara sat on the toilet seat.

"Nice job getting her out. That was daring." Mara seemed to be sobering up.

"I'm glad it worked." Tierney sighed. "We're next."

Mara looked sheepish. "I'm sorry I mouthed off earlier. That was stupid. I made everything worse. It's the alcohol talking. Craig has been wanting me to get help for my drinking. I'm not an alcoholic, though. Really. My booze-filled days have just been a way to cope with the depression. Unsuccessfully, I might add." She reached into the magazine basket on the floor, moving aside some *Real Simple* and *Martha Stewart Living* issues, to reveal a near-empty vodka bottle.

Tierney smiled inside. *A weapon.*

"But I don't need to be doing this anymore." Mara tossed it into the wastebasket. "What I need is to not dwell on the past and things out of my control, and to be there for Max and Craig. I've been so horrible to them. I need to move forward with my life and focus on my boys." She looked down at a four-inch-long scab on her left hand. "And to stop doing stupid things like cutting my hand on wine glasses I attempt to wash too late into the evening. So dumb. I could've lost the feeling in my hand this last time." She began to cry again.

"I'm so sorry you've been struggling."

"But that's not all of it. I'm the reason why Max is repeating kindergarten. I wasn't there for him. Just so focused on myself. I'm even the reason we had to change soccer teams early in the season. I ran into the coach when leaving a dinner in the city with Craig, soaked in chardonnay, and verbally attacked him for not giving Max enough play time and—"

"Listen, the positive here is that you clearly have many people in your life that adore and support you—family and all these friends here tonight."

Mara nodded. "Life is too short to not be living it, you know? I just need to find more meaning in my days."

Tierney quickly turned away from Mara and put her ear against the door again. But it wasn't a sound from outside that had struck her. It was the sound of Mara giving voice to her own feelings, and it took Tierney's breath away. She pressed her hands into the wood and closed her eyes for a moment, leaning in for support.

"I know I've overshared," Mara continued. "I mean, we don't really know each other. But what if, what if this is the end?"

Tierney gulped in a breath and turned around to face Mara. "It's not the end. We're getting out of here. And it's okay to share in a trusted space." BB's advice filtered in. *But with Mara?* Tierney swallowed and her words flowed. "I've been battling my own demons. For the past eight years, actually."

A kind look set into Mara's eyes. "I'm so sorry. Trying for more children, too?"

The comment surprised Tierney—how one sees things through their own lens of life experience. "I'm not sure I could handle more than one child with the baggage I've been carrying around. No, it's the death of a close friend I couldn't help save."

"That would be hard. Eight years?"

Tierney nodded. "And I've been doing everything in my power to bury it, deep inside. But if there's anything I've learned in the process, it doesn't help. It just prolongs the inevitable." Tierney paused, this time from sounds of a struggle in the kitchen.

"Here I'm going on four years since Melody's passing and have pretty much lost my mind. I've even been assigning parents volunteer roles they didn't express interest in, or given them nothing at all. I thought, if I couldn't have something I wanted, why should anyone else?"

What?

"It's shameful." Mara averted her eyes from Tierney's. "And Regina's been causing problems, too. But I'll fix it."

"It's okay, Mara. Secrets can be toxic," Tierney said with an understanding smile, and lowered her voice further. "They make people do irrational things."

Mara looked up at Tierney.

"I'm serious. Grief can unhinge a person. And for me, it's time I face things head-on and reclaim my life, too. I know it's what my friend would've wanted for me."

"That's a healthy attitude."

Tierney said in the slightest whisper, "Would you believe I finally scheduled an appointment with a psychologist? I have an appointment on Monday."

"That's wonderful."

Tierney felt lighter with her honesty, yet distracted by the sound of activity rising in the kitchen.

"Maybe if we get out of this mess tonight, you can give me their contact info."

"Don't worry, we're getting out of this mess," Tierney said as a shadow appeared under the bathroom door. "Just please follow my lead, okay?"

Mara crossed her heart. "You say that like you've done this before."

"Guess I forgot to mention that. I used to be a hostage negotiator in Ireland for a few years before getting into baking."

Mara's eyes doubled in size as she watched Tierney retrieve the vodka bottle and tuck it into the back of her pants.

The conversation in the kitchen grew heated, with Natalia's sobs increasing in volume.

Get the group back together. That's the goal. Get all three of us in the kitchen so SWAT can hone in. "Let us out," Tierney yelled while banging on the door. "We'll help you look. It will go faster."

The bathroom door burst open. "Both of you. Out," Ruby said. "And stand next to this one where we can see you."

Tierney and Mara took their places next to Natalia. While walking over, Tierney caught a glimpse of a SWAT team member's shoe peeking out from behind a box. *They're in position. Wait, is that the sound of a helicopter overhead?*

"Check the toilet tank, Ruby," the man said, taking the gun back from her and aiming it at his hostages. "If it's not in there, you three are getting busy. Drawers, cabinets, until we find it," the man continued.

Just then, a cell phone rang. It was Ruby's.

"Don't answer it," the man yelled.

Bell. Trying to make contact. Jennie must've helped ID the woman.

"We're not talking to anyone. Shut it off," the man yelled, his voice losing confidence.

"Nothing in there." Ruby returned from the bathroom and silenced her phone.

The man looked up to the sound of helicopter blades whirling above the house.

Nothing like having wealthy men's wives in danger to activate resources. Tierney heard a loud pop—the safety being disengaged. *His hands are shaking. He's starting to lose it. We have a short window before he does something irreversible.*

"Can you think of where else Tatyana might have been?" Tierney asked Natalia.

"No," she sniffled. "Just here up at the counter to help Max with homework." Natalia pointed in between heavy sobs.

"My God, would you stop crying," Ruby yelled, and backhanded Natalia across the face.

Mara grabbed the vodka bottle from Tierney's pants and swung it at Ruby's head. She missed and the bottle released from her hand, flying across the room.

Dammit, Mara!

Ruby glared at Mara just as music blasted throughout the kitchen: Kool & The Gang's "Celebration."

"What's happening?" Ruby frantically looked around the room for a music source. Amplified from within an empty water glass in the kitchen sink, Jennie's phone ringtone blared.

Nice work, Bell!

"Calm down," the man yelled at Ruby, now frantically waving his gun around, not knowing where to focus.

Just enough of a distraction for the SWAT team to launch.

Tierney yanked Mara and Natalia down to the floor with her.

"Drop the gun," an officer yelled as the team flooded into the kitchen, multiple guns drawn. Tierney glanced up to witness the defiant man now aiming his gun directly at an officer.

Oh, God.

Bell appeared in the kitchen from the front door entrance where she had been holding position. The man re-aimed at her and she fired a single shot to his shoulder. He dropped the gun and pulled up his other hand to the now gushing wound as his knees buckled in pain.

"Miguel!" Ruby ran to his aid.

Tierney lunged across the floor to reach the fallen gun and slid it across to an officer. Another officer jumped Ruby before she reached Miguel. In an instant, both perps were held down, cuffed, and read their rights. *That beautiful sound never gets old.*

As Tierney stood, she realized she couldn't move her shoulder. She looked around at the "party of the year," as "Holly Jolly Christmas" played throughout the kitchen.

—

"Let's get that arm checked," Bell said to Tierney. The two exited the house and approached one of the ambulances while Mara and Natalia joined officers standing by their gathered partygoers near the black-and-whites, including husbands—all now cheering loudly.

Tierney witnessed the neighborhood scene as the EMT evaluated her shoulder, and thought of how grateful she was for everyone's children to have been with sitters. What looked to be the entire guest list from Ian's poker game was now standing on the front lawn. How could they not have noticed the commotion of SWAT cars shooting past their event?

"Nice work in there. I recognize you now from the pool," Bell said. "I'm DEA Agent Mok."

"Tierney Gillespie. It took me a moment to recognize you, too, in uniform," she said, breaking a smile.

"Say, I could hear you talking from outside the kitchen door while I held my position. Where did you learn those tactics?"

"I used to be a hostage negotiator with the Crisis Intervention Squad in Dublin, Ireland."

"Ah. You're one of us."

"Years ago, but looks as if the skill set stays with you, even from the other side of a situation room."

"We were lucky to have you in there tonight."

"I suppose."

"We've been watching Schick for months. We believe they've had a cocaine operation running out of both locker rooms as a distribution channel. We caught insight into their operation when one of their dealers—a bike messenger—was hit by a car and we found his bag at the scene filled with the purest coke we'd ever encountered around here."

"Wait, the guy on the news in the coma?"

"One and the same."

"The one that protesters were using as part of their crosswalk safety campaign?"

"If they only knew, right? But we've successfully kept the biking accident details out of the press. Wanting the perps to think someone must've just stolen their drugs from the scene without police suspecting anything. They've been distributing to some affluent community members."

Tierney's thoughts shifted to Ian and the mom at the soccer field. "And to think the transport was all out of Schick. In plain sight, right under swimmers' noses," Tierney said, and winced as the EMT wrapped her arm. "Never would've guessed Tatyana was in on anything shady, though. Seemed like a sweet person when I met her on that plane."

"It's more plausible that she stumbled on the operation while cutting open a locker a swimmer had mistaken as her own, and then made some dangerous choices. We think these perps here tonight have ties to a drug ring in Mexico."

"Gotcha. I eventually recognized Ruby and Miguel from the pool. Assume you did, too?" Tierney was surprised by Mok's candor, but maybe she was fishing herself.

"Yes, although we didn't know exactly who from the pool we were dealing with until tonight. My team has been watching Popov's boyfriend, a Josh Jeffries, to see who'd show up at his apartment in hopes they'd mess up. Jeffries cracked under pressure and these two led us straight here."

"Surprising to think the Wrights' house was somehow involved."

"There may very well be drugs inside that house," Mok said, pointing at Mara's. "Although their au pair, Natalia, checks out. We don't think she had any knowledge of what she was being asked about tonight. Tatyana had acted alone, most likely on the advice of the doofus boyfriend, whose been picked up for further questioning."

"And Brad?" Tierney wondered aloud, remembering he was being held for Tatyana's murder. "Could he even be capable of a drug ring operation? You must've seen him regularly at the pool, too. He was lucky to get dressed in the morning."

"I'm afraid I can't comment on that piece. Probably shared too much already," Mok replied. "But our drug detecting dogs will be arriving soon to check the house. I'm hoping we'll uncover evidence to clarify remaining questions."

"I hope you find something."

"By the way, while we were watching this house tonight, you came outside for a bit. Why? Because if you hadn't returned, this evening could have taken a dark turn for your friends."

"Oh yes, that. So random. I had forgotten to bring my sweater inside and—" Upon the realization of her words, Tierney started to laugh.

"What's so funny?"

"It's just, this is the first time my being forgetful has ever been helpful."

Mok looked perplexed by Tierney's remark but the distracting activity taking place on the driveway drew her attention. Tierney followed her gaze to the two men parking an unmarked sedan with a donut spare tire on a rear wheel. *Sutton and his partner.* Sutton exited the vehicle first and surveyed Mara's property. As he turned their way, he broke into an impressive jog for a middle-aged man. His partner followed closely behind.

"You alright? I told you this was dangerous business," Sutton asked on approach, slightly out of breath. A look of deep concern washed across his face as he embraced Mok.

"Hey partner," Mok said, not pulling away until he did, and then straightened her stance. "Took you long enough to get here."

"Very funny, Irene. I was roped into some Police Chief business and then we got a flat. Otherwise, I would've been here sooner."

"Maintenance was never your strong suit." Mok turned to Tierney. "Tierney Gillespie, meet our Interim Police Chief, Howard Sutton, my former partner."

"Former partner?" Ayala looking baffled.

"Oh, Chief of Police now? Yes, we've met," Tierney said to Sutton, connecting the dots from her cookie delivery at the station.

"Indeed, we have, Ms. Gillespie. Nice to see you again." Sutton smiled but redirected his attention to Mok. "You never answered my question. You alright? Any injuries? I knew this undercover narcotics gig was risky."

"Too risky for a woman to handle, you mean?"

"I didn't say that. I've just been worried about you."

"I'm fine. Anyway, Tierney here is our woman of the hour."

"Why am I not surprised," Sutton said, sounding more composed.

Tierney blushed, not only at the compliment but the amorous vibe between Sutton and Mok.

"And you must be Ayala." Mok extended her hand.

"Yes, nice to meet you."

"Great work putting the DEA file I left on your desk to use."

"That was you?"

"Couldn't have left it on Sutton's. He would've seen me all over that."

Sutton nodded.

"But hey, tonight's recap will have to wait." Mok slid off the ambulance's back bumper and onto her feet. "The dogs have arrived. How's Claudia, by the way?"

"Still keeping the kibble industry afloat. But the happiest pup I've ever had."

"You have a dog?" Ayala asked.

Sutton nodded again.

"He's a tough nut to crack, Ayala, but he's working on being more open." Mok offered an encouraging smile and turned to Tierney. "Thanks again for your assistance tonight and the Schick insights." She reached over and tapped Tierney's damage-free arm, and Sutton tipped an imaginary hat her way.

"Don't be surprised if we call on your services sometime," Mok said over her shoulder.

Tierney took in the comment and watched as Mok directed the canine unit towards Mara's house.

"Let me guess, Irene was the driver of the VW Scirocco that disappeared. The piece you kept brushing me off about?" Ayala asked.

"Sorry, kid. Couldn't risk blowing her cover," Sutton said. Their voices trailed off, as the two men joined the crew loading Ruby and Miguel into separate cruisers.

—

Laura, Mara, and Jennie each took turns for a gentle hug once the EMT finished with Tierney's shoulder. Mara shared that Nat was now being looked after in another ambulance—the evening's ordeal causing her to go into shock.

"You were amazing in there," Mara said. "I don't know how you could've been so calm, but sounds as if you have an impressive past. I'd love to hear about it sometime."

"You're welcome. And I'd like that, too. Maybe somewhere with more ambience than a locked bathroom."

The women shared a laugh and Tierney noted the irony of her recent wish to somehow get Mara inside a windowless room.

"I'm just happy things turned out the way they did," Laura said.

Tierney was relieved, too. "And how are you feeling, Jennie? That was a stressful directive to have been given to walk out on your own."

"Moms are built tough." Jennie rubbed her belly. "Don't give me another thought."

"You're a town hero," Mara said to Tierney. "If I can ever return the favor, please let me know."

A smile spread across Tierney's face at the open invitation.

"And thank goodness for Jennie's ringtone," Laura interjected.

"That was awesome," Tierney replied. "Who thought to give officers the number for creating a distraction?"

"No one. It was a coincidence that Jennie's husband called when he did," Laura responded.

Tierney turned to Jennie with raised eyebrows.

"Can you believe he was calling to ask if I knew where Lilibet's favorite bedtime binky was?"

"No way," Tierney said.

"But speaking of bedtime, now that I've given my statement, I'm going to catch a ride home. Take care ladies, and I'll see you at yoga. Lord knows I'll need it after this."

Tierney, Mara, and Laura looked out at the flashing lights and activity in the street, including a news van that had just parked. Party guests were beginning to leave with their husbands.

"This evening has been full of surprises. And lessons. I won't let it be for nothing," Mara said.

"I couldn't agree more," Tierney replied.

Mara held up her right hand. "I hereby vow to do a better job of keeping life in perspective and to no longer be so uptight, like when friends want to bring chocolate chip cookies to my parties," she said and smiled at Laura, "and a host of other things, including keeping promises to myself." She winked at Tierney.

Tierney smiled her understanding. *Maybe BB was right about this confiding thing.*

"Well, gals," Mara exhaled deeply, "this looks to be wrapping up."

"And I should call Sean before he sees all this on the news."

"Oh, gosh. You wouldn't want him to worry," Laura said.

"I'm going to package up our cookies for the officers to take back to the station. It's the least I can do," said Mara.

The three parted ways and Tierney walked over to a nearby tree to place her call to Sean. Before dialing, she saw Craig running towards Mara as she neared their front door, which was being taped off with bright yellow *Crime Scene Do Not Cross* tape.

"Mar, wait," Craig said as he caught up, hugging her for what must've been the third time since exiting the ordeal. "Officers need more time to process the scene, but you're not going to believe this."

"What could I possibly not believe after all this?"

"The dogs found cocaine in the house—an estimated street value of over a million dollars."

"What? But where? Wouldn't we have noticed?"

"The dogs led them straight to the kitchen and into the pantry. Your big pull-out bins with the scoops, for flour and baking powder? Filled to the brim with cocaine."

"So, wait, I was baking with cocaine earlier? The oven wasn't broken?"

"Exactly."

"Holy shit. Isn't cooked cocaine like the same thing as crack?"

Craig laughed. "Not entirely sure of the chemistry behind that. Maybe? But I actually have another surprise I've been wanting to talk with you about. I've lined up my next project, one I'm really excited about."

Mara looked into his eyes. "Well, if you're excited, I am, too," Mara said, and the couple kissed.

—

Back at home, Sean was still reeling from Tierney's account of what had transpired. Their kitchen phone shrilled nonstop once Tierney had silenced her cell. It was mostly reporters on the answering machine, but some community members, party guests, and parents from school were leaving messages, too. Sean finally thought to take the phone off the hook, but not before a call woke Finn.

Tierney hadn't intended to share the ordeal with her son, but still believed honesty was the best policy when it came to parenting. At least the kindergarten version of honesty.

"I'm so glad the bad guys didn't get you," Finn said, arms wrapped tightly around her.

"We all are," Sean said, leaning into the family hug.

"Will you be on TV?" Finn asked.

"Oh, I doubt that." Tierney headed over to the couch and sat down, exhausted and mindful to not move her shoulder too much. She felt lucky it was only a bad bruise this time.

"Why don't you get your bathrobe, and you can sit with us for a while," Sean said to Finn.

Finn flew down the hall, excited to stay up a bit longer. He wouldn't be able to fall back asleep so soon anyway.

"I'll flip on the TV to see if anything has hit the news yet," Sean continued. He clicked the remote and stopped by the bar to pour two glasses of Macallan. "They had a bit on earlier about the Police Chief collapsing at the station today. A detective named Sutton is taking over."

"I heard about that on Mara's lawn. Police Chief Marks is taking early retirement after a health scare. It wasn't a heart attack, just indigestion, but his tests apparently ID'd some underlying concerns."

Louie jumped on the couch's arm and went straight for Tierney. Her furry masseuse, purring and kneading his paws methodically before nestling into a supportive position under her sling.

"The police department has certainly been busy. I got a call tonight from Dean about our meeting next week. Said he's now getting it from all ends of the law. A detective apparently contacted him a few days ago about the lifeguard murder. Turns out he was the host dad of the victim, and was asked for his whereabouts on the night she was killed."

Host dad? Thank God Sean was still facing the bar or he would've seen the her look of astonishment. "You don't say."

"He had an alibi. Was at Stanford Hospital being monitored for chest pains."

Tierney breathed a sigh of relief that Sutton had been thorough. "What a night."

Sean handed her a glass and sat beside her. It was the first time she could process the scene at Mara's in her mind. Maybe the broadcast would help piece together the evening's other details Bell had shared. Make that Irene Mok. How unfathomable that she'd been undercover all those months, but questions remained.

"So, the guy actually waved a gun at all of you and—" He halted his question as breaking news-themed music played.

"Tonight, in Park View, a typically quiet town experienced an event of epic proportion as a murder investigation came to a head during an annual holiday cookie exchange," the broadcaster began.

The studio cut to a live scene. A reporter was standing on Mara's front lawn and proceeded to relay the evening's turn of events. Photos of six culprits now in custody, a few of them cousins, appeared on screen.

Six?

Miguel—the man shot in the shoulder by Mok, an alleged dealer working for the drug ring that had taken up residence in the area;

Ruby—Miguel's sister, the woman captured in Mara's kitchen, working side-by-side with her brother as a drug trafficker. A snake tattoo was visible on her neck in her mug shot;

Carlos—Miguel and Ruby's cousin, and the man still awaiting questioning while in a coma at Good Samaritan Hospital, yet an assumed drug trafficker based on the recent ID made by his cousins in exchange for more lenient sentencing;

Enrique—a Facilities employee with the City of Park View allegedly responsible for placing drugs in various lockers during his late-night shifts—for distribution into the community. Ruby and Carlos had shared his whereabouts with authorities;

Josh—a locally-known weed dealer with involvement in recent cocaine sales; and, finally,

Brad—the man still in custody and charged with the murder of Tatyana Popov, believed to be the leader of the drug ring's operation—code name Yuri.

Yuri? Come on, Sutton. And no way it's Brad.

"A drug operation going on so boldly within the confines of the men's and women's locker rooms at Schick Pool," the reporter continued. "Drugs that had been placed in lockers and moved secretly out into the community to those who could afford the high-end cocaine."

Such a bustling place Schick was, but Tierney was surprised to think of all that going on. "I guess I find all this plausible," she said to Sean, "but not the Brad component. Him calling the shots of a cocaine ring? Having a code name? Murdering someone? I mean, you met the guy over summer. He's a trainwreck."

Sean nodded while looking at the screen.

Tierney recognized the man named Carlos, the swimmer she'd seen over summer who did dry land routines with his two cousins in between deep dive swims. Maybe Carlos was the ringleader—this Yuri person, and Miguel took over after Carlos' accident? Or Yuri was Enrique? Either made more sense than Brad. Sutton was hopefully thinking the same thing. Carlos was in a coma, though, so investigators wouldn't know for certain unless new evidence came forth, or he finally woke for interrogation.

The reporter continued, "and with details provided by Josh Jeffries, investigators have confirmed that Popov had simply happened upon the drug ring and began skimming for herself a few weeks prior to her murder."

The reporter passed the report back to the studio anchor, and the broadcast turned to Tierney. Up came her old badge photo from Dublin.

"Oh, Lord." Tierney now watched through splayed fingers.

"Finn! Come quick! Mom's on TV," Sean called out, and took a drink.

"DEA Officer Irene Mok, working undercover on the Popov case, shared that her team was lucky to have had a hero in their midst—a former hostage negotiator in attendance at tonight's cookie exchange," the news anchor said.

Sean reached for Tierney's hand as he watched the screen and Finn joined them.

"Tierney Gillespie, parent at Park View's Apricot Grove Elementary School, would unknowingly be called from civilian duty this evening, back into her role as a former member of the Crisis Intervention Squad in Dublin, Ireland. Her cool, level head and use of deactivation tactics are being lauded for ensuring no civilians were harmed, or worse, during tonight's hostage situation. A hometown hero. Ms. Gillespie, currently with family, has been unavailable for comment," the anchor said.

"My mom is a superhero, which makes me one, too!" Finn pulled off the cape over his head and draped it across Tierney's shoulders.

"Thanks, buddy. Won't you be needing it?"

He shook his head. "The police have all the bad guys."

Tierney smiled and wrapped her arms around him. She hoped they did.

SUNDAY, DECEMBER 2

Sutton perused the cookie bins taking up all useable space on Joelle's side table. He had already sampled a few from the dozens in the staffroom, pausing at the fortune cookies from his favorite Chinese restaurant in San Jose: Chef Chin's. *Did a mother try to pass those off as her own? The people in this town, I swear.* But that didn't stop him from enjoying one.

He returned to his desk with a Finnish Ribbon Cookie. It was the one Mara Wright said had swept all three competition categories, per the votes she was cleared to tally while waiting for the crime scene to be processed. Sutton dipped it into his coffee, and his tastebuds did a little jig.

He continued to review Tierney's details on his screen, still in disbelief at what Irene had shared. But for a stay-at-home mom with some past training in crisis intervention to have maneuvered the way she did? It explained her keen eye around town and the call-ins, but an ability to maintain a level head in a situation? His team had barely done that. Hell, his people hadn't been able to get hostage takers on the phone.

As Sutton scrolled, he found nothing of note. Her position with a bakery in Seattle. *Queen Anne & Magnolia News* articles, including a marriage announcement and her son's birth announcement. But then he paused at the sight of her driver's license. *Duh. Maiden name.* He brushed crumbs from his fingers and typed in Tierney O'Shaughnessy, her birth date, and hit enter.

Paydirt.

Line after line populated his screen. Trinity College educated. Sergeant in Dublin. Newspaper and magazine articles, Crisis Intervention Squad incident reports—all recounting successful hostage negotiations as the junior member of Dublin's Dream Team, with a partner named Norah Boyce. *Dream Team?* But then the articles just stopped.

He scrolled back up to the beginning of the last article, from *The Irish Independent* in 1999.

Dream Team Tragedy at Embassy

During a gala to celebrate Dublin's women in law enforcement, a sniper with IRA ties enacted a revenge mission for the death of his cousin—the gunman killed in last month's heist at the International Financial Services Centre. Two deaths resulted in the ordeal, including Inspector Norah Boyce and the sniper himself.

The sniper, identified as Shane O'Neill, was believed to have maneuvered his way onto Embassy grounds via a paving construction crew, smuggled in a loaded sniper's rifle and climbing gear stashed within the crew's equipment, and hid in wait on the roof until the evening of the gala.

While the event was under way, an eyewitness on Embassy grounds alerted officers to a gunman cabling down the structure from the roofline with a rifle strapped to his person. As O'Neill neared the window of the Grand Briefing Room, he blasted through the glass, killing his intended target, Inspector Norah Boyce. Before he was able to flee via suspension cable, an elderly female guest—a retired Garda officer—mortally shot him. O'Neill's intentions had been a targeted murder. No hostage-taking plans were evident.

"This was an evil act of violence," said Kenny Kelly, Chief Inspector. "The Squad has lost one of its finest, but her legacy will live on."

"I just assumed he was talking smack," said Brennan Rooney, barman at Violet Malone's pub downtown, who overheard

O'Neill's scheme a few days prior during a drunken rant. "But when I saw the news report on the telly that the guy actually pulled it off, I called the Garda right away."

The "scheme," according to Rooney, was to seek revenge on Inspector Boyce who had been the lead hostage negotiator calling the shots that resulted in his cousin's death. "He thought women in law enforcement were a joke. Said that shrew's tactics not only cost his cousin's life, but millions for his personal business," Rooney shared.

Inspector Boyce's partner, Sergeant Tierney O'Shaughnessy, had been scheduled to present with Boyce at the gala, but was a late arrival. O'Shaughnessy remains hospitalized for unidentified injuries and unavailable for comment.

A private graveside service will be held for Inspector Boyce at Glasnevin Cemetery at 3 p.m. on Thursday.

Sutton's eyes fell to the article's lead photo, of the deceased: Norah Boyce. He couldn't imagine what it must've felt like for Tierney to have a partner murdered. Something like that could mess a person up for life; he would die if anything happened to Irene. But what an idiot, that bartender. Threats of such a violent nature should always be taken seriously, and reported.

He popped what remained of the Finnish Ribbon Cookie into his mouth and shook his head at the current state of things. Irene was doing fine in her new role with the DEA, without him, and how he had underestimated Tierney, profiling her as just another busybody Park View mom. Maybe he could use some female intuition of his own.

Police had found over a hundred thousand dollars' worth of cocaine in Josh's apartment last night, and the punk had agreed to share what he knew about Tatyana's time leading up to her death in exchange for a lighter sentence. Sutton rewound the tape recorder from Josh's late-night interrogation and hit play again.

SUTTON: Let's see if what you have to say is worth a trade.

JOSH: It will be. Look, Tatyana wasn't a bad person. When she discovered a brick of cocaine in that old lady's locker, she knew the right thing was to contact the cops. Said that's what any moral citizen would do, the moral citizen she came to America to be. But instead, she snapped and took it. The au pair thing hadn't worked out, and she was tired of hitting dead ends. So, she decided to do what she knew best. Cocaine running was apparently in her DNA; she had been trained by her family back in Moscow. She thought finding the drugs had been a sign—that it was time for her own survival.

SUTTON: And you just went along with it? Didn't try to do the moral thing yourself and call authorities?

JOSH: I couldn't rat her out. And no cop has ever cut me a break, so I just went along with it. It was all her plan. She told me that night at my apartment, "Joshy,"—that was her nickname for me—"it's crazy what's going on here and we can leverage it with your weed business." She said that first take was worth at least $250k, and we hid it in my PlayStation box in the closet until we could make a plan. But when I sampled the high quality of her find, man, I kinda freaked.

SUTTON: That someone dangerous would really care it's gone?

JOSH: Exactly. I told her to back off for a while. I knew this world from the outskirts. Things could get dark fast.

SUTTON: So, you just sat on it?

JOSH: Well, she couldn't just leave it in the pool locker. And why shouldn't we benefit instead of someone else? There were multiple lifeguards working shifts so no one could be certain it was her who'd taken it. Plus, she had challenging fingerprints.

SUTTON: The scarred fingers.

JOSH: Yeah. It was eerie, like some weird initiation-ceremony thing into the family business.

SUTTON: She said that?

JOSH: Basically. Anyway, Tatyana agreed to take a break from the lock cutting until she figured out the operation's flow. In the meantime, she learned my routes, and expanded them by selling to wealthier clients she'd met through her au pair connections. Rich parents and their friends. Even some of their highschoolers.

SUTTON: So, it was just her selling the coke and not you?

JOSH: Exactly. I just sold weed. If someone asked for coke, I'd link them up with Tatyana directly. And for the first time in weeks, she was happy. Said she felt financially secure. But then she got annoying.

SUTTON: How so?

JOSH: She started talking about marriage, that I owed her citizenship for all she had done for my business.

SUTTON: How do I know you didn't just decide to get rid of her then? Kill her at the pool. And that this is all bull?

JOSH: I've got my issues, but I'm no murderer. Check my record. I've never killed anyone, right? But I owed her nothing. If anything, she owed me for letting her tap into my customer base. But the situation fixed itself.

SUTTON: Go on.

JOSH: After intercepting transfers in the pool lockers for a few weeks, she panicked. She thought someone was following her back to my apartment. And she was right to be worried. One night, I looked out the window and saw that guy Miguel, the same guy in the cell with me tonight? He was on to her.

SUTTON: So, what then? You and Tatyana amicably parted ways?

JOSH: Sort of. I told her I wanted the coke out of my place. She promised to find a better hiding spot if she could still live with me. I told her okay, but we had to split a few times when we heard people breaking in. We crashed at my friend's condo for a while, but Tatyana kept her promise and hid the remaining coke at that rich family's home where she was a math tutor. Her friend, Natalia, was apparently easy to deceive. And that's all I know.

SUTTON: The location of the remaining coke, minus a little cut for yourself.

JOSH: Yeah, dumb to have kept some. I know. But I'm turning over a new leaf in the new year. Actually, starting now.

Sutton stopped the tape and stared at the machine. What was it Tierney had mentioned at the florist? Sensing Tatyana was running from something in Moscow? And had a bunch of cousins? Maybe it could be a family drug ring like Josh implied. It still didn't sit right to have Brad in custody for the murder. He really was too lame to have been the ringleader. And maybe the case had fixated on finding the killer quickly and not enough time considering Tatyana's identity. She had doctored up her work visa. What else had she lied about?

Sutton opened a new screen on his computer and logged into the Interpol site. His old pal from the academy still worked there. Maybe he could help shine some light on this Tatyana Popov.

* * *

Tierney woke Sunday morning later than usual and felt rested. It was the first time in she couldn't remember how long that she'd slept through the night, and her thoughts weren't foggy. But the name Yuri—she couldn't stop thinking about it.

After breakfast, Sean offered to take Finn to the mall for Christmas shopping so Tierney could decompress. He said his paperwork could wait and that work commitments would be taking more of a back seat after what had transpired last night.

When he opened the garage door, two reporters were loitering in their front yard, hoping for a Tierney quotation. Sean's height could make for an intimidating presence when necessary, so it was no surprise they respectfully vacated upon learning there would be no statements.

Once her boys departed, Tierney showered, dressed, and styled her hair. The layers from her recent cut had grown easier to tame. As she looked at her reflection, she felt more together than she had in years.

Tierney heard a knock at the front door and her thoughts momentarily swept back to Mara's wide-open entry, then the reporters. But she collected herself and peeked through the front shutters. *Gem.*

"Wow. Just wow. I mean, so happy you're okay, but I clearly missed the soirée of the year!"

"That it was," Tierney replied. "But first, how is your mom?"

After hearing that an X-ray showed nothing fractured or broken, just badly bruised, and that Gem's mom was resting comfortably, Tierney relayed the previous night.

"I knew you had some kind of hostage negotiator background, but who would've imagined it coming in handy at a cookie exchange?"

Tierney agreed with how outrageous it sounded.

"I can't believe I missed all that. I mean, happy to not have been in danger myself, but how cool to have seen you in action. Parents are excited to learn we've had a powerhouse in our midst all along." Gem gestured around Tierney.

"I've been surprised myself—mostly to discover my training would've filtered back."

"Well, so thankful it did."

"And speaking of surprises, Mara isn't the evil gatekeeper I thought. We unpacked quite a lot in that bathroom."

"Honest to goodness?"

"Let's just say I've learned that people are more alike than different." Tierney chose not to delve into the specifics of her conversation with Mara; none of it was hers to share. She instead just mentioned that Mara, too, had struggles like everyone else.

Gem nodded her understanding. "I also learned something positive about Mara."

"Oh?"

"Laura called this morning. She had the Wrights over quite late last night until they could re-enter their house. Regina apparently scurried off after seeing all the cops in the yard. The whole experience freaked her out for some reason."

"That's kind of Laura. It would've taken a while for officers to wrap things up."

"Well, in addition to Mara staying the course with that allergy safety campaign at school, she's decided to leverage her Junior League connections and create a new philanthropy—by women for women, to help mentor, acclimate and educate young au pairs who want to remain in America at the end of their assignments. I think she's calling it Melody's Place? And they're looking for inaugural members. She plans to include anyone interested. Super inclusive."

"That's awesome. Women helping women is something this town needs more of," Tierney said, recalling Mara's comment about wanting to find more meaning in her days.

"Natalia will be her VP of Community Outreach. After what happened to Tatyana, she wants to help provide an extra level of support for au pairs in the area."

"It's good to hear positive things coming from all that's happened." Tierney thought of her own opportunity for closure.

"And I guess the most positive thing is that everyone involved in this murder case is finally behind bars." Gem exhaled in relief.

Tierney could understand why community members would feel at ease with the recent arrests, but she still had doubts.

—

After her visit with Gem, Tierney returned the landline to its cradle and listened to message after message—from Apricot Grove parents, partygoers, and a few of Mara's neighbors—all personally thanking her. Many had been surprised to learn of her past career. *Should they?* Numerous moms at Apricot Grove had impressive pasts—Silicon Valley was literally swimming with them.

There was also a call from a reporter with the *San Jose Mercury News*, still looking for a quotation. Tierney opted to remain unavailable for comment and let law enforcement handle professional communications.

She headed into the bedroom where her cell phone was charging to see if Sean had called. There was one missed message, from Detective Sutton—make that Interim Police Chief Sutton. She sat down on the bed and hit play.

"Ms. Gillespie. Thanks again for your efforts last night. I wanted to see if you're available next week for a meeting at the station? I'd like to talk with you about a programming idea. Hoping to start my new gig on the right foot." He laughed awkwardly. "As I'm sure you could see, the department—and probably all towns in the vicinity—could benefit from some training in the hostage handling department. Thinking a workshop led by you would be worthwhile. I'm about to hit send on an email that outlines my thoughts so you can peruse the idea. Let me know? You have the number."

Tierney's face lit up at the idea of a workshop, and helping law enforcement hone their skills. Maybe she could do that in addition to the baking business? Or instead of? Either way, she'd have something interesting on the calendar to do around Finn's school schedule.

Already close to 1:00 p.m., she headed into the kitchen for lunch and Louie followed. She selected leftover chicken sandwich makings while Louie eddied around her legs, mewing excitedly at the open fridge's scents.

"You already had your bowl of kibble," she reminded him. *Kibble.* Tierney's thoughts circled back to her last visit to the pet food store. *Wait, that's it.* The Daisy Caps and their dog. The name on the computer screen being engraved onto the dog tag when she passed by: Yuri. Should she share that with Sutton? But it was a dog's name.

She pushed the idea from her mind and shut the fridge. Her attention returned to sandwich prep, but her intuition swirled with each spread of Dijon. Could the grandmas have somehow been involved in Tatyana's death? She stopped moving the knife as other data points from the past few weeks pulled focus. Surely Sutton would at least hear her concerns this time, but she'd need to tread lightly.

She found her phone, purse, and keys. It was a ten-minute drive to the station.

—

"Thanks for seeing me on short notice," Tierney said to Sutton as he took a seat across from her at the station's conference room table.

"To be honest, we hope to be seeing more of you around here. Assume you got my message? This talk could've waited until next week, you know. I gave my partner the day off. I'm sure he'd like to join us for the talk on curriculum ideas."

"Oh, that. Yes, I am intrigued by the idea of leading a hostage handling workshop, thank you. But that's not why I'm here."

"I see. Well, what can I do for you?" Sutton sat back in his chair and crossed his arms behind his head like he was settling in to watch a show.

She took in a deep breath. "This Yuri thing, on the news last night? I have a theory."

"A theory. Okay."

"Or intuition. Whatever you want to call it."

"I'm listening."

"There are two elderly women who frequented the pool together. They have a little chihuahua named Yuri."

Sutton raised a curious eyebrow. "So, Yuri is a dog, that is involved in a drug ring?"

"Yuri is a dog, yes. I saw his ID tag. But I think it's a code name the elderly women chose for their cover. Perps would sometimes come up with code names when I worked in the Squad. A game they'd play. The elderly women were at the pool regularly for water fitness. I never spoke with them, but they were allegedly Hungarian. But I think they might have been Russian. At least one of them. There's something that's just not right about them."

"What exactly doesn't sit right?"

"They'd take the class, but never really listen or participate. They'd keep to themselves, yet observe everything going on around them. They lived close to the pool, and I saw them at Schick the day after Tatyana was murdered. Returning to the scene of the crime, as they say. In addition, I have a friend whose au pair speaks many languages. That young woman assumed one day at the pool that an elderly swimmer was Russian, which caused a ruckus when she tried to engage."

"You witnessed this 'ruckus'? It was violent in nature?"

"Not exactly violent. And I wasn't there. And I'm not one hundred percent sure it was the same elderly woman, but pretty certain. I was hoping you could contact my friend's au pair and ask her to come in, on official business, and look through photos for a possible ID of the Russian woman?"

"You have a photo of the elderly Russian woman for the au pair to review?"

"Um, no, but as I mentioned, they lived nearby—in the apartment complex across the street from the pool. I'm hoping the property manager would have some paperwork from them, a signature, perhaps their walk-through materials might have a fingerprint that could lead you to a photo in the Interpol database? Or even a fingerprint still accessible in the apartment they rented?"

"I see. That's a lot of speculation you've just shared," Sutton said with a smile.

"Yes, I know." Tierney leaned back in her seat. She'd embarrassed herself.

"I'll tell you what," he said, putting his elbows on the table. "I have a newfound appreciation for intuition since taking on this case, and a desire to be more thorough in my role as chief than my predecessor. I've had my own recent findings regarding the true identity of our victim, Tatyana."

"Really?"

He nodded. "Because of your civilian status, I'm unable to provide details. But let's just say that the essence of what you've shared warrants investigation."

Tierney's eyes took on a silvery luster and she stood to shake Sutton's hand. "Thank you for taking me seriously. I'll go track down the name and number of that au pair for you."

"You can just bring it with you tomorrow morning when we have that meeting about the workshop." Sutton's smile grew wider. "Sound good?"

"I have therapy at nine a.m., but am free after that." Tierney stood motionless at the moment of honesty she'd just had in a police station.

"Great." Sutton looked down at his desk calendar. "Assuming that's about an hour, let's say eleven a.m?"

"I look forward to it." A sudden lightness swept through Tierney's body, and she headed outside. She glanced down at her watch and would still make it home before her boys.

She slipped into the driver's seat and her cell phone rang.

"Keats!" BB boomed into the receiver.

"So great to hear your voice."

"I've been dying to find out. How was the cookie exchange?"

She paused, not knowing where to begin. "I survived," she said, and turned on the ignition.

Epilogue

Sasha and Olga lived together unassumingly in the apartment complex across from Schick Pool. The roommates, widows and old pals, were always first to offer a smile and sweet wave to neighbors. Regulars at water fitness, they donned plastic daisy-adorned swim caps upon arrival, and pixie hairstyles at departure. Their gentle manner made up for the language barrier since their English wasn't strong.

Their English was excellent.

The women had married into the same family over forty years ago. Their husbands, brothers, had ensured their wives' education and language skills early on; they had ensured many things.

"You must blend. Become one with any community in which you find yourselves. Be out in the open, right under people's noses, and no one will suspect a thing." The men had many business insights, as drug kingpins with the Red Mafiya—the Golubev gang. And before their double murder years ago in a botched job at the hands of the competing Petrov gang, they had armed their wives with the knowledge and skill set to survive in any country. And a comfortable life at that.

The widows bade farewell to Russia after the death of their husbands. There had been no children; those were called leverage in their circles. Petrovs were naive that way.

The elderly women had settled on California for their latest venture, determined to enjoy their golden years. The one-year anniversary of their operation in Silicon Valley was within sight. There had been a few hiccups, including Carlos' unfortunate biking accident—although his resulting coma proved beneficial in keeping him from deal-making with police, and a nosy swimmer who overheard their murmurs in Russian. Olga had squelched that one in her special Olga way. But overall, business had run smoothly until Tatyana meddled. And to think she was from their homeland. But no matter they all shared Russian blood; Tatyana's relatives had been responsible for their husbands' deaths so she was deemed expendable. *Popov. She could've been a bit more creative with the name change.*

Her fingertip scars had been the first dead giveaway when they had seen her lifeguard training at the pool one afternoon—*such an unnecessary ritual instead of traditional tattooing used by other families.* But the widows did sense Tatyana was trying to create a noble life for herself among her peers—until the day they overheard her whispers on the phone in Russian. Assurances to her mother that an engagement was within reach along with a lucrative business—that she'd send for her soon when it was safe to reveal her location. But Sasha and Olga's cocaine operation was their own creation at the modest community pool in Park View. And theirs it would remain. Unfortunately for Tatyana, "women helping women" was not a practiced concept in the Russian mob.

An impressive Russian drug ring in the traditional sense, the pool scene would appear to outsiders as Mexican-controlled—more believable to California authorities—should trouble arise. Carlos, Miguel, Ruby, and Enrique had all been anonymously recruited while swimming at Schick with the help of mysteriously placed burner phones in their gear. All instructions were texted and no one would ever meet their employer, Yuri.

Carlos had been the leader of the pool's operation and Miguel was in training when the bike collision occurred. It was then up to Ruby to help Miguel reset the flow, which she had done seamlessly.

Sasha and Olga sent locker numbers where drugs had been stored by Enrique after hours, along with lock combinations, during his night shifts as a janitorial worker. It was also he who had the initial task of deactivating the property's CCTV cameras. He wasn't the most thorough team member.

The district's facility office deep in San Jose was where fellow nationals filtered the drugs via the shuttered warehouse at the back of the property located behind the newly built one. The cocaine would simultaneously be placed in both women's and men's locker rooms; otherwise a cleverer trafficker might've suspected their leader to be female. Having the handoffs occur when the pool was most crowded had been a perfect front. And Brad, poor Brad, had been left anonymous stashes of quality vodka in unspoken exchange for his silence should anything be observed.

The elderly women's role had been simple beyond the texts—basic surveillance and management—keep a watchful eye on the cocaine transfer in mid-afternoon once per week on rotating days. The two would watch all goings-on from the comfort of their water fitness class or apartment balcony, both of which offered ideal views of the surrounding property. Burner phones were swapped out frequently in the same swim bags containing the drugs. Golubevs were thorough that way. The rest of Sasha and Olga's time was spent monitoring and playing an active role in the community while filtering profits through offshore accounts.

"Where there are young people, there are drugs. A simple mathematical fact. Build on an established platform and you're in business," had been Boris Golubev's drug running advice. And the eldest kingpin had been correct.

At dusk every night, the widows walked their dog—a Russian toy terrier assumed by most unversed in the canine world to be a chihuahua. Securing their perimeter was the true purpose of the evening strolls, while speaking strategic bits of Hungarian to passersby. But on their way home that late November 15th evening, the air had grown thick as the cloud layer blew in. The dampness helped Olga with her cough, something worsening over the years.

The widows and their pup had almost returned home when Olga noticed a dim light at the closed facility near the smaller pool where they enjoyed class. Olga nudged Sasha in the direction of the light. The two slowed their pace, making their way around the jasmine-edged walking path towards the metal safety gate. The shrubbery, long overdue for a trim, provided the necessary coverage to watch without being watched.

The dim light was enough to illuminate Tatyana's face for an instant as she propped up the vinyl cover of the unused ADA pool lift. Olga looked at Sasha knowingly. *Damn Petrovs.* They had verified their breach. The girl might've initially intended to break from her family ties and establish honorable roots for herself in Silicon Valley, but, as Americans say, the apple didn't fall far.

Sasha and Olga continued to track Tatyana's every move as she reached high up into the pool lift with the help of the bolt cutters to retrieve a large package—the brick that had gone missing from the women's locker room just yesterday.

Tatyana dropped the cocaine into her duffle bag with a clonk—an audible reminder of how much the girl was costing their operation. The elderly women had joked that their stupid thief never thought to look for the same operation running simultaneously in the men's locker room, which is what had kept their business afloat the past few weeks. But tonight, they would put an end to the interruption.

With a sigh, Sasha acknowledged the inevitable. She continued along the walking path with the leash. Olga, the more heartless, slipped on the latex gloves she never traveled without in her back pocket and stealthily passed through the black metal Emergency Exit Only gate. It could be relied upon to be unlocked—typically with a rudimentary use of chewing gum or tape. The widows had watched irresponsible lifeguards time after time leverage the gate when arriving late for a shift or sneaking out for a quick hit or sale.

Sasha and Olga knew they had been lucky again that night— that DEA Agent Mok had not been staked out in the pool's parking lot. So silly Mok's cover had been to them anyway. Not only could they sniff DEA from a mile away, they had observed her out of character from their balcony when she assumed no one was watching.

Little did Tatyana know that Sasha and Olga were watching her, too, that evening, while Brad was predictably passed out on the office futon—a now regular occurrence.

Tatyana zipped her duffle shut and repositioned the chair's cover. Unfortunately, her adrenaline high was too distracting to register the quiet footsteps approaching from behind. As Tatyana picked up the bag, she reached over for the bolt cutters to return to the mechanical room and hesitated; the tool was no longer where she'd left it. As she glanced around, the metal swung swiftly across her temple—a spot Olga had discovered long ago to be the most effective way to quickly end a "situation."

Tatyana's lifeless body dropped to the ground, and Olga pushed her into the pool with a single shove of her boot. Keeping up her strength through water fitness had come in handy. Olga grabbed the duffle and headed back toward the gate. She looked over at Brad, passed out, through the office window and closed the gate behind her. *So horrible what addiction did to people.*

As she exited, she caught Sasha's surprised look and glanced down at her own hands. She was absentmindedly still holding the bolt cutters. Perhaps age was starting to take its toll. She checked for onlookers before tossing them into the public garbage can where they would easily be found by law enforcement—along with Brad's fingerprints, as the only employee besides Tatyana to ever use them. She rejoined Sasha on the return walk to the apartment at their standard strolling pace.

The fact it took so long for police to discover the murder weapon was due to an odd turn of events. While the widows returned to their apartment, a weathered-looking elderly male bike rider (with plastic bags and a wire basket filled full of cans and bottles for recycling) was on his way home when he saw the tool's handles peeking out of the garbage can. He retrieved it, balanced it across the basket behind his seat, and pedaled home. The following morning, after finishing the liter of gin he'd started the night before, he began his daily collection route back down the path. As he brushed hair away from his eyes with his dirty, gloved hand, he swerved and course-corrected, but not before the bolt cutters flew out of his basket and into the dense jasmine near Schick Pool—a location searched by law enforcement first.

As the widows reached their apartment, Sasha couldn't help but consider Tatyana's situation. What was the girl thinking to have gotten involved? She should've been smarter. Sasha remembered her twenty-year-old self wanting to come to America so desperately. She would've been an art teacher, and a mother, if she'd had the choice. Having achieved neither goal, however, didn't stop her maternal instincts. Sasha was going to miss Park View; her brief interactions with children around the park and pool had been her favorite part of the area, especially on Schick's Olympics and Field Day.

Olga could sense Sasha's sadness as they entered their apartment. "Stop being so emotional," she snipped in her native tongue. "You know there was nothing else we could've done. Consequences are consequences."

Sasha nodded. She felt for Tatyana's mother, but knew it was time for them to move on. They'd be packed and on a flight within thirty-six hours. A pity, too, as Silicon Valley had been a viable market. But the women weren't concerned. They'd always moved stealthily under the radar. After all, how well does anyone really know a person who never shares much of anything?

Olga selected a bottle of their finest vodka and poured two glasses. "To a long overdue vacation." Olga raised her glass to toast her sister-in-law.

"The family villa in Tuscany would be lovely this time." Sasha sipped from the Dyatkovo crystal and was reminded of their estate's interior decor, riches that would make the curators at State Hermitage Museum in Saint Petersburg drool. "Sound good, Yuri? You're the boss."

He yipped excitedly and nuzzled her leg in loving approval.

"Tuscany it is," Olga said, with a laugh and a cough.

THE END

Photo credit: Sari Singerman

ABOUT THE AUTHOR

ELIZABETH KEMP was born and raised in California, and lives in Silicon Valley with her high school sweetheart husband. She studied public relations at the University of Southern California, earned an MBA from Santa Clara University, and led a successful career in high-tech marketing communications before becoming a stay-at-home mom. That decision helped rekindle her love of reading for fun, and enabled her to pursue writing full-time. When away from her laptop, Elizabeth enjoys lap swimming, hiking, pickleball, and golf. *Tread Lightly* is her first novel. Visit her at elizabethkempwrites.com.

ACKNOWLEDGMENTS

Tread Lightly began as a spark of an idea while on an Alaskan cruise to celebrate my parent's wedding anniversary. I have many to thank for helping me keep that spark alive while finding time to write in between the cracks.

At Sibylline Press, special gratitude to Julia Park Tracey, for seeing something special in my manuscript; to Vicki DeArmon, for believing in me as a debut novelist and answering all of my questions so quickly, to Suzy Vitello, Maxfield Fulton, and Nancy Townsley, my incredible editors, whose excellent instincts made this story stronger; to Alicia Feltman, for her talent in designing beautiful covers, and to Anna Wilhelm and Hannah Rutkowski, for their marketing expertise.

Thank you to Ellen Sussman for her motivational style of teaching in *Jumpstart Your Novel*, her creative writing course with Stanford Continuing Studies. And thanks to Karen Conley, fellow classmate, for reading my earliest chapters and lending an expert eye as I plotted the first three-act structure I'd written since undergrad.

To Heather Lazare, my first developmental editor, for her keen insights, industry knowledge, and guidance on what I called a manuscript, and in telling me, "I know you can do this!" when I needed to hear it most. And to Stephanie Kelly, for her quick and ingenious skill in polishing places that needed it.

A special shout-out to Zibby Owens, the whirlwind of an inspirational human, for being so warm when I met her in person and shared details about my manuscript.

There have been many other supporters along my book journey that it would be impossible to name them all, but below are the rockstars who took time from their busy lives to read my pages. Whether that meant one scene, a chapter, the first fifty or the whole enchilada, I am so thankful (in alphabetical order) to: Sharon Barnes, Kate Connors, Marcy Dermansky, Barb Eckstein, Becca Funke, Laura Grodrian, Shannon Hancock, Kara Herren, Celia Johnson, Julie Lunn, Lisa Manterfield, Andra Miller, Elizabeth Murdock, Jordan Rosenfeld and Jenny Troxler.

And no writer can make progress without conversation about the publishing industry itself. Whether that was in person or online, a big thanks to Heather Lazare (again!) and her Northern California Writers' Retreat *Book Journey Club*; Valerie Saul for our lovely check-ins and her knowledge of Sibylline Press; Shirin Yim Leos for her monthly guest interviews and ultra-supportive Greater Group; Cynthia W. Gentry, and Annemarie O'Brien.

I'd also like to credit the organization responsible for giving me what I call my mini-MFA, the Kauai Writers Conference Online community. To its talented faculty, speakers and members, I am truly grateful. Your weekly Sunday sessions since COVID have been a bright spot.

I am also indebted to the authors who took the time to read and blurb *Tread Lightly*. You are all amazing, and I'm honored to have your words on my book.

In addition, the following books were useful to me in writing this novel: *Never Split the Difference* by Chris Voss and Tahl Raz; *Apples Never Fall* by Liane Moriarty, and *In the Woods* by Tana French—for inspiration to create a fictional Crisis Intervention Squad in Dublin in the same vein as her Murder Squad.

Then there are my amazing friends, who offered genuine excitement surrounding my debut novel. Whether in the form of coffee meet-ups, long walks, "thriving" gatherings and geta-ways, delicious meals together (sometimes with a frightening gift exchange in the mix), rounds of pickleball and golf, book club evenings, or lovely salon appointments, my heartfelt gratitude to you all for every moment.

Thank you also to my wonderful Kennedy family, for their unwavering encouragement, even when I didn't have new book scoop to share at our birthday and holiday gatherings.

Lastly, to my very special Team Kemp. My loves. To my husband and best friend. For always believing in me and supporting my pie-in-the-sky dream of publishing a novel. To my fabulous daughters, my biggest cheerleaders, without whom none of this would be worth it. They all read pages of Tierney's adventures at various stages (sometimes twice!), and motivated me to keep going.

And one final thanks—to the universe, for enabling me to demonstrate that a stay-at-home parent can still get back in the game and succeed in any career path.

STUDY GUIDE QUESTIONS

1. Have you ever felt like a fish-out-of-water in a new environment? What are your thoughts on how Tierney handled her own experience in Park View?

2. *Tread Lightly* examines the topic of female friendship. The narrative is at times propelled by relationships between women, including: the budding friendship between Tierney and Gem, the found-family friendship between Tierney and BB, the professional friendship between Tierney and Norah, and the rocky-start friendship between Tierney and Mara. Which friendship did you find most relatable? What makes relationships between women special or challenging?

3. The author explores the push-pull of motherhood—that balancing act between having children and a career. Was it wise for Tierney to continue being a stay-at-home mom once Finn started elementary school, or should she have chosen a different path from the onset?

4. We are profoundly shaped by our childhood experiences. In what ways was Tierney both positively and negatively shaped by her police-family upbringing? What are your thoughts on how she perceives therapy?

5. Discuss the lifeguard murder mystery. Were you surprised by who the victim really was and who the perpetrators turned out to be? Have you ever realized that something was going on right under your nose without knowing?

6. Tierney chose not to share her concerns about Dean Javitz being a potential suspect with Sean. Was she right to keep

that from him, and not add unnecessary stress to an already overwhelming job, or should a healthy spouse relationship include sharing everything?

7. For years, Tierney credited Norah for the level of confidence she had obtained. Have you ever relied on another for feeling confident in yourself? Do you know someone who has?

8. Did you see any similarities between the Sutton-Irene professional relationship and the Tierney-Norah one?

9. Based on your familiarity with Tierney's character by the end of the book, what do you think is her next best act—accepting Sutton's offer to lead a hostage negotiation workshop, pursuing the baking class route, some combination of both, or choosing an entirely different path?